For Grace and Eleanor Wyld
and Emily Robey

Dear Diary,

Wednesday the 4th of September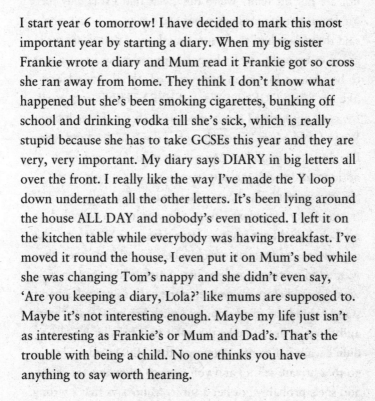

I start year 6 tomorrow! I have decided to mark this most important year by starting a diary. When my big sister Frankie wrote a diary and Mum read it Frankie got so cross she ran away from home. They think I don't know what happened but she's been smoking cigarettes, bunking off school and drinking vodka till she's sick, which is really stupid because she has to take GCSEs this year and they are very, very important. My diary says DIARY in big letters all over the front. I really like the way I've made the Y loop down underneath all the other letters. It's been lying around the house ALL DAY and nobody's even noticed. I left it on the kitchen table while everybody was having breakfast. I've moved it round the house, I even put it on Mum's bed while she was changing Tom's nappy and she didn't even say, 'Are you keeping a diary, Lola?' like mums are supposed to. Maybe it's not interesting enough. Maybe my life just isn't as interesting as Frankie's or Mum and Dad's. That's the trouble with being a child. No one thinks you have anything to say worth hearing.

Dear Diary,

Still Wednesday the 4th of September

Have just been next door to see what Clare is going to wear
on the first day back at school but she won't tell me. She
says I'll copy her, when how is that like even possible when
she buys really expensive cool designer clothes and we
don't?? But the really weird thing was that I was only there
for about ten minutes when her mum sent me home. She
said that Clare had to do some maths and that Clare was
going to be really, really busy from now on so I was going
to be seeing a lot less of her except at school. But Clare's
like my BEST FRIEND! We do EVERYTHING together!!
I was so upset that I ran home before she could see me cry.
When I told Mum I cried though. I don't understand what
I've done to offend her. Mum went mad. She says it's
nothing to do with me and everything to do with 'that
ghastly woman'. She hates Clare's mum. She calls her HND
(it stands for Her Next Door). She was like so offended on
my behalf and kept saying, 'How dare she? What a terrible
thing to say to your own child's best friend,' and then she
wanted to go round and see her, which is like really not
what I need before we've even gone back to school. I had to
stand behind the front door and push her back really hard
and shout at her to make the point that I really, REALLY
didn't want her to go. Mum says that HND wants Clare to
go to a private school and you have to sit exams for those
and she's probably got her a tutor. Mum says that's wrong,
that she's just trying to buy her a better future. I don't see

why that's so bad if she can afford it. Mum's obsessed with HND. Whenever I ask her to do something for me like buy me new ~~knickers~~ nickers or trainers she says things like, 'If the surgery's not too busy, darling,' or, 'Maybe at the weekend,' which means never. But then she doesn't just leave it at that. She has to put herself down for not having the time to be 'The Perfect Mum', unlike HND who doesn't work. When to me she is the perfect mum because she's mine. But if it's true, that Clare's mum's not going to let us hang out together much, then this is going to be a really, REALLY bad, sad year at school because she's been like my best friend forever, since reception.

From: Sue James
Sent: Wednesday 4 September 21:52
To: Angela James
Subject: Checking in after a fab two weeks in Greece . . .

Dearest, one and only sister . . .

I may be middle-aged with saggy knees, three kids and a marriage which can at best be described as stagnant but hey! let's live a little . . . That's my new mantra for life anyway because how else do you endure a moody teenager on her GCSE year, a tween who feels inadequate because she can't wear Prada, a surprise late baby and an adulterous menopausal husband? Go on holiday all together, that's what you do. Flying anywhere with babies is always fun. The more kids you have the easier it is to forget one. Left Tom behind in the departure lounge because it's so long since I've had a baby that I just got up and walked to the gate when they called our flight. Then concussed him in the plane, banging his head against those panels just above the seats as I stood up to take him to the back to change his nappy . . . forgivable usually in a mother, but NOT when that mother is also a doctor . . . so that was two points down on the holiday scorecard of marriage before we'd even got there. Managed to raise it sky-high again through waterskiing because I can still do it and Matthew can't. He tried several times and strained his groin.

Matthew couldn't understand why none of us wanted to accompany him on visits to ruins in temperatures close to forty degrees. (You're used to this sort of heat down under but for us Poms just moving from the pool into the shade required Herculean effort.) The one time I did go with him we got lost up a dirt track. He refused to stop to ask a man on a moped the way because he can't speak Greek and being a man couldn't even begin to communicate. So I got out of the car and established where we ought to be, which of course made Matthew even crosser because he now felt humiliated. When we finally reached the 'sight' it was the most unprepossessing pile of stones I have ever come across and I was just grateful that we had left Frank and Lola behind.

Another significant highlight was discussing feminism with Frankie over a bottle of retsina. Matthew, Lola and Tom did 'Row Row Row Your Boat Gently Down the Stream' so many times I wanted to capsize them. And then, as they were doing it one night for the 900th time, Frankie said, 'What IS feminism, Mum?' I nearly jumped out of my skin with excitement. Frank's conversation for most of the holiday up until that point had consisted of one of three phrases – 'I miss Chattie SOOOOOO much,' 'Am I brown enough?' and 'I think I'm gonna DIE of BOREDOM spending TWO WHOLE WEEKS WITH YOU TWO' – when she wasn't listening to her Walkman, so feminism burst on to this scorched desert like an oasis. It's a relief to know she can still think.

Matthew tried to pour water on decades of female achievement with 'a load of old bollocks'. Frankie claims it's redundant now, so there was plenty of scope for conversation from then on. I know sexual politics still burns as bright as ever amongst the young. It's just that they talk of it in terms of boys being 'only interested in one thing'.

Lola spent the best part of each day jumping in and out of the pool with a girl she became best friends with. So weird seeing her displaying the beginnings of womanhood – she's budding pert little breast sacs beneath protruding nipples and even a few wisps of pubic hair and my beautiful child is disappearing in front of my eyes – and yet she still behaves like a child. There she was playing with this other (far less developed) ten-year-old, diving through rubber rings, rescuing orphaned fish and pretending to be a mermaid. She's not even eleven, yet she seems more of a teenager than Frankie. She's leggy, moody and stroppy – lippy Lola – and answers back all the time. 'So-o-r-ry' is now her favourite word, making it quite clear that she isn't at all.

So it's the start of a brand-new 'school' year and getting Lola into a decent secondary school is going to be about as easy as springing a mass murderer from Broadmoor. You either need to lie about where you live or become terribly devout to even stand a chance. There isn't a sibling policy at Frankie's school, and we live 1.6 miles away. It's such a popular school that they now say that you have to live less than half a mile away to get in. HND is of course going private – chippy bitch. And she's so competitive about it – upset Lola today by telling her that she couldn't see Clare outside school because of course the child is so bloody dim she's going to need round-the-clock tutoring just to be able to understand what's written on the exam paper. Even if I believed in that as an option, Lola would never pass the exams – her spelling's atrocious and I'm not prepared to sacrifice Lola's health on the altar of ambition. So it's going to be a tricky time. Frankie is unbelievably moody, determined that nobody has ever had it so bad and is already jostling for position at the start line. She told me last night that GCSEs were much the most important thing a child ever did, much harder than moving to secondary school and that she deserved – yes DESERVED – a massive prize at the end of it!

Not looking forward to going back to work tomorrow. It's been so wonderful not having to touch the squidgy bits of complete strangers. And it means having to deal with Ian Bryson again. Ian is good-looking, charming, charismatic. His queues at the surgery are always the longest because he has this knack of making every patient feel special, plus the women love to linger for a last look and he fancies himself as a Dr Finlay. But he takes a fiercely moral stand on everything. He's against abortion and laughs at any form of 'alternative' medicine. Such practitioners are all just quacks as far as he is concerned and he doesn't even believe that there is much of a link between mind and body. We crossed swords on my last day because I saw one of his patients and he had written 'Deranged Alternative Hypo' across her notes because she'd asked for allergy testing. I foolishly challenged him about it at lunch and we had a massive row in front of the receptionists. Then in the afternoon had a lovely old dear lying on the table for a 'down below' – suspected incontinence. I always say, 'Give me a cough' to see if there is any leakage but instead I said, 'Give me a kiss.' She was so deaf and batty that she didn't hear but I got the giggles so badly that I had to leave the room. I stood bent double, weeping with laughter in the corridor, where Ian saw me so word soon spread round the office. For the rest of the day everyone just said, 'Give me a kiss,' when they saw me . . .

Kate Figes

After two weeks in any other working environment the episode would have been long forgotten. But at this practice ANYTHING is possible with Ian around.

Tons of love, Sxxxxxx

What About Me, Too?

Dear Diary,

Thursday the 5th of September

My new teacher is called Miss Jennings, although she's not coming in until next week so we had a supply teacher called Mr Burt. Kieran and Tom are already messing about, winding him up by pretending they don't understand really simple stuff. I'm sitting next to Camilla, not Clare, which is so unfair if I'm not going to see her much outside school. Maybe her mum feels that our house isn't good enough for Clare to come to (which it isn't).

Clare, of course, has brand-new trainers and D&G jeans for the first day of year 6 and a mobile phone which rang three times in lessons – her mum checking she was all right. Mr Burt said that if she didn't turn it off he would konfiscate it and then she spent the rest of the day complaining about how unreasonable he was. I think she just wanted it to ring because it made her feel more important. She also had this amazing new pencil case with compartments and a really cool eraser pen which she said she'd let me borrow, only that's hard because I'm not sitting next to her and when I asked her at break time if I could have a go she just ran off with Tanya laughing – TANYA, THE MOST HORRIBLE GIRL IN THE WHOLE SCHOOL!!! They were whispering today and giving me these evil stares like they were talking about me behind their backs. I don't know what to do at break time without Clare, we always sit together beneath the apple tree and talk and I felt kind of stupid sitting there all on my own.

We ought to be able to sit next to who we like at school and nobody really likes Camilla because a) she's fat, b) she was born without a foot and has to wear a false one which means she can't run or do PE properly which is why she's fat, c) she tells lies to make people like her, d) she farts, a lot, and she never brushes her hair so she's definitely got nits. Mum says I have to be nice to Camilla and that the teacher will move us all around again at half-term, but that's ages away and she doesn't have to sit next to her all day long, scratching away.

From: Sue James
Sent: Saturday 7 September 22:12
To: Angela James
Subject: Re: How is marriage stagnant exactly?

He's angry, sullen, argumentative, moody and accusing –
permanently. I'm insulted daily either as a 'fool' or a 'nag' or,
worse still when he's in a really bad mood, as a 'stupid bitch'.
If he comes home irritable, which is most days, he picks on the
kids, but mainly Frankie, for the simplest things. If they do
something which falls below his standards of behaviour it's all
my fault; yet when they're good or succeed at something it's
because he's been such a positive influence on their lives. I am,
of course, irrelevant. I feel like I'm walking on eggshells and
never know when I'm going to say something that'll trigger a
fight. Lola is always his darling girl. She can do no wrong. But
Frankie gets it in the neck for everything although I do have to
admit she has attitude with a capital A. He's now started on the
'you'd-better-really-knuckle-down-to-those-exams-this-year-
and-get-good-grades-unless-you-want-to-end-up-on-the-dustbin-
of-life' line, which isn't even true. He had to resit A levels
before they would let him into law school, and what a mistake
that was.

    Dr Ian 'Finlay' Bryson has gone on the offensive. He's
started filling my in tray with research papers that cast doubt
over alternative medicine. He wants a competition, but I haven't
got time for this so I just scrawled, *'The art of medicine consists*

of amusing the patient while nature cures the disease' (Voltaire).
Who cares how they feel better so long as they DO' in red felt-tip
across the top of today's offering. Thirty-fifteen.

Sx

What About Me, Too?

Dear Diary,

Sunday morning the 8th of September

Dad said he'd take me to the common with my bike but that's not gonna happen now because it's raining and they're rowing again. So I'm lying in my room with the door shut and a pillow over my head so that I don't have to hear them shouting at each other quite so loudly. Tom's teething and grisly, Mum's walking around with her eyes half shut and telling Dad what to do because she's too tired to do it herself and he doesn't ever like being told what to do. Mum never learns. How long have they been married? Doesn't she know anything?

They managed to get on all right last night over supper but that was probably because Frankie was doing all the talking. She was meeting Chattie (her boyfriend) to go to a club and had her hair done up in a stupid bun on the top of her head with extensions of the wrong colour sticking up like a volcano and she looked really stupid with much too much make-up on. Dad managed not to say anything at all about how she looked for once, but started on GCSEs, his pet subject of the moment. So boring when who cares whether or not she passes? I don't, anyway. Frankie sat there talking constantly about Chattie – how he's been an animal-lover since the age of five, how his mum and dad have a waterbed and take him on really exotic holidays like boat trips down the Amazon (they'd never go to a boring Greek island and lie on a beach), how his mum is such a great cook and he's thinking of painting his room a deep purple colour. We just sat there eating and listening. Tom chucked food onto the floor beneath his high chair and then peered over to have a look at it, while Frankie talked and talked and talked and hardly ate a thing. I mean I really like Chattie but she seems to think he's some sort of God or something. Why does she have to talk about him ALL the time?

I went into her room this morning to take back some of CDs which she's always stealing, and do you know what? Chattie was in bed with her and she's not supposed to do that. Mum says he can't stay the night until she's sixteen and she's still only fifteen. I went into her room and saw him there asleep, which means she sneaked him upstairs. Frankie heard me come in and pulled me towards her by the neck of my ~~peejarmers~~ ~~piejarmers~~ peegharmers and said that if I told Mum she'd take all my Sylvanians to the charity shop and that if I didn't tell Mum she'd let me borrow her make-up. What choice do I have? That's so unfair it's practically blackmail. But actually the only reason I'm going to keep quiet about this is that I like Chattie. He's really nice to me. In fact he's nicer to me than anyone else in my whole family, except Toyah (she's our au pair and she knows some really cool card games) only she's not family. And if I told, Mum might not let him back here and then Frankie would really get nasty or split up with Chattie and that would be terrible.

What About Me, Too?

Dear Diary,

Sunday evening in bed ✏️

Waiting for Mum or Dad to come and kiss me goodnight only they seem to think it's more important to shout at each other. He says she never considers him and that she's a selfish bitch. She says she never has the time to even consider herself these days and that he's a selfish bastard. They shout so loudly at each other that the whole street can practically hear. It makes me feel all shivery. I just want to dive under the duvet. If they start to talk about divorce I'm going to have to think seriously about running away to stop them. I could go to Granny's if she wasn't in a home. I wouldn't want to go to Granny and Grandpa Wilcox because they're so mean they'd send me straight back, and anyway they live in Yorkshire and I don't know how to get there. Clare's house is too close and I'd have to hide in their Wendy house so that her mum wouldn't find me. That's the trouble with being a child. There's no place else to go. But if I did run away like Frankie did it would make them work together to find me, rather than argue like this all the time. Anything's got to be better than this.

From: Sue James
Sent: Sunday 8 September 22:15
To: Angela James
Subject: Re: Not in front of the children

You're right and we try (although it is hard to put a lid on your emotions and delay rowing until they're out of earshot), but children are also much more resilient than adults usually give them credit for. Tom's too young to understand and Lola just bubbles along with her friends (both real and imaginary). But Frank does worry me because she's so moody and volatile, this is her GCSE year and the events of last spring still haunt me. HND won't let me forget anyway. She cornered me in the playground on Friday morning and pressed this leaflet into my hand about a series of workshops on managing difficult teenagers. 'I thought it might be useful,' she whispered conspiratorially, 'and how is Frankie at the moment?' (There was then this pause when she almost said, 'Still shoplifting/binge-drinking/bunking off school?') As if I'd tell her. Do you think you can get ASBOs served on your neighbours for being nosey? So I lied and said she's been predicted with a fistful of As and A*s and had she seen the latest medical research which suggests that eating at least two pineapples a day improves the cognitive abilities of children. That got her thinking. I could see her eyes sparkle with ambition. The woman's so stupid she believed me and now poor Clare, who won't touch any form of fruit or vegetable, will have to endure her mother's force-feeding. Hopefully we'll hear a few more rows coming from her side of the party wall as Clare resists. And then imagine all that sticky mess! HND can't even stand crumbs. She'll be bulk-buying detox and redecorating the house before Christmas . . .

The main problem with Matthew is that even though he is back, it's hard to feel he really wants to be here, with me, rather than with the fresh young thing he fucked repeatedly when I was pregnant. He's back in body but not in spirit and spends most of his time jogging or reading the newspaper, rather than helping out with Tom. Having a baby is never easy, but when you're over forty, working and have two other children . . . It is so much harder than I ever remember it being last time. Someone always gets forgotten. I left Tom strapped into his buggy on the front path for nearly an hour this morning because the phone rang as we came in and the wind blew the front door shut. I'd been up half the night on call trying to calm down a woman with indigestion who was convinced she was having a heart attack and I was just so deranged from sleep deprivation and eager to load up the washing machine that I completely forgot I had a son until Lola said, 'Where's Tom?' Things should improve on the call front next month. We're about to hand our 'call' system over to council management – dynamic new practice manager is putting much more efficient systems in place – and I can't wait. I'm too old for it. The younger doctors who need more work to pay their mega first-time-buyer mortgages can do it. I never want to have to walk through poorly lit estates in the middle of the night again, worrying about whether I'm about to be mugged by some moron in a hooded sweatshirt who thinks (mistakenly) that I'm carrying drugs.

We're more like two old warring friends sharing a house, squabbling over who last cleaned the communal kitchen or bought the milk, rather than a married couple sharing a life. Whatever we say to each other – even the simplest things – get misinterpreted. It's as if there's more now that has to be left unsaid than said to keep the peace and that just widens the distances between us. It's like I don't really know him any more, I don't know what he's thinking about, what's going on in his life and, you know what, Ange, I miss being how we used to be, curled up and carefree. I miss feeling cared for, I miss laughing with him. I miss the way we used to talk late at night in bed when the children were small and we still held all those illusions about the immutable rock-solid nature of family life.

I don't feel sexy any more either, which is not something I could admit to anyone else. Frankie just oozes sexuality at the moment. She looks fantastic and when Chattie's around they can't stop touching each other, which is lovely (I don't *think* she's actually sleeping with him yet – she did promise me that she'd wait until she was sixteen), but their ebullient sexuality just makes me feel like a dried up, fat old hag. Although it is hard to imagine the dried up stick insect next door shagging on the dining-room table. She doesn't even eat off it. In fact, does she even eat? Imagine depriving yourself of one of life's greatest pleasures ALL THE TIME and then having to run up a sweat on one of those stupid gym machines AT LEAST THREE TIMES A WEEK so that you can defy the inexorable way time slaps fat upon your bottom and stay sexually appealing and then not even get laid . . . I bet she finds doughnuts more sexually arousing than Robert . . . Now there's a thought – he's much too nice for her . . . only joking . . .

What About Me, Too?

It's late and I'm knackered and I really ought to go to bed. It's just comforting talking to you this way. I think emails allow us to say things to people that we would find hard to vocalize face to face or on the phone. A bit like writing in a diary only this one is two-way. Even though you're not with me, we can stay close. I can't really talk about this to anyone other than Julie, who's being a complete brick, such a loyal friend, but promise that from now on my emails will NOT WINGE. It's shameful really, when we're lucky to have so much.

Much love to those precious nephews of mine. JPEG a lovely pic of them and I'll get it to Mum, which reminds me that we must actually think about whether we're going to keep her at North Butting, but I haven't got the energy for that now. I'll ping you in the week. Planning to go see her next weekend.

Much love,
Sxxxxxxxxxxxxxxxxxxxxxxxxxxxxxxxxxxxxxxxxxxxxxxxxx

Kate Figes

Dear Diary,

It's hard sometimes to see the point of boys or parents. They're arguing so much that maybe they really were happier apart. Lola's so pissed off with them that she said, 'I really don't know HOW I can go on living with you,' at supper tonight and Mum just laughed, which of course just pissed Lola off even more. I mean, don't they know anything? And then boys just give us more grief. Why is love so difficult exactly? I mean, I love Chattie, I know I do but I don't wanna be with him like every minute for the rest of my life. And then when we're not together he texts and calls me the whole time, asking me what I'm doing and it feels like he wants to hoover me up, like I can't even think my own private thoughts any more without telling him. I couldn't believe that I was actually pleased when he went to Scotland this weekend and I could spend some time with Ruby. There was this really fit man at the club who looked like a cross between Johnny Depp and Orlando Bloom and he even took my number but then I felt like so guilty about that because I shouldn't want to even think about someone else if I love Chattie. Is fifteen too young to settle down? Ruby, Fran and the others think so but then they're just jealous and we have been going out for nine months and sixteen days and that's nearly a fifteenth of my whole life so it feels like forever.

I'm starting a diary again to try and work out what I really want from life and love because I just don't understand boys. They're like so weird. We want them to like us so that we feel real but then when they get too close it's like being in a crowded room with a whole load of freaks who aren't interested in anything other than sucking your tongue out of your head and squeezing your tits. When I'm not with Chattie, like over the summer when we didn't see each other for twenty-nine whole days, I think I'm going to die I miss him so much. No wonder Juliet killed herself when she discovered that Romeo was already dead. What was she going to do, go back to her family???

Dear Diary,

Wednesday the 11th of September

I asked Clare yesterday if she wanted to come to my house
after school today but she said that she couldn't and ran off
with Tanya. She's probably got a clarinet lesson or a tutor
coming. There's always someone there helping her with
exams papers which is mad because she's always getting
stars for her work and it's always her work that gets read
out in class because it's so good because her mum writes it
for her. Then when I asked her at break time today if I
could borrow her coloured pencils she said no and 'isn't it
time that neglectful mother of yours bought you a crop top
and some sani pads?' and then ran off laughing with Tanya.
THEN at lunchtime today, they were standing by the door
when I was coming out of the toilets, waiting for me and
Tanya said, 'It must be hard having a sister who's a thief
and a drug addict' and I wanted to punch her lights out. So
I shouted 'bitch' back and tried not to cry and she said she
was going to tell Mr Burt that I'd been swearing. HOW
NASTY IS THAT? I don't think she did though because he
didn't say anything. Tanya's horrible. I don't care what she
does but I thought Clare was my friend. Camilla said I
could borrow her pencils all afternoon, but I don't like to
borrow off her because she's so much poorer than we are
and only has one foot.

What About Me, Too?

Dear Diary,

Still Wednesday the 11th of September

Mum and Dad were arguing over supper as if I wasn't there. Frankie was out seeing *Romeo and Juliet* with the school because she's studying it for her GCSEs. Tom was asleep so I just sat there with my hands over my ears, feeling sick and unable to eat. They were arguing about such stupid stuff as well, like who cares about who does what with Tom so long as he's happy, and what does it matter whether or not they love each other provided they're here? When Mum came home tonight from work I asked her if she'd take me shopping at the weekend and she just sighed and said, 'We'll see, maybe,' which means we won't. I'd like to get some baggy tops so that no one else notices that I'm growing breasts. When Frankie's here, which is almost never, I do at least feel as if there's someone else to talk to, someone to take the rap before me. But when she's gone it's just me and them and their stupid quarrels. They don't even think about the fact that I might not want to hear them shouting at each other. Dad gets so angry about things. He gets angry when he can't find a clean shirt in the morning, angry when he trips over Tom's toys, angry when he's late for work, angry when we're stuck in a traffic jam. The worst though is when he gets angry with me just because I've asked him to help me with something and he hasn't got the time to help me or he doesn't know the answer and won't admit it. I don't see why he has to get cross about it. The very VERY VERY worst though is when he gets so cross that he makes Mum cry like he did when he left. I really, really hate that. It's so scary. Mum always had a rule when we were younger. No fighting in the car because it's dangerous and she didn't want to have to hear us. Well I don't see why I should have to listen to them fighting while I'm trying to eat my dinner. When it looked like it might be getting to the point where Mum was gonna cry, I pushed the plate away, got down from the table and ran up to Frankie's room. I don't think they even noticed that I'd gone.

What About Me, Too?

From: Sue James
Sent: Friday 13 September 22:16
To: Angela James
Subject: Re: Her cheek is gobsmacking

HND has been round this evening stirring . . . She claims that Lola called Clare a 'fucking bitch' at break time yesterday. I wanted to say, 'She has a point, she must get it from you,' but managed to bite my lip just in time. They've only been back at school a week and already she's started on a brand-new season of perfectionism – ironing and labelling Clare's socks, writing and correcting homework before it's handed in, testing her spelling in the bath and indulging her every whim, for Little Miss Perfect must have everything her perfect mother wants. The summer holidays are such bliss because there's nobody around to judge your children or your failings as a mother. But as soon as they go back to school everything is on show – the contents of your lunch box, faded, tatty un-ironed clothes, last year's trainers, dishevelled hair. All of these things just scream one thing to the mothers at the school gate – crap working mother; poor neglected child. I refuse to let the anorexic food-deprived bitch make me feel guilty, though. So I stood there with my arm firmly braced against the front door so that she couldn't come in and see the pile of dirty dishes in the sink or Tom, still up and smashing wooden bricks against the sitting-room window, and told her that it was important to take everything kids say with a pinch of salt.

'They all say things they shouldn't in the playground. That's just what children do.'

'Well, I think she should apologize to Clare and that you should punish her.'

'Do you?' I replied. 'And what did Clare do to provoke this insult?'

'Clare? Nothing! Nothing at all!'

Of course, Little Miss Perfect can do no wrong. It's never her child, always someone else's. So I said I'd have a word with Lola in the morning (I could hear her listening through the banisters on the landing) and shut the door firmly in HND's face. Lola denies the whole incident and seemed upset by the fact that Clare had even said such a thing. It's hard to imagine Lola saying anything like that to Clare when she adores her. So we put 'Dancing in the Street' on at top volume, pressed the speakers close to the party wall and danced and screamed along to make sure she got the point that we didn't care. Thanks for the pics – love the one of you and Spike hugging in the garden – you look so happy and so well. Will try and ping in properly over the weekend.

Sxx

What About Me, Too?

Dear Diary,

Saturday the 14th of September

Yesterday was Friday the 13th and so of course it was unlucky. Clare's Mum's been round and said I swore at Clare and used the 'F' word, which is like the worst thing anybody could ever do according to Clare's mum, that and having sex with a woman. She also said it wasn't surprising, given how much Frankie swears. But I never did; I may have called her a bitch because she was being really horrible about Camilla and laughing at the way she smells and limps but I would never have called her a fucking bitch. It's now totally obvious that Clare doesn't like me any more. She's never told her mum anything like that before. She told her because she wants to make her fight with my mum.

From: Sue James
Sent: Sunday 15 September 23:12
To: Angela James
Subject: Re: Re: Her cheek is gobsmacking

Ange darling,

I know, new mums are dreadful when it comes to judging each other, and it gets even worse once their kids go to primary school. But then HND is not normal. How can any woman who spends the best part of each week in beauty salons having bikini waxes and her lips plumped with botox be normal? She's been round this morning to fan the flames rather than extinguish them and maintains that Lola has stolen things from Clare's pencil case and that was what has provoked the row. The very idea that Lola would do such a thing is laughable. She even said that she thought Lola should pay for the replacements. Not only has Clare's mother decided who the criminal is (out of a class of thirty), she has also decided on the punishment. No wonder Lola called her daughter a 'fucking bitch'. The words were on the tip of my own tongue.

Glad you and Spike are happy – that's as it should be. He's lucky to have you and should cherish you . . . and you may be right that this is just what happens to a couple when they have been married this long, but if that's just the way things go then it's awful. How can any two marriages remotely resemble one another when it's made up of two distinct individuals, and the chemistry is bound to be different in each one as a result? All I know is that what we had once was very good and that somehow seventeen years later, three children, conflicting work pressures and middle age have come between us. Maybe we do just have to tread water for a while to get through this bit. What I resent is being at the other end of his bitterness at life and growing older and feeling trapped. Everything is my fault. Everything.

He's also drinking too much and last night's display on about a gallon of gin was further than he's ever gone before. Frankie had Ruby and Saskia here. Chattie was away with his parents and she wanted a girly sleepover with a couple of videos. When they were in the kitchen, Matthew kept standing right behind Saskia (who is tall and very beautiful) and nudged her in this excruciatingly embarrassing horseplay way with his shoulder, giggling like he was a teenage girl himself, trying to get in with them. Then when they were in the bathroom, mucking about with make-up and having a lovely time, Matthew barged in too and cranked up the flirtation by calling them 'sex kittens', commenting on their bodies and touching up Saskia's bum. Frankie had the sense to shout at him, kick him out and lock the door, but it was bloody embarrassing for her and if Saskia's parents ever find out I expect the police'll be round. His flirtations with her friends when he's sober are bad enough, but last night's behaviour was offensive. When I tried to talk to him about it this morning (after his jog, of course), we had yet another row and he told ME to stop being such a fussy old woman and that Frankie had known it was just a harmless bit of fun.

Then in the scale of life and death, how important is this? All that matters is Matthew. Out there in the rest of the world life goes on, or tries to anyway, against all odds. Last week I had one death of someone not yet forty, one suspected case of domestic violence, two hernias, five cases of genital warts and about 16,000 squillion tummy upsets in children who didn't want to go back to school. On Friday I had a distraught woman in my surgery who clearly had a large breast tumour, almost certainly malignant. The hard-nosed bitch in me wanted to say, 'Oh well, never mind, it's curtains then. Have you made a will? Organized counselling for the kids yet?' because it was obvious that this woman's life was swiftly drawing to a close. Her lump was massive. But actually I had to calm her down with fake reassurance: 'It's probably nothing, most lumps are benign but we'll make you an appointment at the breast clinic just to make sure...' And then yesterday I went to visit eighty-two-year-old Fred who is dying of lung cancer. He hasn't been to a doctor in forty years and then gets me. Lucky him. He has no one really in the world, doesn't say much and since he's hardly been a drain on health service resources I felt he of all people deserved more of the caring, sharing side of me. So I put on my halo, sat by his bed, held his hand and said, 'Is there anything else I can do for you?' trying to sound like I really cared.

'Short of a fucking miracle, no,' he replied. I laughed all the way home because for once the patient had the last laugh. Pretty hard to be loving and wifely then to Matthew because he's pulled a ligament fucking jogging...

Escape looms on the horizon. There's a two-day conference on euthanasia in Paris next month and none of the other partners can go, except, of course, Ian Bryson who is fervently anti – so I made damn sure I was the one who got to go.

What About Me, Too?

I might need it myself sooner rather than later. Seriously, it's going to be so damn good to be alone again with nobody to think about for a whole forty-eight hours other than myself, AND it'll be my first night away from Tom – hard but it's gotta be done. Every now and then, usually when there's a boring patient droning on about such unspecific ailments that it's hard to know what to diagnose them with, I drift off and fantasize about these forty-eight hours of escape – early morning breakfast on Eurostar . . . read every page of the paper in peace . . . a little shopping . . . good night's sleep in a hotel . . . perhaps even with a strange Parisian (do you think I dare after all these years?) . . . interesting, poignant subject for a conference which is of direct relevance to us (when do we kill off Mum?) . . . I'm going to see her after work on Wednesday and will try and give you a full breakdown of her ailments then.

Much love, Suexxxxxxxxxx

Dear Diary,

Clare is a complete liar. I never NEVER NEVER NEVER took anything from her pencil case. Why would I do that? I can't believe she said that about me. All I ever wanted was to be her friend. What's really totally horrible about this situation is that it means I can't ever go over and see her like I used to and they've just been in their garden with her mum fussing over her the whole time about wearing a hat and putting suncream on and sitting in the shade because it's been a really hot weekend, and Clare could see me through the fence in our garden but she never said a thing. It makes me feel so alone. We were best friends. And now if we're not any more I don't know what to do, who to be with.

What About Me, Too?

From: Sue James
Sent: Wednesday 18 September 23:56
To: Angela James
Subject: Mum

She seems very frail, complained a lot about her joints aching and laid on the guilt about how nobody comes to see her much. She claims that the old lady in the next room has her entire family visit her every Sunday. Not sure whether to believe that. Anyway, I gave her a quick once over – pulse and blood pressure fine, but her throat's red, glands slightly inflamed and I think she had a bit of a temperature so asked Matron to get her some antibiotics.

She's miserable, that's the honest truth of it, Ange, and I just feel so bad about her being there, surrounded by incontinent, batty old women. I have to hold a scarf over my mouth for the first ten minutes I'm there to get used to the smell and, given how much I have to smell in my line of work, that's saying something. And that's just the people. The smell of lunch makes me want to throw up. Crap pap without a single vitamin. It's got to be the most depressing thing on earth for her knowing that this is it, her last home, when intellectually she's still all there. The painting keeps her amused but it's not enough. Almost everybody she's ever known is dead, which must make her feel very lonely. She said on Sunday that she couldn't remember what Auntie Mabel's brother was called and how there wasn't anybody around to ask any more, nobody to

33

remember old times with so what was the point in living at all. I tried to reassure her that actually it didn't really matter what Auntie Mabel's brother was called, but I can see that if you have no one to share the past with then you don't have much future.

I think we should move her. Actually, we're all she has left. There's Uncle David but he's next to useless and uninterested in her, and I know she can be the most infuriating person on earth at times but who knows how much longer we'll have of her? If she was closer, I could sort of pop in more. I'm going to do a search of available places nearer us this week and let you know what I come up with.

Other than that everything's fine. Frank seems much more settled and happy although she's been out a lot and came back at one in the morning on Tuesday. I hadn't a clue where she was and her mobile was off so had to lay down the law a bit there — she has to be in now during school nights to revise and out only on Fridays and Saturdays, unless there's a birthday party or something special in the week, which will of course happen surprisingly often. I ask her occasionally if she's up-to-date with her coursework and just get 'Fuck off,' or 'Mind your own business,' so who knows how it's really going.

Woke to ominous rattling of the letter box. Relations with HND are rock-bottom — got a letter from her complaining about Tom's toys in the garden (she says the plastic looks garish) as well as the noise (presumably she hears the rows or is it the music? I make a point of putting on 'Dancing in the Street' at top volume now every evening about five minutes after I spot the tutor arriving). Well fuck her. I am still so incensed by her accusing Lola of stealing that I want to firebomb her entire house but Frankie just said we should

frame all her letters and hang them in the downstairs bog for a
laugh. Brilliant idea, I think. Let her rant and have a heart attack
– the woman's bonkers anyway. I seriously think she's got
Munchausen's by proxy. She thinks she's doing the right thing
by her daughter but actually she's turning her only child into a
spoilt brat who will be unable to relate to the rest of the
normal world as an adult. That child has more money than she
knows what to do with. She ought to start saving it up for all
the drugs she's going to want in a few years' time just to be
able to cope with the fact that she has a mother like that. Clare
already looks pale and haunted with dark rings under her eyes
from all the extra work and pressure involved in getting her
through the entrance exams. Lola says she has a tutor every
day and that she's not allowed to watch any television at all.
Apparently they're reading *Pride and Prejudice* (or is it *Sense and
Sensibility*?) together in bed at night so that Clare can talk
knowledgeably about adult literature at interviews. She is the
sort of mother who believes that her child is so special that the
rest of the world has to be bored by her accomplishments. You
don't have to meet her to know her. Framed photographs of
every different stage of her development line the hall walls and
her mother has been known to make her perform excruciating
pieces on her clarinet in front of dinner guests. So I guess she's
perfect fodder for private education as well as anorexia and
heroin addiction, and even though I'd rather die than
compromise my principles by sending Lola to anything other
than a state school, I do wonder sometimes whether I'm
holding her back.

If anything it's easier this way with a full-scale war because I
don't have to make the effort to be nice to that ghastly woman,

but I do worry about Lola. I keep asking her how things are with Clare and I just get 'fine' in return, but I sense it isn't. There's not that constant chatter with her or about her. Whenever anything happened it was always must tell Clare, must show Clare, or can I go to Clare's and I haven't heard that once since term started.

Anyway, yawning now so must abed.

Much love, Suexxxxxxxxxxxxxxxxxx

What About Me, Too?

Dear Diary,

I hate Dad almost as much as I hate Mr Toogood. Too bad he has a name like Toogood and has to teach PE. Mum says she had a teacher once called Mrs Titcomb. Imagine that in our school. She'd have to change her name to Jones. Mr Toogood caught me bunking off PE today and when I told him it was because I had history coursework to catch up on he said that was irrelevant and gave me a detention. Well how is PE relevant when I don't even have to sit a GCSE in the poxy subject anyway? And DAD! First he behaves like some sort of sex maniac around my friends and then when he talks to me it's always about exams like they are the only thing in the whole world that matter when I would have thought world poverty and the AIDS crisis in Africa were far more important. He can't stop going on about them, talked the whole time about the importance of spacing revision at supper tonight, so now I feel really stressed about it when they haven't even started yet because he like EXPECTS me to get As and A*s when I'm not even sure I'll be good enough to even pass. I wish he'd just lay off me, lay off my friends and think of ways to help me like giving me more money, buying me the right books and generally improve the quality of my life. And stop rowing with Mum. She may be unattractive with crap hair but she doesn't deserve this sort of treatment. He ought to show her a lot more respect. So we had a big row about that and now my throat's sore from screaming and I hate him.

Dear Diary,

Monday the 23rd of September

Dad took me out today. He got me some clothes at Gap, which I really like, and a pencil case just like Clare's and then he took me out for some spaghetti carbonara and a Coke, which is great because Mum never ever buys Coke at home. She says it's bad for us, full of sugar and caffeen. It's nice to be out alone with Dad, much better than going ANYWHERE with Mum who is just so embarrassing. She always talks in this really loud voice so that EVERYBODY looks at us and then when we're shopping she's always so mean, complaining about how much things cost and fishing around in the bottom of her (tatty) purse for change so that she doesn't have to break into ten-pound notes. But it's also kind of scary being out with Dad because he used to take me out on my own for treats when he moved out. He went all gooey while I was trying to eat and put me off my food by telling me how much he loved me even if he was fighting with Mum, which makes me think that he might be about to leave us again. Even if they're rowing, it's better for all of us if he's here. Mum can't cope without him.

Clare and Tanya have started wearing large hoopy earrings like they're twins or in a club or something, a club I'll never be able to join because Mum'll never let me have my ears pierced. She says it's barbarik and that if I really want to do it I can have them pierced when I'm a teenager and pay for it myself. Like I'm ever going to be able to do that with my huge collection of money, I don't think. When

What About Me, Too?

Clare saw my new pencil case she accused me of copying her which is like soooooo mean and then she said she was going to get her Mum to buy her a different one at the weekend and I wasn't to copy her. She thinks she's so cool just because her mother buys her stuff, anything she likes, but she isn't, she's just spoilt and even if we were richer and I got loads of pocket money I wouldn't drop my best friend like she has.

From: Sue James
Sent: Wednesday 25 September 20:32
To: Angela James
Subject: Re: Mum

Dearest Ange,

Just a quick recap on the mother situation. The options seem limited. Three out of the four homes that I've tracked down near us I saw last time and didn't like them much then. So I've made an appointment to see a new home (which has just opened on the other side of Richmond Park) on Saturday. It's more expensive but if it's at all nice I'll start working on her about moving. The change will be difficult but exciting too, give her something to focus on, plus it really is less than an hour from here, which will make all the difference. I can even cycle there and turn into a new slimline me. If it's no good I'm thinking of going back to see two of the ones I've seen before. The third was so awful I still feel bad about not having reported it – grotty, damp, probably wouldn't pass a health and safety check and everyone looked even more miserable, starved, heavily sedated and dead than Mum. I've talked to her at length three times since the weekend about all this but she keeps forgetting and then when the penny drops she says she's only going to move to Australia to live with you and gets cross when I tell her that's not possible. This evening she even had the nerve to say that I never cared for her as much as you do, which made me so mad I think I would probably have smothered her if I'd been there (suffocation by binliner, I'm told, is the most effective method). Would I be doing all this research into a home nearer here if I didn't care about making her life nicer???

I'll let you know the latest at the weekend.

Hope all's well. Sxxxxxxxxxxxx

Dear Diary,

Friday the 27th of September

Sorry I haven't been able to write in you all week but it's
been a busy time. Miss Jennings finally arrived on Tuesday
and I really like her. She's tall and pretty and much younger
than any of the other teachers and she's changed everything
immediately. She's reorganized all the desks into a large
circle, with hers at the top, which means that I'm not sitting
next to Camilla any more. It goes girl/boy/girl/boy now and
I'm between Mickey (yuk) and Kieran (yuk! YUK! YUK!).
I ~~think~~ know absolutely certainly that I'd rather be next to
Camilla, because Kieran has behavioural problems. He finds
it really hard to concentrate and keeps rapping his ruler
against the desk. Miss Jennings makes us discuss things a
lot more and at the end of each day we have to hold hands
and say a sort of prayer, thanking each other for the day
and promising to give our best the next day. I don't like
having to hold Kieran's hand (yuk) but I kind of like it, the
words I mean. And when Clare's mobile went today, her
mother once again checking up on her, Miss Jennings
konfiscated it for the rest of the day. YESSSSS! Clare was
furious and says she hates her now and no doubt her mum
will be complaining on Monday.

Miss Jennings wants us to start a project on what life
was like for Victorian children, which is really interesting.
I've found 3,212 websites on Google to go through already!
I think I'm going to do something on poor children because
they had such difficult lives and had to look after

themselves. Gangs of children roamed the streets just like they do now and they didn't go to school, they didn't HAVE school (lucky them, they didn't have to suffer people like Tanya). But poor them, they had to work in factories from five in the morning until nine at night and they were so tired when they got home at night that they collapsed on their beds, too tired to eat. And then the really poor ones roamed the streets looking for work and stealing and then if they got caught by the police, for stealing or sleeping in barrels, they were sent to PRISON or places called workhouses where they were beaten and treated very badly. But they all had each other, like in *Oliver Twist* and made really good friends. And sang about soup.

Dear Diary,

Saturday the 28th of September ✏

Mum's gone to visit a new home for Granny with Tom, Frankie is asleep and Dad has gone jogging AGAIN. I haven't seen him all week because he's been working late and now he's gone jogging which means he'll come back all sweaty and disgusting and tired so he's not going to be much fun. He says he's training to run in the marathon but he just looks SO disgusting in those giant trainers with that stupid sweatband around his forehead that I never ever want to be seen out in public with him looking like that. What is the point of jogging anyway, because you don't actually run anywhere, you just roam the streets and the common looking like some disgusting outsize schoolboy with hairy legs, like some sort of disgusting peddle file. Honestly, he's worse than Kieran.

I just heard Frankie laughing with Ruby in her room so I went up to talk to them, but she shouted at me to go away and told me to leave her stuff alone. I've decided to spy on them and then if they say anything interesting I'll write it down and leave this diary around so that Mum might just happen to read it.

What I Have Found Out, Which Is A Lot

1) Frankie has had sex with Chattie, but thinks that's OK because they are in a loving stable relationship. (Mum definitely doesn't know this.)

2) It hurt at first (yuk).

3) Ruby hasn't had sex yet because she hasn't even had a boyfriend but she's thinking about finding someone to have sex with so that she can know what it's like.

4) Saskia has finally started her period. But she probably won't be having another one because although she says she's on a diet she actually has anorexia because of her mother who is an obsessive apparently. Frankie says she's much too controlling and obsessed with her own looks and that that gets transferred down (so no danger of that here 'cos Mum's hair is a scruffy mess and she doesn't even wear make-up to cover up the bags under her eyes). Ruby disagrees and says you can't blame everything on her mother, when Saskia never takes any responsibility for anything she says or does.

5) Hayley got really really drunk last night and was vomiting all over the bath at this party and they had to take her outside and walk her up and down the street about 600 times so that she sobered up. Ruby and Frankie were really bitching about her, said they couldn't believe how Saskia and Hayley always drank so much (like they don't, oh yeah???) and how trashy their clothes are becoming and if they weren't careful they were gonna end up pregnant and disowned by their parents before they even took their GCSEs, which they will probably fail anyway. But they did think that it was a good idea to buy some fake ID off the Internet so that they can get into pubs and clubs. Saskia and Hayley have and it works. Mum DEFINITELY doesn't know this.

For breakfast they ate six doughnuts, a packet of Jaffa Cakes and a carton of juice. They complained that the milk was off. Then Dad came back from jogging and started having a go at them about the state of the kitchen. So they pushed off (don't blame them) but without clearing anything up, which made him even more cross. So I made Dad a cup of tea to try and keep him happy, just how he likes it – warmed the pot and used real tea because Dad thinks that tea bags taste disgusting and Mum never has the time to make a proper pot. I left it to stand for exactly three minutes and then poured it through a strainer. He seemed really pleased with it and gave me a huge sweaty cuddle but then he left it on the table to go cold because he spent hours texting someone who kept texting him back and then he got himself a beer out of the fridge.

What About Me, Too?

Dear Diary,

If Dad's so neurotic and obsessed with health that he has to go jogging all of the time then he ought to know that it's stress that kills people and he's stressing me out. I'm the one with the exams. I'm the one who needs his undivided support and attention so that I don't stab myself with a kitchen knife in a pit of gloom, but what does he do? Shouts at me for not wiping the table. (How much does a table really matter? More than your own daughter?) He shouts at Mum when she's stressed out enough from work and Tom as it is (if it weren't for Toyah I'd be the one doing EVERYTHING around here), while spoilt, precious Lola can do no wrong. He's the one who needs to go back to school and study psychology because even Saskia's dad knows that you're not supposed to favour one child over another, and he's an idiot. Sometimes this house makes me so MAD that I want to kick in the walls. No wonder teenagers drink themselves stupid. With them rowing all of the time, stressing each other out and stressing me it's kind of hard to concentrate and then Mum wants to know why I'm out all the time – ANYWHERE but here. What really gets me is that he thinks he has the monopoly on stress when from where I stand he has a great life – he has money, a job, he knows what he's doing with his life whereas I have huge loads of information chucked at me every day, information I'm supposed to remember and I'm constantly being told that what I do now could affect my whole life. Imagine Dad having to live with that! He'd be lean all day as well as all night.

From: Sue James
Sent: Sunday 29 September 10:16
To: Angela James
Subject: Re: Re: Mum

Dear Heart,

Clarice's nursing home is practically palatial – incredibly expensive but so nice I'd like to book myself in for a week or two of institutionalized respite care. Major cat fight last night over a bloody mobile phone! Frankie couldn't find hers and wanted to go out so the whole house had to be overturned looking for it. First she accused Matthew of stealing it (she thinks her text messages are *that* interesting), then she had a go at me about the house looking like a rubbish tip which was why she couldn't find it and then the harmless question, when had she last seen it, provoked a torrent of expletives and explosive anger because the fact that SHE had lost her own mobile phone wasn't the issue here, everybody else was to blame. Were we like that? I suppose we were. It's funny how she seems perfectly sensible and grown-up one minute and then becomes an irrational, certifiable monster the next. Mind you, I suppose you could equally well apply that description to Matthew and me at times.

Turned out that Lola had it all along. She was lying on her bed playing games on it and made out that she hadn't heard the rest of us taking the house apart to find it. Frankie snatched it from her, Lola claimed she'd hurt her in the process and then said she was deprived because she hadn't got one. DEPRIVED! The very idea of a child in primary school having a mobile phone makes me feel ill. They definitely aren't good for us; ear, nose and throat doctors say that they are seeing a rise in the numbers coming in with tumours, and we're surrounded by microwaves now with all these wretched masts. Incredibly, there's even evidence that the youth of the future will have larger than average thumbs! At least there's a point with teenagers in that you feel they're safer with them than without them. I expect Clare's got one, naturally.

Anyway, Clarice's ... There's a lovely sitting room overlooking a well-stocked garden, lunch smelled delicious and the bedrooms were light and spacious – plenty of room for all Mum's pictures and things. Only trouble is the cost, practically double what we pay for North Butting, but I figure it's worth it just for the peace of mind. After I've paid out for Mum and Toyah there's next to nothing for me, but actually I feel so guilty about Mum, I'd rather know she was being well looked after than buy a new dress. Obviously it's hard for you to judge without seeing it but maybe have a think about what you feel about this financially and let me know ...

Bell just rang ... HND round to ask me what I thought of the new teacher, who of course I haven't had time to meet, but then she only arrived last week. For one awful moment I thought she might have got wind of the fact that I left Tom behind in the playground when I dropped Lola off at school on Friday morning. I was busy chatting with another working mum (always a relief to have an ally at the school gate). I kissed Lola goodbye when the bell went and then walked out in 'going to work' mode. It was only when Karen (the lawyer I'd been talking to) came hurtling out of the gate, wheeling Tom's buggy in front of her and collapsed in a heap of laughter when she caught up with me on the corner that I realized what I'd done – again! Honestly, if I had four kids (and believe me, I never will!) I'd be in real trouble with the social services. So I put on my best face with HND just in case she had seen this appalling incident and was about to use it against me, but oh what joy! She just wanted to discuss how worried she is about the new teacher's working methods – she makes them sit in a circle to say a New Age prayer at the beginning and end of each day and she's already confiscated Clare's mobile phone (hooray, so she DID have one), when Clare apparently needs it on permanently so that her Munchausen's mother can keep tabs on her the whole time. Now apparently the teacher plans to take them on a team-building activities week after half-term which is *exactly* when Clare will be sitting grade 605 in clarinet. First I've heard of it, the trip, I mean, clearly not the clarinet, because of course the child's a genius. Must go through Lola's bag and see if there's a letter hiding in there and see what she's on about . . .

Sorry to hear that Stan's been quite poorly, high temperatures can be really worrying and yes, it probably is only a question of time before Ollie gets it too, but you could be lucky. Tom has been surprising well so far, no change-of-season cold yet. He just gets fatter and fatter and shows no interest in learning to crawl at all. He sits there like a little Buddha, clapping his hands, babbling away on his teething ring, waiting for the next meal. But what is it with boys, sis? Yesterday he picked up a paint brush, pointed it at me and very clearly said 'BANG'.

Much love, Sxxxxxxxxxxxxxxxxxxxxxxxxxxxxxx

What About Me, Too?

Dear Diary,

Wednesday the 2nd of October

It's Tanya's birthday today and she's having a party on
Saturday. All the girls in the class are invited except for
Camilla and me, which means that Clare's mum is going to
let her go, but she won't let her come over to my house
which is just next door. I know I shouldn't mind because
you can't have everybody in the class to a party but it seems
a bit mean to leave two out. I didn't invite her to my
treshure hunt last year but it's just that they're all talking
about it – she's having a disco and Clare makes a point of
saying how much fun they're going to have in front of me
so that I hear and feel left out. Today she and Tanya and
Britney were playing this game in the playground,
pretending to be grown-ups, and when I asked them if I
could play too they said no because I haven't got my ears
pierced. So I went off to play with Camilla. We pretended
we were poor Victorian children without any parents,
scavenging and stealing from a rich family and that we had
to turn invisible to do it, which was fun because I thought I
was the only one who likes to play imaginary games. Clare
just likes to talk about clothes and teenage stuff and all the
things she's gonna buy which just makes me feel small. But
then when Clare and Tanya noticed that we were having
fun they started following us around and imitating us and
laughing and taking the piss out of us, which is just so
unfair. They wouldn't let me play with them and instead of
leaving me alone they had to ruin our game.

From: Sue James
Sent: Thursday 3 October 21:13
To: Angela James
Subject: Re: Re: Re: Mum

I know she could live for another ten to fifteen years and that would bankrupt us but that's very unlikely. In fact, moving her could kill her. And there's a waiting list so by the time she gets to the top she could be dead anyway. However, if you can stretch to it (and if there is one advantage to being married to a banker rather than a lawyer it has to be access to money), I think we should go for it. I can't really ask Matthew to help with Mum, he has his own parents to think of in the years to come and I certainly wouldn't want to have to help him out with *them*, but you're right, he should be contributing to the cost of Toyah and he isn't at the moment. Haven't seen much of him, he's been coming in well after ten most nights. Big case on, apparently. I'll raise Toyah, diplomatically next time he's in a good mood and I'm awake, so that'll be sometime after Christmas.

Frankie's been on the phone for an hour and a half and is driving me MAAAADDDD!! She dyed her hair pink last night, as well as all the towels and the walls in the bathroom – there are pink splashes everywhere and neither Toyah nor I can get them out. AAARHHHHH!!! Fucking teenagers and their image problems . . . how insensitive of me. I know I should be much more understanding, doctor and all. Those irritating parenting handbooks for teenagers say things like, 'Keep calm and phrase things so as to make it clear why you are unhappy with their behaviour/attitude, etc.' So you're supposed to say calmly, 'I'm really upset by the way you have got pink hair dye all over the towels, the walls and the carpet. Next time will you please consider the effects of your actions,' when all I want to do is scream 'YOU SELFISH, STUPID BITCH' but that's childish apparently and likely to set back relations with an adolescent by months. It's hard to be understanding when everything I say or suggest gets trashed as 'stupid', and what would I know anyway? Every sentence Lola utters gets said slowly and broken up as if to accentuate my stupidity so it's 'So-r-r-ry' if I tick her off, 'S-o-o-o-?' if I pass comment on something and 'He-l-l-l-o-o' if I ignore her for just a minute. This morning when Lola got into bed with me, instead of cuddling up affectionately she turned her back on me and said, 'Your eyes look like deflated balloons and your breath stinks.'

Still only two weeks to go till Paris. A man resembling Sasha Distel keeps coming into my dreams . . . do you think he'll be there on the train? And then sometimes I wonder what would happen if I just didn't come back. It would be so easy just to take a train south. Disappear for a while and invent a new life. How long would it take, do you think, before they even realized I'd gone?

Dr 'Finlay' Bryson is clearly jealous that I'm going and he isn't. He's now emailing me with links to euthanasia research papers and wacko individuals/groups who bung up anti 'murdeous death by injection' stuff on the web. I'm just ignoring it. And then every now and then he likes to stick the knife in with, 'Give me a kiss.' So today I just said, 'Any time.' Honestly,

I'm at least fifteen years older than him . . . so if this is genuine sexual tension, come and get me, babe . . . I could teach you a thing or two . . . Do you think he could actually be trying to come on to me? Kind of exciting if he is, in that attraction of opposites sort of way . . .

Sx

What About Me, Too?

Dear Diary,

Sunday the 6th of October

Saw Clare leave for Tanya's party this afternoon looking just like her mother with her face all made up, her hair up in a bun, a brand-new coat which I've never seen before and these amazing high heels, which of course Mum thought were a health hazard. Her mum dragged her by the arm across the road to the car, while Clare looked back at the window and waved to me. I waved back. She waved nicely, not in a I'm-going-to-a-party-and-you're-not sort of way, which means that maybe she does still like me. When she's not with Tanya, that is. And then she tripped over (maybe Mum's right and they are a health hazard).

Mum's gone shopping. Frankie's asleep. Dad's grumpy. He's hardly said a word to me all morning except for when I was playing on his mobile phone, when he got so cross anyone would think I'd lost it or broken a window or something. Then he spent the whole time texting on it until Mum came back.

Dear Diary,

Tuesday the 8th of October

It's been a really terrible day, one of THE worst EVER.
First of all I was late for school because Mum was on the
phone to a patient and then she couldn't find Tom's
snowsuit coat thingy. I told her that I could get there on my
own but she wouldn't let me and then when I said that I
thought I was old enough to go on my own she shouted at
me for being 'lippy', whatever that means, when I was only
trying to help. Miss Jennings told me off twice, once for
being late and once because I'd forgotten to write down
some notes on the Victorians. I really like her and want her
to think well of me so it was kind of awful to be humiliated
in front of the class like that. Then at first break Kieran and
Mark started following me around the playground saying
things about my breasts like, 'Nice pair, can I feel them?' so
I punched Kieran and got into trouble with Miss Lawrence
who was on playground duty, only I wasn't going to tell her
why I punched him, and THEN at second break, when it
came to lining up to go back into the classroom, Tanya was
behind me in the line and gave me such a massive push
forward that I fell over and pushed over Camilla too, which
is not good news because of her leg situation, and THEN
when I was playing on Dad's mobile phone while he was
watching the football this text message came through which
said, 'cnt wt, need u, call me, xxxxxxx.' Can't wait for
what? It sounded really urgent so I told Dad he had a text
message and he got really cross with me, said I wasn't ever

to touch his phone again. So I read through every single one of his text messages while he was having a bath and there were literally hundreds from the same number, from someone called Laura, and all of them had kisses on them. I don't know what to do. I can't tell Mum because if Dad has got another girlfriend then she'll only get sad again. And now I can't sleep. He's gonna leave again, I know he is.

Dear Diary,

Thursday the 10th of October

Haven't seen Dad since he left for work yesterday. Mum and Frankie had a fight about money. Frankie says she needs more than Mum gives her and Mum thinks what she gives her ought to be enough. Then Frankie had a go at me about the way I apparently always put OK at the end of every sentence which is just so, so untrue and she only turned on me because she hadn't won with Mum, so I kicked her. I decided not to make things worse for Mum by telling her about Laura. I made a pot of tea instead to try and calm everyone down but it looked a bit watery. It's not my fault I was born second.

What About Me, Too?

Dear Diary,

Saturday the 12th day of October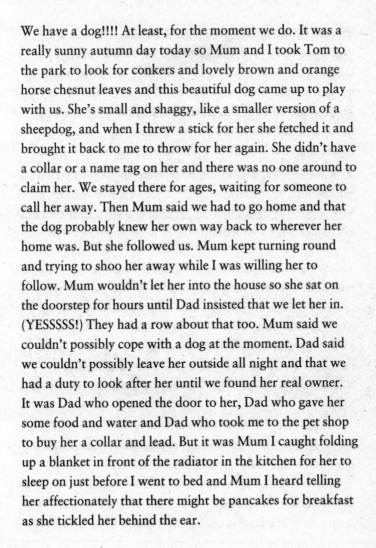

We have a dog!!!! At least, for the moment we do. It was a really sunny autumn day today so Mum and I took Tom to the park to look for conkers and lovely brown and orange horse chesnut leaves and this beautiful dog came up to play with us. She's small and shaggy, like a smaller version of a sheepdog, and when I threw a stick for her she fetched it and brought it back to me to throw for her again. She didn't have a collar or a name tag on her and there was no one around to claim her. We stayed there for ages, waiting for someone to call her away. Then Mum said we had to go home and that the dog probably knew her own way back to wherever her home was. But she followed us. Mum kept turning round and trying to shoo her away while I was willing her to follow. Mum wouldn't let her into the house so she sat on the doorstep for hours until Dad insisted that we let her in. (YESSSSS!) They had a row about that too. Mum said we couldn't possibly cope with a dog at the moment. Dad said we couldn't possibly leave her outside all night and that we had a duty to look after her until we found her real owner. It was Dad who opened the door to her, Dad who gave her some food and water and Dad who took me to the pet shop to buy her a collar and lead. But it was Mum I caught folding up a blanket in front of the radiator in the kitchen for her to sleep on just before I went to bed and Mum I heard telling her affectionately that there might be pancakes for breakfast as she tickled her behind the ear.

Dear Diary,

Sunday 🖉

Frankie wants to call her Dogged Dandy, which is a
disgusting name and bound to get shortened to Dandy or
Dog. I want to call her Chloe because I wish that was
my real name. Mum says we're not to name her at all
because she belongs to somebody else and already has a
name and she'd only get confused. So at the moment she
is 'the dog' but I call her Chloe. Dad took her out for a
walk this morning when he went jogging round the
common so he could send lovey-dovey texts to Laura.
Checked his phone while he was in the bath. She puts
at least 3,000 kisses on the end of each message AND
they're going to the cinema together on Wednesday night
which Mum of course doesn't know, which makes me feel
really bad. What's really scary, though, are his messages
to her. He says things like, 'not long now'. Not long till
what? Till he runs away with her? They must be planning
something and I don't know how to stop them. And then
there's this really weird one that I don't understand –
'Claus lusts for Fifi'. Who are they? I am desperate to tell
Mum.

Frankie lets Chloe eat all the leftovers off the plates,
which makes Mum scream at her because she says its
~~unhigeenik~~ dirty, and Tom pulls her fur whenever he
can get near her which makes Mum nervous, but Chloe
hasn't barked or snapped back. She's very patient, it's
almost as if she knows that Tom is just a baby. I've

been playing ball with her all afternoon in the garden.
I hope she stays. I think she's really good for this family.
Dad laughs when he plays with her. I really hope she
stays.

From: Sue James
Sent: Sunday 13 October 20:48
To: Angela James
Subject: We seem to have acquired a dog...

Dear Heart,

Yes, it is so ... the damn thing followed us home from the park
yesterday and I can't get rid of it. Frankie and Lola would
probably leave home if I tried. She's smallish and very pretty,
black and tan sheepdog type with intelligent eyes but a bit of a
bark which is going to piss off HND. Good. Tom insists on
grabbing at her, which means it's only a question of time before
she sinks her teeth into him and I'm up at A&E for hours
waiting for a tetanus jab, AND she'd crapped on the kitchen
floor this morning. Luckily it was a hard stool. I've put up some
'DOG FOUND' posters in the local café and at the library so
hopefully some small child will come and claim her soon so that
Lola understands that she has to let her go. But in the
meantime the whole family, including Matthew, have gone soft
in the head. I think he's doing it just to annoy me. He knows
I'm not keen on dogs and sees her arrival as a timely way to get
at me. Haven't exactly found the right moment for a
conversation about money but have decided to put Mum down
on the waiting list for Clarice's anyway and see what happens.
There's still quite a lot of her stuff in storage and she'd have a
bigger room at Clarice's. So she could take more of her things

with her and it might be time to go through the rest and either distribute to the family or sell so that we don't shoulder the cost of storage any more. I know we didn't want to do that when we moved her into North Butting because it felt so very much like killing her off before she was dead. I could go through it with Mum. It would give her something to think about and might even give her some pleasure, you never know with her. The blackest things seem to amuse her . . .

Frankie is lobbying heavily to go to something called the Virgin's Ball. Don't ask. Lola's only comment on the subject was that she bet most of them weren't. It only costs £25(!) to get in and apparently its clientele is 'exclusive', from all the 'best' London schools (which means private – good hunting ground for better boys, I suppose, as well as higher quality E and vodka). I had a look at the invite and it does look like great fun for teenagers – bands, light shows, a strict no drugs/drink policy (oh yeah?), goody bags and model scouting agencies, which means every girl'll be walking around looking gaunt and interesting in the hope of being spotted (you'd have loved it, Ange). It doesn't finish until 1.30 a.m. She says we can send a taxi to collect her. When I didn't respond with an immediate and enthusiastic 'Why, of course, dear' but stood there thinking about it, looking at the card, she lashed out with, 'You never want me to have any fun, you just want me to stay home and work. Well, I need some way of relaxing with my GCSEs coming up and I could just lie to you, you know, and stay at Ruby's and go anyway. You should be pleased that I'm actually asking your permission.' But she was only asking me in the first place because she wanted me to pay for it, only I didn't say that because I know now that only makes her storm off. It was the accusation that all I cared about was her working that really stung because of course she's right, so I said it looked fun and then she played the sympathy card by telling me that her science teacher called her 'stupid' today in front of the whole class and chucked a pen at her when she got an answer wrong. Frankie then stormed out of the room crying and got a detention for not being in class, which seems a little extreme. I thought teachers weren't allowed to do that sort of thing any more, chuck stuff, so I said yes, of course she could go to the ball and promised to ring her head of year to complain (which I'm dreading).

Time to go and turn Lola's light off and make her stop reading, which sounds ludicrous, doesn't it? Matthew took her to the library yesterday to find some books on the Victorians for her school project and she's been engrossed in them ever since. She was curled up with Chloe (ghastly name but that's what she wants to call the dog) on the sofa for most of the afternoon with her nose in a book. Occasionally she would lift her head to tell us things she thought we didn't know and ought to, such as poor children didn't go to school and had to work sweeping streets and chimneys . . . but then every now and then she would come up with something I didn't know that is really interesting. Did you know that *Oliver Twist* was one of the first novels to have a child as its central character and that when it was written policemen had been on London's streets for less than a decade?? I didn't. She's probably absorbing the high rate of venereal disease amongst child prostitutes so I'd better go . . .

Over and out, Sxxxxxxx

What About Me, Too?

Dear Diary,

There are basically three types of teachers: teachers who are so timid they can't keep control, teachers who shout all the time and then the REAL weirdos who want to be your friend. So it becomes a matter of honour to make life as difficult as possible for them to see how long it takes to get them to cry or leave. I mean if you're not actually any good at teaching then why do it? Why not go and do something else more useful? What we need are the really good ones like Mr Hollis who doesn't shout and expects respect and is basically just so nice and normal that you WANT to be good. Humming makes life difficult for some teachers because it's irritating and they can't see where its coming from. The year 7s have started doing this really cool thing, which is that whenever Miss Kelly goes SSSSHHHH! (she does it all the time), they all take off their jumpers at the same time. Then when she's really cross and goes SSSSHHH SSSSHHH twice, they put them all back on again. And then when she's scribbling rubbish all over the board someone at the back smacks their lips into a 'p' and the person at the next desk goes 'e . . . nis'. That was jokes.

Chattie and I have just had a row about this. He thinks we are immature and unkind. Well, so what? It's unkind to lock healthy, active children in these dumps and HIS trouble is that he needs to lighten up. Just texted him to say sorry and that I love him. Waiting for him to text back.

Dear Diary,

Wednesday the 16th of October

Miss Jennings has started talking to us about the activity week in Wales and it sounds really, really good. Each day we're going to have to do a challenge and we won't know what that is until the morning, so it could be to climb a mountain or to build something and we're going to have to work in teams to achieve our objectives. I think that means tasks. I hope that means I get to be in Clare's team WITHOUT Tanya. We also get to sleep in dormitories – one for the girls and one for the boys, which is going to be so cool, like one big sleepover FOR FOUR WHOLE NIGHTS!!!!

I set my alarm for three last night so that I could sneak down and check Dad's mobile for messages but I couldn't find it. I couldn't find his briefcase either or his coat so I tiptoed into Mum's room and he wasn't there either. He didn't come home last night which means he's with Laura. Mum was so fast asleep that she didn't even know that Dad wasn't there beside her. Perhaps this is it, he's left us and Mum's going to wake up in the morning and pretend that everything is normal. I went back to bed and couldn't sleep. I cried a bit, quietly so that I wouldn't wake anyone up, and then just lay there trying to imagine just what this evil woman could look like and thinking of all the ways in which she could die a horrible death. It's so lonely knowing something this important but not being able to tell anyone else. But the really good news is that Chloe is still with us and Mum has begun talking to her like she talks to Tom, which means that she's falling in love with her, so maybe, just maybe, she'll stay.

Dear Diary,

Thursday ✎

Everyone's talking about Wales. Camilla rang me last night to ask me if I would be her partner on the coach and I didn't know what to say because actually I want to be Clare's partner, so I said yes because I didn't want to upset her and then when I put the phone down I felt bad about the fact that I might have to let her down. I rang Clare and asked her if she'd be my partner and she said she'd think about it. Mum took me to see a secondary school today. Not the one that Frankie goes to but the one that's nearer to our house. It was massive. You could easily get lost there, all the corridors and rooms looked the same. But I really liked the girl who was showing us round and they had this really cool common room place where you could go and hang out with your friends, and they have hot chocolate machines!!!! We sat in on a maths lesson and I knew some of the answers! Clare says that her mum says it's full of people who take drugs and don't do their work but they all looked perfectly normal to me. Clare and her mum didn't even come and look today so how would they know anyway? Chloe is still with us. No one has come to claim her yet. She loves toast and barks for it at breakfast and it's soooo sweet when she rubs the end of her nose between her paws. She's really good at catching balls too. She's clever. Mum let her curl up next to her on the sofa last night in front of the telly . . . YESSSSS!

What About Me, Too?

From: Sue James
Sent: Thursday 17 October 23:03
To: Angela James
Subject: That's easy for you to say when you don't have to walk it or pick up the s . . .

Because of course nobody else does it, although Tom would love to if he could get his hands on it. He's at that stage when he wants to shove everything into his mouth. You're right, it is good for Frankie to have something to hug other than Chattie and yes, I did buy her a ticket for the Virgin's Ball. No need to have a go, sis, point taken. I'm bending over backwards trying to be supportive and slipping her extra tenners every now and then works wonders.

Why do so many schools resemble Victorian workhouses? Took Lola to the open day at the local sink school which, please God, is not destined to be our fate. Ghastly place, like a prison really, with high barbed-wire fencing surrounding large sixties concrete blocks, with cracks in the walls. It seems like such a grim, grey, crumbling, bleak place and then to lock children inside such forbidding architecture??!! Too many of the kids looked bored and either malnourished or obese. There wasn't a single tree or even a plant in the concrete playground and there's a sodding great phone mast just across the road. It makes my blood boil to think that this is Lola's only option for the next five years unless she gets into Frankie's school. I think we may have to consider moving into another catchment area, or consider more drastic measures like having her baptized in the next ten minutes so that she can apply to a Church school, or remortgage the house to pay exorbitant independent school fees. Not that she's likely to get in with *her* spelling, plus you need special coaching in French and music theory from the age of six months. It's equally bleak at the other end of the life spectrum. Went on from there to Clarice's to fill in the forms for Mum. Doesn't look likely that she'll get a place before early next year. She's about number fifty-two on the waiting list which means that fifty-two people have to either move or die, so start praying for a vicious epidemic of Hong Kong flu in Richmond.

THEN onto North Butting to persuade her. Matron took me to one side before I was practically inside the front door to tell me that Mum has been playing up. She's been refusing to eat, hurled her pudding across the dining room yesterday and said it 'smelled worse than cow dung' (she's right, it's pigswill). She rang the police four times last week and the fire brigade once and things have gone missing. Last week they found most of their dining-room forks in Mum's bathroom.

When I broached the subject with Mum she said they were exaggerating. I think she's just bored. She's always had a wicked streak. But it was a good moment to tell her about Clarice's and I think she liked the idea, particularly when I mentioned that the food smelled delicious and that we could get some more of her things out of storage. Then back home up the M40 in time to catch Frankie gripped by a gruesome documentary about cosmetic surgery when she ought to have been in bed. How anyone can consider putting themselves through surgery unnecessarily beats me, even if you do end up with a flat stomach and fewer wrinkles. (I expect HND is already saving up for her facelift. Suspect she already has some sort of treatment to burn off the epidermis because her skin looks so waxy.) So I switched off the set, heaved Frankie off the sofa and up into the bathroom and took Chloe out for a short walk up the street before putting her to bed too. She likes to be wrapped up in a blanket in front of the radiator in the kitchen. Ah ... I hear Matthew's home, so better go and express some sort of interest in his life.

Much love, Sx

Kate Figes

Dear Diary,

Friday the 18th of October

Clare was being really horrible today about her Victorian
project. She was boasting about how they were going off to
museums and things to get postcards and posters to make
her project looked really good so I'm going to work hard all
weekend to try and get most of it done.

Things I have found out:

1. The poor areas of London were really crowded because lots of people
moved into London from even poorer areas looking for work. But they had
nowhere to live so the really poor parts got more and more crowded with
whole families living just in the corner of one room without any heating or
running water. It got really smelly and dirty and there was lots of pollution
and smog and poo in the streets, and diseases spread by the poo so the rich
people NEVER went there in case they should get sick too. Sometimes the
stench and poverty were so awful in these places called 'rookeries' that the
police wouldn't even go there. They were beyond the law. Mum says that
sounds a bit like one of the estates she has to visit when she's on call.

2. Poor children in Victorian times had very few toys unless they made
them – footballs out of tied pieces of rag and bats from pieces of wood.
Imagine Clare trying to cope with that! She'd die without her iPod or her
bags of nail varnish and lipstick and her bed full of cuddly toys.

3. Lots and lots of children didn't go to school. They roamed the streets
begging or selling things like matches or cleaning up horse poo. Lots of them
went to work in factories from dawn until dusk and then would collapse at

72

home, too tired to wash or eat, and then if they got injured by the
~~mashinry~~ ~~marsheinry~~ masheenary (I wish I could spell properly) and
couldn't earn money for their families any more they were chucked out
onto the streets to look after themselves. Their parents either didn't want
them or couldn't afford to look after them. So they slept in barrels or
doorways and then if they got caught for as little as stealing carrots from
a market stall they were sent to PRISON!!! Henry Mayhew, who was a
good man, says that some children were even put in prison for throwing
stones and playing cricket on the streets! They wouldn't do that now,
although Chattie did get a pink warning slip from the police last week for
skateboarding in the city. Frankie couldn't stop going on about how unfair
it was and how the streets were meant to be for the people and how they
just ban everything that young people like doing, like having a laugh with
your friends on the streets, and you can EVEN get sent to prison for
writing grarfeetee when Frankie says this is art.

4. Children who lived on the streets begged and did tricks for money and
were taught how to steal stuff and pick pockets. Victorian street children
didn't know right from wrong because no one ever taught them. They were
dirty and swore all the time because the grown-ups didn't care enough to
teach them any better, or maybe they just thought that was OK for them
because they were never going to get anything better out of life, and
instead of doing anything about it, the rich people were so shocked by the
behaviour of orphans and street kids that they tried to shield their own
children from the poor. Mum says that still goes on today and that's why
Clare's mum wants to send her to a private school, so that she doesn't have
to mix with those who are really hard up.

From: Sue James
Sent: Saturday 19 October 17:12
To: Angela James
Subject: Re: Clarice's

No, I doubt it's Alzheimer's – she's been batty for years. She just gets naughtier as she gets older. It'll probably happen to us too. Already has with me. I lie awake sometimes plotting about all the nasty things I could do to irritate HND and then think, 'This is the stuff of playgrounds. Must at least try and be a little more grown up.' Let's hope this move to Clarice's comes through soon. I know you came at Easter, but if there is any chance of making some sort of vague plan for coming again sometime during the next year that would help.

HND knocked loud and furiously on the door this morning. Chloe dug under the fence into her garden and has been crapping on her lawn. Good for her! I apologized but apparently that isn't enough. She says she's going to complain to Environmental Health and wants the dog taken away and put down like that ghastly spinster woman at the beginning of *The Wizard of Oz* who turns into the Wicked Witch (Oh no, please, Auntie Em, don't let her take Toto!!!!! as Judy Garland snatches him up into her arms . . .) I just smiled and told her we'd fix the hole. Honestly, that woman! Caught Lola watching them wistfully through the window as they left to go somewhere in the swanky Merc. She was hoping that Clare would wave or smile or something but she didn't even look up at the window.

What About Me, Too?

My heart breaks for her. I so want to be able to sort things out for her, but ten-year-old girls can be such bitches.

My social life advances. I never realized how much having a dog means you make friends without even trying. When you cross the common with a baby, everybody gives you a wide berth and ignores you. With a dog you are surrounded by people from the moment your foot hits rough ground. Attractive men fall to their knees and lavish affection on your mutt. Children talk to you. Other dog owners welcome you warmly to their club. I now take Chloe every morning at eight when Toyah arrives and usually bump into at least one of the following – Mildred from the estate with three lurchers, Happy Homosexual Harry with 'Salt' and 'Pepper' (a West Highland White and a Scottie), Julia (with the very well turned out poodle) and, if I'm REALLY lucky, Mark, divine Mark the architect (with the black Lab). I get such a flutter when we do meet I'm speechless, but it does at least prove that I'm not sexually dead yet, just dormant.

Tom's finally walking and Lola and I have spent most of this afternoon moving everything dangerous up to a higher level and of course discovered all sorts of things that have been missing for weeks in the process, like the list of Frankie's coursework delivery dates, the letter from Miss Jennings about the Victorian project saying 'Parents are asked to help their children with research.' We also found an entire pile of clean laundry that no one has remembered to put away – Frankie has been screaming at me that she hasn't got enough pairs of the right tights when they're all here – and we found the copy of Charlotte's Web that Lola had been reading and so enjoying and then lost, which really cheered her up. We're going to start reading it again after supper. The great bonus of the day is that now I don't have to do any washing! I was wondering how long I was going to last at work wearing today's bra and knickers. What if Bryson decided to corner me by the cupboard full of urine sample bottles to press his manly body against mine? What if Mark just happened to drop by the house to see if I wanted to walk the dog with him???

Much love,
Suex

What About Me, Too?

Dear Diary,

Sunday morning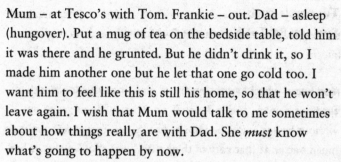

Mum – at Tesco's with Tom. Frankie – out. Dad – asleep
(hungover). Put a mug of tea on the bedside table, told him
it was there and he grunted. But he didn't drink it, so I
made him another one but he let that one go cold too. I
want him to feel like this is still his home, so that he won't
leave again. I wish that Mum would talk to me sometimes
about how things really are with Dad. She *must* know
what's going to happen by now.

I had another good look at his mobile while he was
asleep and she's sent him two text messages this morning
alone. So I sent one back: 'It's over. Don't wnt 2 c u again.'
And then I switched his mobile onto silent mode and hid it
in the bathroom so that Laura would get really upset at him
not replying. That should sort it.

From: Sue James
Sent: Sunday 20 October 21:19
To: Angela James
Subject: Re: The pink or the green one?

You know what? I've always hated pink, it always looks either sickly or chintzy, and it depends on what shade of green but without having seen your house I can't say. You always were so much better at that sort of thing than I was. You've always had the knack of presentation (do you fancy helping with a project on the Victorians?). Do you think our technology is up to webcams??? You could walk round your house with a camcorder and talk me through it! And could be a fab way for me to keep up with Stan and Ollie . . .

Frankie has been out most of the weekend (as has Matthew). Her mobile's been off (says she forgot to take her charger to Ruby's and the battery went dead on Saturday). I really hate the idea of her just cruising round London all weekend, eating junk food and never really touching base at home OR doing any coursework. So we've had a furious row about that and now I feel bad because she's screamed at me for not trusting her when she's doing so well (which is true). But then she's not sixteen yet. She says that she needs to have fun in order to be able to cope with studying, now that I'm not letting her out in the week. But to be out all weekend? And nearly every weekend??? She just follows her instincts with that wonderful spontaneity that is the privilege of youth. She can't seem to see beyond the next hour. Matthew wasn't there to hear the beginning of this conversation. He's not even aware of how much she's out or whether she's doing enough work because he isn't here enough himself to monitor that, but he comes in during the height of the row and has the nerve to take her side, fanning the flames between all of us by telling me to 'relax and let her live her own life'. AAARGH! Tonight he said she has to take responsibility for herself and that if she fails or does less well then she has to live with that and do the resits, etc – a very different line to the one he has been punting up till now. He was just siding with Frankie to get at me, when what we need more than anything is a united front as her parents to make sure she gets through this year without failing or breaking down. So I left them to it. Asked him to bath Tom and put him to bed, told Frankie to heat up the chicken stew I made for lunch and took Lola to bed with me to read up to the end of Chapter Nine, when Charlotte promises to try and think up a plan to save Wilbur and tells him to get lots of rest and go to sleep while she has a good think hanging upside down. *Charlotte's Web* was my favourite book when I was her age so it was lovely to get lost in it again, cuddled up with my lovely Lola, who is fast becoming leggy, voluptuous Lola . . .

She's asleep now, in my bed. Off to Paris tomorrow, first thing. I'll let you know how it goes. I've packed and repacked several times; it's so exciting. And have even treated myself to some new underwear, face cream, really expensive soap and a brand-new tube of toothpaste! All for me! Pathetic I know . . .

Much love (and let me know which colour you eventually pick).

Sx

Dear Diary,

Monday the 21st of October

Clare brought her project into school this morning even though it's not due in until Friday and it is SO good it makes mine look pathetic. I'm gonna bin it. She's done so much work it looks like a proper book with beautiful large curly letters at the beginning of each section and her pictures are so good she COULDN'T have done them by herself, her Mum did them. Everyone crowded round and said, 'That's so good!' and Miss Jennings propped it up on her desk so that everyone could see – so once again Clare's work is up on display and mine won't be. I came home and looked at what I had done and wanted to rip it up, only Toyah stopped me and said she'd help me make it look really beautiful and drew a picture of Oliver Twist in the workhouse. Mum's away so I can't talk to her about it. Dad's out with Laura probably and doesn't care. I nearly told Mum about her yesterday by ~~aksident~~ accident. She sat down to tell me what would happen while she was away, how Toyah would put Tom to bed and how Dad would be back in time to put me to bed and I said, 'What if he's . . .' and then had to stop myself. 'What if he's what?' asked Mum. 'Working,' I lied. And then she said that he wasn't going to be working and had promised to be home. But he isn't home yet and it's nearly ten o'clock. Frankie's spent about 300 hours talking to all of her friends on the phone and I had to heat the pizza for supper myself. And clear it up.

What About Me, Too?

Dear Diary,

Mum's gone away for just one night to Paris, but from the way she's been going on about it anyone would think she was going to Australia to see Auntie Angela for a whole month. She's pinned notes up all over the place reminding us to do stuff that we know how to do, like clean our teeth and lock the back door and make sure the gas is turned off and that Tom's night light is on, and then when it came to actually leaving the house this morning she kept coming back to remind us about stuff and kiss Tom one last time. Dad had to pick Tom up, hand her her passport which she had embarrassingly left on the kitchen table and kick her out the door into the taxi so that she wouldn't miss her train. I mean we love her and all that but how difficult is it exactly for any of us to cope for just one night? Dad hasn't come back though, which is pretty mean of him, and Lola's really upset about it. If he IS bonking someone else again he could at least have the courtesy not to do it tonight, although I can't tell her that obviously so I just keep saying he'll be home soon.

From: Sue James
Sent: Thursday 24 October 22:10
To: Angela James
Subject: Paris was bliss . . .

No Sacha Distel sadly, but the anonymity of hotel life, a stroll down the Boulevard St Germain with those massive golden autumnal trees glinting in the sunshine and some decent coffee was all it took to remind me that there's a big wide world out there. Just being alone for a while without demands from patients or children was all I needed. Interesting conference too. Dr Ian 'Finlay' green eyes Bryson wants to have lunch with me 'sometime' so that I can tell him all about it. He thinks euthanasia is licensed murder and we'll all turn into Harold Shipman types, bopping old ladies off because we think they're better off dead. Maybe they are. Have a great story up my sleeve though, thanks to Jane in reception. He gave a patient a really heavy-duty lecture on the dangers of smoking, went on and on about it and then stood up to see him out and a packet of fags fell out of his pocket! So the next time he says, 'Give me a kiss,' I'll say, 'You can have a blow job if you give me a fag,' which should sort things. Lots of us help the dying on their way with large doses of morphine when people fight against the dying of the light – 'I'll just give her something to help with the breathing,' when the death rattle is so loud its practically knocking the pictures off the walls.

Then home to domestic chaos. HND has sent Lola into a

total spin of self-doubt about her Victorian project because Clare's is good enough for permanent exhibition at the V&A. HND must have been working hard on it for weeks. If that's how she wants to spend her days, fine. I have more worthwhile things to do tending to the sick, poor and hypochondriac of south London, but the vindictive cow had to bring the damn thing in almost a week before the deadline so that the rest of the class felt inadequate before they'd even finished. HND managed to move the goalposts in injury time so that no one else even had a chance of coming close to equalizing. That's either just stupid (possible) or worse, taking competition to its most extreme form of cruelty (also possible). She practically scratched my eyes out last Christmas when Lola was chosen to be Mary in the nativity play while Clare was just a pesky common sheep. HA! She did make sure though that Clare was the best dressed sheep on stage (and probably got her a tutor on 'baaing' as well). Anyway, Lola has been in tears while I've been away and darling Toyah has been drawing pictures, researching Victorian children and mounting her work – what a girl, and I THINK Lola is now happy enough with it to take it into school tomorrow.

But then when it came to the briefing meeting for parents after school today about the activity week in Wales after half-term, I really did begin to wonder whether HND is in fact mentally ill. The rest of us sat there listening to Lola's teacher who I'd not met before and liked enormously. She's young and lively and clearly passionate about the kids. But HND doesn't trust her or like her teaching methods and was rude and disrespectful and it was really embarrassing. There are kids in that class from the estate who have probably never even been to the countryside before, let alone gone somewhere where they get to canoe, sail and pony-trek in the Black Mountains. Their parents were probably worried sick about things like spending money and the cost of equipment. But HND couldn't keen her mouth shut about safety measures, security, what food they would be eating, the ratio of workers to child, the weather and wasn't it going to be too cold and did the coach have seat belts and were there evacuation procedures if a child got homesick because Clare had never been away from home before! All perfectly legitimate questions, I suppose, but they were fired at the poor teacher with the velocity of an automatic machine gun. Poor Miss Jennings gave as good as she got but looked a little upset by the end of the meeting. Lola says that the boys tease Clare in the playground about going to a posh school and being a baby and needing a bottle at night (which just might be true). Just imagine what life will be like for the poor child if she does get homesick and needs to come home. She'll never be able to live that down.

I think I might go out into the garden and encourage Chloe to dig a hole under the new nine-foot-high fence that she's had swiftly erected along our garden party wall and crap on her back doorstep. I've already trained her to piss against the tyres of her Mercedes. Revenge is sweet.

Much love, Suex

What About Me, Too?

Dear Diary,

Friday night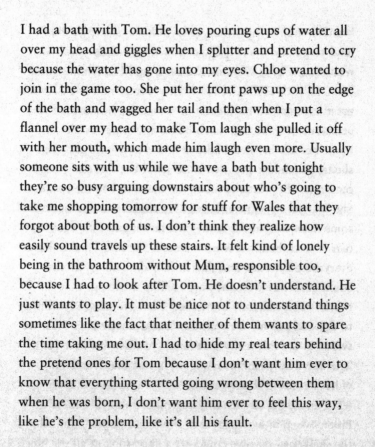

I had a bath with Tom. He loves pouring cups of water all over my head and giggles when I splutter and pretend to cry because the water has gone into my eyes. Chloe wanted to join in the game too. She put her front paws up on the edge of the bath and wagged her tail and then when I put a flannel over my head to make Tom laugh she pulled it off with her mouth, which made him laugh even more. Usually someone sits with us while we have a bath but tonight they're so busy arguing downstairs about who's going to take me shopping tomorrow for stuff for Wales that they forgot about both of us. I don't think they realize how easily sound travels up these stairs. It felt kind of lonely being in the bathroom without Mum, responsible too, because I had to look after Tom. He doesn't understand. He just wants to play. It must be nice not to understand things sometimes like the fact that neither of them wants to spare the time taking me out. I had to hide my real tears behind the pretend ones for Tom because I don't want him ever to know that everything started going wrong between them when he was born, I don't want him ever to feel this way, like he's the problem, like it's all his fault.

Dear Diary,

Saturday the 26th of October

Went shopping with Mum today. I kept saying we didn't
have to go and that I could cope with the shoes and
trousers I've got. We took the list from Miss Jennings and
GOT EVERYTHING ON IT! Even brand-new socks! Mum
must have gone a bit mental or something because we've
got loads of scratched lunch boxes and water bottles at
home but she insisted I needed brand-new ones and then
she let me choose my own rucksack. I got this really cool
pink one. She's usually much too mean to buy me new stuff.
She bought me some amazing Caterpillar walking boots and
some new jeans and a really cool jacket and I kept saying I
didn't need them but Mum insisted. She said I had to have
everything I needed and that in four days all my clothes
could get really wet. She keeps telling me things that she
thinks I don't already know, like I have to hang my stuff up
to dry and put my dirty clothes into a carrier bag. Then we
went out for this really nice lunch, just her, me and Tom.
The only really embarrassing thing was that it was only
when we got to the restaurant that we realized that we'd
left Tom in the kitchen department of John Lewis. He'd
fallen asleep in his buggy and Mum had pushed him behind
the shelves so that we could get a good look at all the lunch
boxes. It wasn't until we sat down and looked at the menu
and Mum said, 'What would Tom like?' that we realized
and had to run out of the restaurant without paying for my
Fanta – SOOOOO embarrassing – but he was all right. Still

86

fast asleep behind the lunch-box rack and nobody had even noticed him. Mum keeps leaving him places. Dad says it's because she never really wanted him in the first place, which is the sort of thing he likes to say just to get at her.

Dear Diary,

Monday the 4th of November

On the coach to Wales and I can't stop worrying about Tom. He was crying as the coach pulled away. If Mum and Dad keep on rowing while I'm away as badly as they have been rowing this past week then he's gonna start feeling like it's all his fault because I won't be there to protect him and Frankie couldn't care less about anybody but herself. Sorry if my writing is a bit wobbly. I'm sitting next to Camilla who is feeling a bit carsick. Gr8. Clare is in front of us, next to Tanya and they keep whispering to each other so that we can't hear what they're saying. Gr8. Mum and Tom took me to school this morning with all my stuff. There were loads of parents hanging around on the pavement by the coach, helping to load on the bags and wave us off. Clare's mum handed her a huge bag of sweets (which she is refusing to share with anybody other than Tanya) and then ran along beside the coach, waving goodbye. How embarrassing is that? I'm so glad she's not my mum.

A bit later at the centre.

It's like a giant house or even a hotel beside a lake. My bed is between Clare's and Tanya's. Miss Jennings said she was going to decide who slept where to prevent any arguments and now they're trying to get me to swap but why should I? I don't want to get into trouble. And then when we unpacked our bags I was really proud of my brand-new Caterpillar boots and Clare just slagged them off

as hippy boots and said they were the sort of boots that
drug-takers wore, when how would she know that? SHE
produced a ~~moscito~~ moskito net to cover her bed with,
which made Miss Jennings laugh, and a wind-up radio with
a torch. Why does she always have to have the coolest
things?

Dear Diary,

Tuesday night

I'm so tired I can't keep my eyes open, and a bit shivery even though I'm in bed. Clare and Tanya kept talking over me last night and kept me awake. They were saying really horrible things about me as if I wasn't there, but I didn't want to make them hate me even more by saying anything and pretended to be asleep and was really pleased when Miss Jennings came in and told them to shut up. I wish Mum was here to hug. We've been outdoors all day long doing an assault course. We had to work in groups of eight and help each other get up and over scaffolding and across a river using planks which were really heavy, and I'm now lying on my bed writing this and waiting for my turn to have a hot shower. Camilla was in our team and she found it really hard to do the climbing because of her leg situashon so that meant our team was the slowest but I don't mind because she was so happy to be able to do it at all. I want to try and be alone in the bathroom so that no one can see me. It's bad enough having to change into my ~~peejarmas~~ piejarmers in front of everybody else. I miss home but I mustn't think about it too much in case I cry. I miss hugging Chloe, the smell of her fur and the way she licks me when I come home from school and wants me to play ball with her in the garden. We're going pony-trekking tomorrow so that should be less tiring.

What About Me, Too?

Dear Diary,

Wednesday night

Got a letter from Mum today which was gr8 because we're not allowed to phone home as Miss Jennings says some people will get upset and it's better to just forget about home until we go there on Friday. She says that one of the toughest things in life is learning how to enjoy each day for what it is. But that's hard.

I loved the trekking. My pony was called Dusty, I think because she's a smokey, greyie sort of a colour. I felt so free, like Dusty and I could ride off together and be all right. They let us have a trot which was really exciting but not canter. Clare says she can ride and has had lessons and complained about not being allowed to canter, but what about everybody else who can't and might get hurt or fall off (like she did!).

Dear Diary,

Thursday ✐

Well, it's been a bit of an eventful last day. I can't believe
we're going home tomorrow already. Clare and Tanya got
up last night while everyone else was asleep and went
outside in their ~~peedgharmas~~ ~~piejarmers~~ night clothes with
the wind-up radio and torch and started dancing to music
on the lawn beside the lake. They were pretending to be
moon goddesses, doing weird dances and they were
laughing so loudly that they woke up Miss Jennings who
has confiscated Clare's radio. Clare rang her mum in the
middle of the night (she brought her mobile even though
she wasn't allowed to) and now her mum has rung the
centre and complained to Miss Jennings who looks furious
and has given Clare and Tanya one of the worst jobs –
putting all of the equipment away at the end of the day –
which means they'll be last to get to the bathrooms, for
once. Clare's mum is so cross that her precious daughter
has been told off (Miss Jennings doesn't know that Clare
has her mobile with her) that she has been threatening to
drive up to collect Clare today, which is just soooooooo
embarrassing. I heard her begging her mum not to in the
loo this morning because it would just be the worst thing
if she did come.

There's a disco tonight. Clare and Tanya have been
trashing it, saying it'll probably be pathetic but how many
discos have they actually been to exactly?

What About Me, Too?

From: Sue James
Sent: Thursday 7 November 20:48
To: Angela James
Subject: How awful it is here without Lola

She's on an activity week in Wales, back tomorrow in time for
our fireworks party (why didn't I just say 'no' when Frankie
asked?) and I can't wait to see her. I always thought of Lola as
the quiet one, but now I'm beginning to wonder whether she
isn't actually the glue, keeping this whole family together. Tom
gabbles away in his high chair, but without Lola singing songs or
spoon-feeding him his tea with rocket and airplane sounds, his
chatter is a bit subdued and he keeps asking for her: 'OOOLA,
OOOOLA!' Chloe spends most of the day curled up at the
foot of Lola's bed, Matthew and Frank are too self-absorbed to
even notice that she's gone, but I miss her so badly that it
hurts. Took her shopping the Saturday before she left to make
sure she could match Clare on the goods front because that
must matter so much more when you're away from home.
She's never been away for more than a night before.

   With Tom in bed and Lola away, Frankie basks in the
knowledge that she is an only child. She spent four hours
walking round the house last night with the phone clamped to
her ear and her mobile in the other hand, texting one friend at
the same time as talking to another. She spends about forty-five
minutes complaining about how Saskia called her a bitch for
bitching about her, when everyone knows that Saskia has a

first-class degree in bitching (the words 'pot' and 'kettle' come to mind). Then she shrieks, 'SHE DIDN'T!!!' and my ears prick up at the prospect of something really revelatory, like who's smoking or doing drugs. Apparently Saskia lays out her clothes for the following day on the floor the night before and told Ruby that it was 'the best bit of the day'. I collapse, disappointed, and run a bath. After about two hours of this incessant chatter she started walking round the house, pacing her territory liked a caged animal, with an ice cube wrapped in kitchen towel, pressed firmly against the top of her nose. Apparently she had dropped her mobile onto her face while she had been tapping out a text message, lying on her bed. The accident didn't stop her conversation though, she kept running to the bathroom and asking Ruby if she thought she might have a bruise tomorrow. Hilarious really. I suppose with two parties this weekend – our fireworks tomorrow and the Virgin's Ball on Saturday – I can see that she doesn't want to look like she's just had her lights punched out.

Thrilling day at work today – I was just drifting off and thinking about what I might actually do if Mark in the Park asked me out for a coffee (OK, I'm no better than my daughter) when I should have been listening to a rather anxious and skinny woman moaning on about her aches and pains when the panic button went and I was able to rush out of my room with great excitement. An addict was wielding a knife in the waiting room and threatening to kill someone unless we gave him drugs. 'Take 'em all and I'll keep the drugs' was my considered opinion. Jane, the receptionist, looked genuinely scared, but managed to call 999. I tried telling him that we never kept drugs on the premises (which is a lie) and that he was better off raiding a chemist's and then Ian Superman Bryson decided to raise his popularity stakes still further by taking the law into his own hands and wrestled the malnourished, desperate junkie to the floor with the sort of gusto usually reserved for giant ten-ton bears. I grabbed the knife (hooray) and then wondered what to do with it. It would have been nice to have turned it on Bryson and demand he recant as a narrow-minded, arrogant, homeopathic-hating womanizer. But the waiting room cheered at this point, Bryson took a bow and yours truly was left to escort the poor kid into a room and talk him down for the ninety minutes it took for a police car to arrive. Still, at least it did mean I could escape from the anxious anorexic. Next time she comes I'll suggest she goes to see Bryson for acupuncture.

Must go — mega delivery of bangers and bakeable potatoes just being delivered by Tesco.com for tomorrow night.

Sx

Dear Diary,

The things that go on when I just go away for just four
days. Frankie's been through every single item of my
clothing and messed up every single drawer. She's got a
dark bruise on her nose and never stops moaning about that
or the fact that she's got a dry patch of skin on her cheek
which is easily fixed with some moisturizer AND she's had
a row with Chattie about the Virgin's Ball on Saturday
night because he's away with his family this weekend and
can't go and doesn't want her to go without him. She says
he should stay and disappoint his parents since he's going to
be sixteen next month and it was about time he did what he
wanted to do, not what they wanted him to do, which is a
little unfair, I think. So she's in a real strop. Tom has nappy
rash and nobody's bothered to clean out the teapot since
I've been away so it's got disgusting mould in it. They're all
so lazy they just use bags, which does NOT make Dad a
happy man. Mum's panicking about whether we've got
enough sausages or plates for everybody and Chloe's pacing
the house because she hates the fireworks that have been
going off every night and knows something's about to
happen, and I bet nobody's bothered to take her out for a
walk. Dad's not home yet and he's supposed to be setting
up the fireworks. At least Toyah's done a good job building
a fire. But it is really good to be home. I just hope that
everybody cheers up in the next hour in time for our
fireworks party.

What About Me, Too?

Dear Diary,

Saturday the 9th of November

Mum's furious because the garden looks terrible. Every single one of Frankie's friends came and drank all the beer. Chattie tried to look like he was enjoying himself but he looked really anxious and then left early when his parents came to pick him up and take him away for the weekend. Frankie looked much happier after he'd gone, like now she could really enjoy herself. They all chased each other round the garden with sparklers, screaming.

Mum spent most of the time in the kitchen talking to Jane and Mary, the receptionists at the surgery. Jane held Tom while Mum fried sausages and shoved them into hot-dog buns for me to hand out. The only person who didn't have any friends at the party was me. Clare's mum wouldn't let her come over because we'd only just come back from Wales, which was a bit unfair since she's just next door and could have come for an hour. I could see her watching us from her bedroom window, because of course she wasn't allowed any fireworks. I waved and she ran away. None of my other friends could come either so I helped Mum with the food, looked after Chloe and helped Dad organize the fireworks. But then when it came to letting them off I was really glad that none of my friends were there to see him go mad.

Ed and Jack from over the road were helping him set up the fireworks with torches in a taped off area at the back of the garden. He'd bought lots so that was really cool. I love watching the way multicoloured rockets explode against the black night sky. But then something snapped in him. It was like he was suddenly really, really angry and he started letting off hundreds of fireworks really quickly, all at the same time, like he wanted to get it over with or he was bored or something, and Jack told him to slow down because it wasn't safe but he wouldn't listen, he just kept on running round the garden with a lighted touchpaper and all the children and Frankie's friends ran screaming into the house to watch from the windows they were so frightened. Mum was furious. So now they can't even have a party without the whole world seeing how badly they get on.

What About Me, Too?

Dear Diary,

I really don't understand what I have to do to make Chattie happy. HE decided to go away this weekend and just because HE's away apparently that means that I can't go out without him, which is just so pathetic. Clearly they've never heard of Germaine Greer in India. Mum gave me one of her books and it's cool. Why does he expect me to stay home in this dump just because he's away???? What does he think I'm gonna do? Doesn't he even trust me? He says he loves me but how can that be if he doesn't want me to have a good time when he's away? It's like he wants to own me or something. So I did have a good time, a really good time, and I've sent him a text saying so and that I wished he could have been here with me to enjoy it too . . . but that's just wound him up, I can tell because he hasn't texted back. That's what he does when he's pissed off with me. Honestly, men are SOOOO pathetic, so childish.

From: Sue James
Sent: Sunday 10 November 22:51
To: Angela James
Subject: parties

Ange Sweetie,

A good party save for a brief psychotic interlude from Matthew. Luckily there were at least fifteen doctors there to administer straitjackets and sedatives if he got really out of hand. Either he's a closet pyromaniac and the sight of all that gunpowder sent him sky-high (excuse the pun) or, and this is far more likely, he simply sensed that he had all the power at that moment and chose to terrorize everyone by running round manically and lighting all of the touchpapers at the same time. It sounded like Armageddon and my roses have been charred to a cinder. But no one was hurt and anything we do that is likely to make HND self-combust with rage is always a pleasing thought. According to Mavis, I got off lightly. Her husband bought a chainsaw, went into the garden and destroyed every single living thing. He made such a huge pile of branches and plants by the back door that he couldn't get back into the house! Who was it who said, 'When women get depressed they eat or go shopping; men invade another country'? So true. The teenagers enjoyed the thrill, screaming their heads off with a mixture of fear and excitement and then descended like locusts onto the food and drink. I overheard one of the boys saying that he thought Frankie's dad was 'safe. He's got a Harley', so Matthew's adolescent outburst must have been completely OK by them. Something they understood – let rip, be dangerous and loud, show no concern for anybody else and make sure they're in the limelight as a result. There's far more similarities between middle-aged life crises and adolescence than meets the eye. Anyway, it was clearly cathartic because he's been quite nice ever since.

The hot news from next door at 8.30 this morning is that Clare has nits (never! I thought she had a special halo of DDT around her head to protect her from them). HND clearly horrified and claims she got them from Lola as they slept next to each other in Wales, which went well I think. Lola's very proud of her new riding skills. So I said, 'How awful! Sorry to disappoint you but Lola's head is clear,' (haven't of course had time to check it). She looked unconvinced and kept trying to peer past me to have a good butchers at the state of our hall. Boots and shoes all over the place as always. Hers are in racks and graded according to size. So I tried to make the peace by apologizing for the noise from the party and sounded really concerned as I said I hoped that Clare had recovered from her fall. 'Lola tells me that riding is not one of Clare's many skills! Let me know if you need me to have a look at her.' This was clearly the first the woman had heard of it. She scurried back next door to grill her poor daughter and check that her three cognitive strengths (playing the clarinet badly, making flapjacks and being nasty to Lola) haven't been affected.

Feeling guilty about Mum, haven't checked in on her in a while but will try to this week.

Love and kisses, Suex

Dear Diary,

Saturday the 16th of November

Only one week and one day until my birthday!!!! Mum says I can't have a party this year because I'm getting too old for them and that I can take a few friends out for a treat or have them for a sleepover. I'm kind of pleased in a way because it means there won't be a scene at school about who's coming and who isn't and the fact that I don't want Tanya to come but I do want to invite Camilla because nobody ever invites her to anything and this way nobody'll know that actually I quite like her.

Me, Chattie and Frankie took Chloe for a walk in the cemetery off the high street today and Chattie suggested that if I take some of my friends ice-skating, he could give them all lessons. That's a really cool idea. Camilla would really love to learn to skate, I know she would. It's just that nobody bothers to teach her those sorts of things because they just assume she can't.

It was really crisp and cold in the cemetery. Frankie thinks the cemetery is creepy but I don't. It's a welcoming place that gives a home to the living as well as the dead, to birds and foxes and squirrels. It's also very beautiful. There are loads of carved angels with their hands pointing up to the sky or to God and to Hope, with ivy wrapped around their legs. There are trees and flowers and benches for people to sit on. And every tombstone has a name so they are never forgotten. Chattie says it's a Victorian cemetery. I wish I'd known about it when I did my project.

Frankie wasn't at all interested in my party or the cemetery. She just sat staring up through the trees at the sky and chucked sticks for Chloe. She's such a clever dog. She always seems to be able to find the same stick even when you chuck it right into the heart of the woods behind the tombstones. They've been having a row and either didn't think I was listening or didn't care if I was. She says he's being too possessive which I think means that he wants to possess her, which is really stupid because nobody owns anybody else, but she feels that way because he wants to know about everything she does and she's obviously getting a bit bored by that but he says that's what people in relationships just do. I think she ought to be a bit more pleased that he cares enough about her to want to know, unlike poor Mum who says she wonders sometimes whether Dad cares about anybody but himself, and when I said that Frankie just said, 'Well what do you know about relationships, big girl?' Sorr-rry! I was only trying to help. We sat for ages on the steps in front of this great tomb with a massive stone lion on the top. He's asleep, protecting the dead beneath with this lovely long swishy tail curled up beside him. Somebody had picked some flowers and left them as a gift between his paws.

Frank says she thinks that maybe Mum and Dad should get divorced, that things never seem to get any better and they never seem to have fun together any more. Chattie said that sometimes it is better to divorce (like how does he know when his parents are married?); he talks sometimes like he knows everything when he can't. I don't see how it can ever be better to divorce when Tom's so small and needs everyone so badly. I don't understand why they can't just decide to get on with each other because of him, if they can't do it for Frankie or me. He is just a baby. I think it's the not knowing what might happen that's the worst thing. I wanted to tell them about horrible pig-ugly Laura and her stupid lovey-dovey text messages but just as I was about to reveal my extraordinary secret and get them to help me to stave off the inevitable, Frankie stormed off in a sulk and Chattie chased after her. I wish I could just tell someone and then I wouldn't feel so bad about having to hold this secret inside of me for so long. I need Frankie or Mum to know so that I'm not the only one. I took Dad's phone off him this morning while he was shaving and sent her a message saying, 'away nxt weekend, sorry xxxxx' because I want to make sure that Dad is around for my birthday.

What About Me, Too?

Dear Diary,

Tuesday. After school

I've asked Clare, Camilla, Polly and Britney to come to my skating party on Saturday. Frankie and Chattie are taking us skating and then we're all going to have pizza at home and sleep over. Tanya pretends she doesn't care but I know she does because she's been being really horrible to me at school. Someone drew all over the painting I did in art last week and I know it was her although she accused me of being paranoid when I asked her. She told Miss Jennings that I had copied from her work yesterday which is just a total lie and she calls me busty all the time in front of the boys so it's spreading round the playground and making everyone laugh. But I did get four stars for my project today and Miss Jennings made me stand up and read it out to the class. I was really, really pleased about that, she said I'd put a lot of intelligent thought into it and that it was really ~~orijinal~~ original, which is cool but it just gave them an opportunity to pick on me even more so I wish she hadn't done it and had just said it was good, like she did with all of the others.

Dear Diary,

Friday night, well Saturday morning actually, and what a night. Not sure I ever want to have to go through THAT again! Hayley got a text from this weirdo she fancies who's really old, like twenty-two or something, and he told her about a raze. So we went. There was nothing else to do. They'd taken over this empty warehouse and it was only £5 on the door and there were literally MILLIONS of people AND music and it was kind of exciting, you could get anything you liked – E, dope, ket, coke. Scary. A smoke would have been nice, only I couldn't because it makes Chattie go mad. Chattie didn't like it much, probably because of all the drugs, and wanted to go home. But I couldn't leave Hayley, who of course never found the weirdo and really wanted to and didn't want me to go or Saskia, who of course got so excited by it all that she drank too much vodka, because she can never wait for the first one to hit before she has another, stupid bitch, and collapsed on the floor. She wasn't just being sick, she was practically unconscious and she went all clammy and sweaty. Chattie wanted to call an ambulance but both Hayley and I knew that would mean her parents would be told and she'd probably be grounded for six months or, worse still, be sent to boarding school. I told him that she'd been this drunk before and been OK. I rubbed her back and tried to talk to her to keep her awake but Chattie insisted she had to go to hospital, he said someone might have put drugs in her drink and called a taxi. Three taxis refused to take her in case she was sick in the back. But the fourth one was a really nice man who had teenagers himself and he took us all to hospital and then waited with us to make sure Saskia was all right. We waited for hours before they did anything – she could have died. They pumped her stomach and called her parents – I had to give them her number, Chattie made me and I still feel bad about that because they're gonna be like so so mad with her. He's right, I suppose, in that they have to know that she's in trouble but he doesn't know what her parents are like. I made sure we left before they arrived so that they couldn't blame ME for corrupting HER when actually it's her and Hayley who're always the first to try anything and lie the most to their parents because they're shit-scared of being grounded. It was like Holby City *in there. Three people with drug overdoses and two with stab wounds – and that was just when we were there! I was glad Chattie was with me. He may be a bit too straight and jealous but at least he makes me feel safe.*

From: Sue James
Sent: Saturday 23 November 23:01
To: Angela James
Subject: Lola's birthday

Dearest, what should I do . . .?

I'm riddled with guilt because I said she couldn't have a party this year. She seemed OK about it at the time but now I'm beginning to wonder whether that was such a good idea. We went to the massive ice rink in Croydon this afternoon (Matthew insisted he had to work, which caused yet another argument because you just don't work instead of going to your daughter's birthday party and I was so incensed I almost divorced him on the spot). Frankie was so tired she was next to useless and sat slumped over a double espresso but Chattie gave them all a lesson which went down particularly well with Camilla who is a sweet girl with a prosthetic lower leg. She was born without a foot and is the only child with a disability in the school so she has quite a hard time, I think. She can't fail to stand out. Chattie worked really hard encouraging her onto the ice – she shies away from most physical activity and isn't encouraged to take part at school. Anyway, we got the skates on and Chattie held her by the elbows and took her round and she absolutely loved the thrill of it, the speed, the chill on her cheeks and she managed several times to skate a bit on her own which made all the kids cheer – they were so pleased for her so that was good. BUT, and it's a big BUT, I said Lola could take four friends – Clare, Camilla, Polly and Britney (amazing, isn't it? She's damn good at impersonating her namesake too). Anyway, yesterday she begged me to let a child called Tanya come as well – said she liked her but *I* never have – and she caused nothing but trouble from the moment she arrived. She fell over repeatedly on the ice rink because she can't skate, but instead of admitting that and letting Chattie teach her she insisted on going it alone and sent several smaller children flying in the process. During supper she didn't like anything on the menu, clung onto Clare like a teddy bear, announced that they were best friends, which was of course meant to be hurtful, and always made sure that Lola felt left out by whispering. She talked about herself the whole time and how great HER party was (which Lola wasn't invited to), and this evening she has managed to trash most of Lola's wardrobe as 'crap' and now says there isn't any room in Lola's bedroom for Lola! She wants to chuck her out of her own bedroom on her birthday sleepover! I've gone in there and rearranged the mattresses and told her to stop being quite so rude but poor Lola is trying hard not to look miserable, jammed up against the wall with Camilla while Tanya, of course, sleeps in the middle with most of the room. I'm so angry I could strangle the child. What a bitch! I know you are supposed to excuse everything in the young but if either of my girls behaved like that I'd heave them straight into family therapy. What I'd like to do is ring her mother and ask her to come and take her mean, spiteful daughter home but of course I can't do that because that would make things even worse for Lola. Any

suggestions if you're out there? I'm so angry I can't sleep, and
neither, it seems, can they . . .

Masses of love,
Sxxxxxxxxxxx

What About Me, Too?

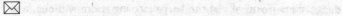

From: Sue James
Sent: Sunday 24 November 09:52
To: Angela James
Subject: Re: Lola's birthday

No, you're too kind. She's just a first-class bitch. Why do we excuse behaviour in children that we would never tolerate in adults? Just because they're children isn't enough of an answer. How are children ever to learn how to behave properly if adults don't correct them? I know that sounds awfully right wing but to excuse bullying behaviour with 'she's probably having a tough time at home' doesn't wash with me. Lola hasn't exactly had it easy this past year with Matthew moving out and Frankie's troubles but she isn't nasty like that to her 'friends', or so far as I know she isn't – if anything she's far too nice to everybody, never wants to make anybody think ill of her by speaking her mind. It's just about power, kids do it because they can. Bullies breed bullies. No doubt Tanya thinks this is how you treat people because her parents chuck their weight around and encourage her to do the same to make sure she doesn't get shat on from a great height by the others. 'Anyone messes with you, you tell 'em they can mess with me instead.' I had a mother like that in the surgery only last week. Her fifteen-year-old daughter had come to see me the day before because she had read about thyroid conditions in a magazine and was worried about her weight. She assumed I'd just give her a test, when she's clearly overweight for the obvious normal reasons. Twenty-four hours later her equally obese mother thinks it's perfectly all right to barge into my room without an appointment to take me to task for seeing an underage girl alone and then castigates me for refusing to give her a thyroid test. I said it wasn't necessary. She said how did I know. I said because she didn't complain of any other symptoms and she then said, 'Call yourself a doctor' in a sarky tone and flounced out of the room!

Anyway, they all fell asleep at about 1 a.m. and it was Chloe who finally made the peace between them. She dived into Lola's sleeping bag and refused to get into anybody else's bed because she's a loyal darling and could almost certainly sense that Lola was a bit upset. Then of course all the others wanted a cuddle so Lola had to get into the middle of the giant bed of mattresses and was finally able to assert her rightful central place as the birthday girl. Thank heavens for Chloe. If anyone turned up now and said she was their dog I think I'd have to lie and say we'd had her for years! I've tossed (yes, tossed, one of my many skills) about 100 pancakes for breakfast (although I did manage to put salt rather than sugar on Tom's one which sent him into the sort of rage we usually only ever see in Matthew), my hair smells of clarified butter and all five of them are now lying slumped in front of Sunday morning telly. Clare was dragged back next door half an hour ago to do some clarinet practice. And, since today is Lola's actual birthday and Matthew is here, we let her open her presents in front of her friends over breakfast. She was thrilled with the digital camera. And perhaps more importantly, Tanya and Clare went 'WOW! LUCKY!' in unison. She says she's going to become the family photographer so expect plenty of JPEGs in the near future.

Masses of love, Sx

What About Me, Too?

Dear Diary,

I've got mocks in seven WEEKS, three pieces of coursework to do by Friday, school's a total nightmare at the moment, Saskia's a complete bitch and spent the whole of today teasing me about the fact that I thought the word derogatory meant to get lost. She laughed so loud the whole fucking playground could hear her. I think she's just giving me a hard time because SHE's getting a hard time at home. You can't just end up in hospital having your stomach pumped and expect parents like HERS to carry on as if nothing has happened, although she won't tell us what they've said. And THEN she started having a go about how science was boring and scientists were nerds and I wanted to hit her because it's not THAT boring. It was a doctor who probably saved her life after all, which Ruby pointed out to her in a rather sweet, loyal way. If I get into medical school and turn out to be the one who discovers the cure for cancer, how nerdish is that?? She'll be the one boasting to all her friends about how she 'knows' me when I'll be the one having dinner with the stars. Chattie's piling on the pressure because he wants me to see less of my friends and spend more time with him (when Saskia's THIS horrible I wonder why I don't). With friends like these and exams, the last thing I need at the moment is divorcing parents. It's embarrassing enough just HAVING parents – THESE parents.

Chattie and I were there for Lola's birthday party and Chattie gave all her friends a skating lesson, but from the way Mum's been going on this past weekend anybody would think I'd done nothing at all, just because we went out last night and I stayed over at Ruby's and wasn't here for her actual birthday this morning. Mum feels it's important for the whole family to be together 'at times like this' when Lola couldn't care less, so why should Mum? She's been giving me a hard time with these narky little comments and she's walking around with the hump when actually what she probably needs is to be humped, only who would want to hump THAT and she hasn't got the slightest sympathy for the fact that I'm fifteen, bored and stressed out. I'm so glad she's not my doctor as well. Imagine that! Dad's on my side on this one. He loves it when we fall out and he has an ally in their stupid little war. Bet Saskia doesn't know what the word ally means. Must remember to ask her tomorrow.

What About Me, Too?

Dear Diary,

Tuesday

My legs really ache and I'm worried that I might have something seriously wrong with me like cancer but Mum just laughs and says it's growing pains. I know she's a doctor but what if she's got it wrong? Maybe I need a blood test. I definitely need a crop top because Tanya and Clare say I do but when I asked Mum if she'd buy me one she laughed at that too and said there was nothing there yet to support, but it doesn't feel that way. They feel huge. I really don't want to go to school but Mum says I have to.

Dear Diary,

Wednesday ✏️

Mum tried to get me to go to school this morning but I cried so much that she had to let me stay. My legs still hurt. When I went to school on Monday, I thought that maybe because of my party Tanya and Clare would be different but they weren't, they walked round the playground whispering with their arms tight around each other's shoulders. I've been taking pictures of Chloe with my new camera. She's been sleeping on the sofa with me. Toyah promised me that she wouldn't tell Mum because she's not allowed on the sofa.

Toyah and I took Chloe to the cemetery for a walk after lunch. I took pictures of all the different types of trees there with my new camera. Most of them have lost all their leaves but the cemetery is still so green because of all the ivy and weeds. We even found some holly. Toyah was really interested in all the tombstones. Maybe they don't have cemeteries in Australia. We walked around looking for our names and found lots of Sues but no Lolas or Toyahs. We found lots of children which is like really sad and one grave where three sisters are buried. One died as a baby in 1901, the year she was born. Her sister Beatrice died in 1899 at the age of four and the eldest one, Jane, died when she was ten. Imagine how heartbreaking that must have been for the parents. I hope they had some more children to make up for all the ones they lost. Life must have been very very hard in Victorian times if so many bad things could happen to children. There was a lot of disease and not many doctors around as good as Mum. All those poor street children who had to look after themselves must have found it very hard not to give up hope.

But Camilla doesn't give up hope, ever. I think she's so brave. I saw her stump for the first time when she came to stay the night at my party. She took her foot off and put it by her clothes and then got into bed! She never ever takes it off at school. I think she just felt so at home here that she forgot – which I'm really, really pleased about. There was like this embarrassed silence when she did it, particularly as the end of her leg looks so, so weird, sort of unfinished with this tiny little stump at her ankle. But then we started to talk about it and Britney asked her weather her false leg rubbed and she said that it had done today because of the skating. That means that Camilla must have been so, so brave in Wales because she never took off her false foot there and we were running about all the time. I'm so lucky. Things may be difficult with Mum and Dad rowing all the time but at least I have two feet.

Chloe loves it in the cemetery. She leaps about sniffing. Toyah says that's because she can smell foxes and rats. You can easily lose your way in the cemetery because there're all these winding paths but I wanted Toyah to see the lion because he's like so amazing. 'Wow! Look at HIM,' she said in that really bubbly way she has of being more Australian when she's excited. 'He's FANTASTIC.' Toyah climbed up onto the lion's back and looked out over the cemetery and said, 'I don't think I'd even mind being dead if I could be buried under him!' which was a funny thing to say but not true. Nobody wants to be dead. I climbed up behind her and squeezed her tight. I love Toyah. Having her around helps because she's always the same, always my friend. I was just about to tell her about Dad and Laura and the text messages because I thought she would know what to do when she screamed, 'Look at THAT!' and jumped down onto the ground. She was peering through a crack in the marble slab at the side of the tomb. I jumped down beside her. We pulled back the slab together and there were steps leading down. Creepy. We held hands and went inside. It was like so, so scary going down those steps and SOOOO dark. Toyah had a Mini Maglite on her key ring and that helped. The steps led down to a large room. There were metal holders on the walls for flares and dirty old mattresses piled up against one wall. But no sign of any bodies or coffins. The room seemed quite clean really, considering nobody had been inside it for like 100 years. But when I said that to Toyah she said that people were living here. She flashed her torch into a corner: 'Look, there's a stash of food and . . .' she flashed her torch into the opposite corner, 'someone's lit a fire over there.' I couldn't believe that anybody would want to live in a tomb. But when I said that to Toyah on the way home she said that nobody would choose that over a lovely warm house but for some really poor hard-up people they have nowhere else to go. She says that they can even be young people, teenagers just like Frankie, who have such cruel parents that they run away and live rough. She said it in a really sad way like she knew it from her own life but when I asked her if it had happened to her she said no. If Toyah is right then there are a lot more similarities between Victorian children and children today than I realized. I wish I'd known that for my project.

Dear Diary,

Friday ✏️

Mum, Dad and Frankie had another one of their massive rows last night. I don't know how Frankie can be so immature when she's fifteen and practically a grown-up when I'm only just eleven and I never row like that with them. She ought to listen to them more, instead of just shouting back. I'd better not tell her about the Lion's Tomb. She does NOT want to be kicked out and have to go and live there. Mum and Dad started it. They were arguing over the video recorder. Dad wanted to watch the football and Mum wanted to watch episode six of *Crime and Punishment* on the other side, and neither of them knows how to make the video recorder work. Frankie is the only one who does but she was on the phone to Ruby, talking about practically nothing at all, except that I did learn one interesting fact which is that Saskia's parents have grounded her for three months because she drank so much she had to go to hospital, so now she's stopped eating and has started puking up in the school bogs to keep her wait down. Imagine that, our bogs stink so much that you don't even need to stick your finger down your throat to feel sick. Anyway, Mum and Dad were shouting for Frankie who wasn't listening, in between insulting each other for being so pathetic that they couldn't work the video recorder. Then they even started arguing about the merits of watching football versus *Crime and Punishment*. Mum said that he could watch the football any night of the week on Sky sports and that she had been looking forward to this all week. He said she could watch the repeat on Sunday and that this was a big match. How pathetic is that? They went on arguing about it for so long that they forgot about Frankie and she forgot about the bath she was running because she was talking to Ruby on the phone and it started flooding over the side and onto the bathroom floor and they only noticed when water started dripping down the cracks in the ceiling into the living room above their heads, and then of course they went even madder and turned on Frankie for forgetting. And I just lay in bed listening to all of this, checking through Dad's text messages, and was pleased to see that my messages were beginning to have an effect and she was cross with him for ignoring her, so I sent another one back saying, 'dnt lve u nemore, got new girlfrend,' so that should sort it for good. I slipped his phone back into his jacket pocket and wondered weather all families were like this or weather it was just my luck to be lumbered with parents who argue like children and an older sister who is a cretin.

Dear Diary,

Why is everything that goes wrong in this house my fault? It's just water but from the way Mum's going on anyone would think I'd set fire to the place, which is what Fran did smoking in her bedroom last week, only her Mum's so cool about everything and chain-smokes herself so she couldn't get cross. You'd think Mum'd be pleased, you'd think she'd appreciate the fact that actually, compared to some of my friends, I'm totally, totally sorted – I don't smoke like Fran any more, well, only sometimes because Chattie hates it so much. I don't get catatonic on drink or drugs like Hayley and Saskia. I LIKE FOOD but all she can do is go on and on at me for forgetting to turn off the bath, when how dangerous is that exactly? I mean how many teenagers drown in a bath each year, huh? AND Dad says they can claim money off the insurance and have the room decorated so actually they ought to thank me for it. The real problem is that their marriage is worse than it's ever been. I suggested to Mum that they ought to go to see a marriage guidance counsellor but she just laughed and said what would I know about marriage at fifteen with only one boyfriend. Charming, when I was only trying to help.

What About Me, Too?

From: Sue James
Sent: Sunday 1 December 21:45
To: Angela James
Subject: What a humdinger of a morning . . .

Matthew stormed into Frank's bedroom this morning looking for his mobile phone and found Chattie in bed with her. Instead of withdrawing politely he stood in her room with his hands on his hips and ordered Chattie to get up, get dressed and leave, which of course was humiliating for both of them. Frankie went ballistic, they had a furious row and then Matthew stormed out of the house for a jog in the pouring rain. Frankie burst into tears and sobbed into my shoulder, great heaving sobs like she was crying about her whole life, not just the fact that her stupid father had lost it. I tried to make her laugh by saying that he was just angry about the fact that someone else was having sex in this house instead of him and that he'd get over it but she just kept on sobbing, which made me want to cry too. Of course she's been having sex with Chattie, why wouldn't she? Though I wish she'd told me. He's gorgeous, but all I could think of to say was, 'Have you been using condoms?' which made her go, 'Mu-um, of course I have.' Mulling it over now, I wish I'd suggested at that moment that she ought to use at least two at the same time, 'one over the other in case one splits'.

I think what really enraged Matthew was losing control. Frank is out there, a sexually maturing adult, being influenced by other men, not just him. This is, of course, a load of patriarchal crap but then I feel a bit funny about it too. I feel complete revulsion imagining them having sex – the idea of your own child being penetrated by someone else makes me feel ever so slightly sick, a bit like it does when it's your own parents. Perhaps that's what he's feeling too only we can't of course talk about it because he's been withdrawn and surly or asleep on the sofa ever since.

Frankie then stormed into Lola's bedroom and accused Lola of telling Matthew and called her some really horrible things, the 'c' word even passed her lips, so that led to another violent, ugly scene, with Frankie trying to pull out her hair and Lola kicking at her shins shouting, 'I didn't I didn't I DIDN'T' so I then had to spend another half an hour calming Lola down. Meanwhile, Tom had spotted these moments with no supervision to try his hand at self-feeding. He opened the fridge and tipped a carton of milk and a pot of yoghurt onto the floor and was busy licking it up with his tongue when I appeared. I hate to think when we last washed that floor, and what with. Honestly, that boy is so greedy but I suppose you have to give him full marks for initiative. Lola's been off school most of this week, says she has a tummy ache and feels sick but she hasn't got a temperature. Her legs ache too, which could be growing pains. Every morning I get her up for school and she complains that her legs ache and cries, saying she doesn't feel strong enough. She just doesn't want to go to school. I've said we'll go in together in the morning and I'll have a word with Miss Jennings.

I'll ping you in the week about Mum. Have a lovely day on the beach.

Sx

What About Me, Too?

Dear Diary,

Dad is the biggest fucking hypocrite that has ever lived. How dare he preach to me about sexual morality when he's been unfaithful to Mum AND they're MARRIED with kids. Chattie and I haven't done anything wrong, even if it's against the law, which Dad shouted about 10,000 times, so loud that the whole street could hear. I expect HND's already been onto the police. WE love each other but he treated Chattie like he was some sort of dirt beneath his shoe, chucking him out like that when he was always happy to watch the football with him before. He secretly really hates the idea of his daughter sleeping with a black man. That's what it is, like the Capulets were about Juliet marrying a Montague, but I'm not going to run off and marry him in secret like Juliet did. He thinks Chattie's not right for me. Well how dare he even THINK he has a right to have an opinion on who my boyfriend is???? I'll never ever forgive him for this, like he thinks he has a right to run my whole life. I HATE HIM I HATE HIM I HATE HIM. I've called Chattie about 100 times but he won't pick up. Honestly, love is difficult enough without parents getting in the way and making things worse. Mum tries to be understanding but because she's a doctor whenever she talks to me it's always in terms of health and REALLLLY patronizing, like are we using condoms – DERRR – when what really matters to me at the moment is coping with Chattie's feelings at being kicked out of my house like he wasn't even liked. I'm worried about Chattie, Dad really offended him and he is so proud – what if he's run off and done something really stupid like get drunk or even tried to kill himself?????

Kate Figes

Dear Diary,

Sunday the 1st day of December and only twenty-five days
to Christmas

I wish I was still a small child and didn't understand
anything. Frankie's being really really horrible and has
blamed everything on me and Mum just fusses around her
the whole time like something really terrible has happened,
like she's broken all the bones in her body when she hasn't,
she's just had stupid sex with Chattie, that's all, and been
stupid enough to let Dad find them. If I were still a small
child I wouldn't care, I could just go off and play with
Clare, but I can't even do that any more. If I was small, like
six, which is a really good age because you can do things by
yourself but people still look after you, I wouldn't notice
that Mum hasn't even been nice to me to make up for the
fact that Frankie has accused me of stuff I didn't do. And I
wouldn't know how to read text messages and have to keep
this secret about Laura all to myself. Whenever I think
about it my tummy aches. I also would definitely not
understand that Mum and Dad have been arguing about
Frankie so they don't have to argue about their own
problems. It's been a real crap day.

What About Me, Too?

From: Sue James
Sent: Tuesday 3 December 17:12
To: Angela James
Subject: Re: Mum

Talked to North Butting at length yesterday. They don't think she's demented, just being difficult and mendacious and they say they rang me with an urgent message to call them back on Friday but I never got the message, because of course they left it with Frankie. They might as well have left it with the dog. What's more worrying though, is that Mum has been refusing to eat so I think I'll go up there on Saturday.

Lola wouldn't go to school AGAIN today so I've come home early to try and get to the bottom of all this. I think she's being bullied by Clare and Tanya but HND, who helped Miss Jennings yesterday on the swimming run, is an EXPERT on all children, and knows otherwise. She rang me last night to say that Lola had refused to swim because she had a tummy ache and Miss Jennings had told her that she often complained of tummy aches. She then suggested that I had her tested for allergies and if it wasn't that it was probably trouble at home! The cheek of her! And I'M the one who's the doctor! The woman definitely has Munchausen's by proxy. She's obsessed with disease. I was so outraged I told her firmly in my 'disassociated from feelings' voice, reserved for the most difficult patients, that an allergy was unlikely and that I suspected Tanya and her own daughter had been bullying Lola. At that she put down the phone. Thank goodness.

Much love, Sx

What About Me, Too?

Dear Diary,

Thursday the 4th of December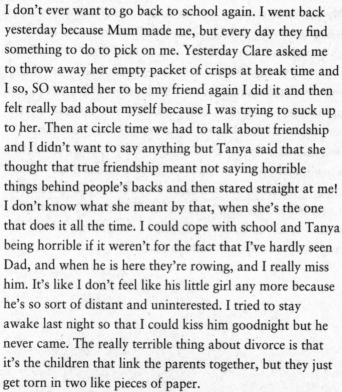

I don't ever want to go back to school again. I went back
yesterday because Mum made me, but every day they find
something to do to pick on me. Yesterday Clare asked me
to throw away her empty packet of crisps at break time and
I so, SO wanted her to be my friend again I did it and then
felt really bad about myself because I was trying to suck up
to her. Then at circle time we had to talk about friendship
and I didn't want to say anything but Tanya said that she
thought that true friendship meant not saying horrible
things behind people's backs and then stared straight at me!
I don't know what she meant by that, when she's the one
that does it all the time. I could cope with school and Tanya
being horrible if it weren't for the fact that I've hardly seen
Dad, and when he is here they're rowing, and I really miss
him. It's like I don't feel like his little girl any more because
he's so sort of distant and uninterested. I tried to stay
awake last night so that I could kiss him goodnight but he
never came. The really terrible thing about divorce is that
it's the children that link the parents together, but they just
get torn in two like pieces of paper.

Mum's been at work all day but Toyah's here so that's
OK. She made me a cheese omelette for lunch because she
knows I love them and when Tom was having his nap she
helped me print off some of the best pictures of the
cemetery. The ones deep in the tomb didn't come out at all,
even with a flash, which was a bit weird – there was this

really bright shading in the right-hand corner of them.
Toyah said it was probably a ghost! I hope she was joking
because if I was a teenager who had run away from home
I would not want to live with a ghost. Even a friendly one.
We stuck the pictures into my scrapbook and Toyah was
being so so nice, telling me stories about when she was a
child and how when her Mum and Dad fought she used to
run away to this den she had made on the beach, and then I
told her. I told her about how Dad was probably having an
affair with somebody called Laura and how I'd read his text
messages and then I burst into tears and she cuddled me
and said that was an awful thing to have to live with all by
myself, and then I felt much better. We agreed there was no
need to tell Mum yet and make her sad. But she said that if
I ever felt sad about it I should say 'lion' to let her know
that I needed a hug. I love Toyah so much. I can't think
how we ever managed without her.

What About Me, Too?

Dear Diary,

Sunday the 8th of December

Mum and her friend Julie went to see Granny today and I
didn't have to go because Dad was going to take me and
Tom to the baby bounce. What that actually means is that
he reads the newspapers and drinks coffee, while I play with
Tom, drag him up the tubes and push him down the slides,
which is OK so long as I'm with him. Then Dad took us to
McDonald's for a Coke and burger, which Mum bans us
from having because she says the food is really, really bad
for us, but Dad says that's wrong so now I'm not sure what
to believe. Then when we went home we passed this young
girl begging in a doorway. She looked really dirty, like she
needed a bath, and so young so maybe she has run away
from horrible parents like Toyah says. Maybe she even lives
in the Lion's Tomb. I wanted Dad to give her some money
because it's nearly Christmas and so, so cold and I know
she really needs the money but Dad said that you shouldn't
give beggars money because it only encourages them and
that she was probably a drug addikt or she'd spend it all on
drink anyway. I said how did he know that, and it wasn't
right not to give her something when we could and we
argued about it all the way back to the car. He thinks that
people have a choice, that they don't have to go out begging
and that they could get a job and that it's all their own
fault!!! I don't see how that can be true, when no one's
going to want to give her a job when she looks that messy
and no one's going to choose to sit in a cold, dirty doorway

begging for money if they didn't need to. But when I said that to Dad he said that I was too young to understand. Well what's to understand? Children don't have much choice, except whether to buy *Bliss* or *Heat* magazine or chocolate or crisps in the sweet shop with their pocket money, which is why it takes them so long sometimes to decide because it's just about the only thing they have to make an important desishon about. Unless you're spoilt like Clare, that is, and can have whatever you want.

What About Me, Too?

From: Sue James
Sent: Sunday 8 December 21:12
To: Angela James
Subject: The mother figure

She's fine, a little thin but mentally all there – in other words, her usual devious, manipulative self, intent upon making as much mischief as possible. At least she's not faecally incontinent, which has to be one of the worst aspects of old age – so humiliating. I got called in by Matron and told that if she didn't behave (which means not spreading wicked rumours about the food) she would have to ask her to leave, which made me want to laugh because if this bunch of hardened battleaxes can't handle old ladies, who can? I felt like I was being told off by a headmistress for misdemeanours usually attributed to my children rather than my mother, which was a little weird. I explained about how we were trying to move her nearer to London and that she was coming to stay with us for ten days over Christmas (yes, TEN WHOLE DAYS – how will we manage? Any ideas?) and that we would feed her up and talk to her about her behaviour then. What I really wanted to say to her was, 'We pay you a ton of money to look after her and at least she has the gumption to be naughty, unlike the rest of the half-dead in here!' What I REALLY don't want them to do is to change her drug regime without consulting me. I don't want them giving her sedatives to keep her quiet and I made her promise me that they wouldn't alter anything until after Christmas.

Christmas, AARGH! Mum's moving into Lola's room on the 20th and Lola's going to double up with Frank, which will not make life any quieter since they argue over everything at the moment, even who has which gloves in the morning – there aren't enough nice ones to go round apparently. And of course, what it DOES mean is that there is absolutely no possibility of any sexual activity in her room, which thrills me but must be pissing Frank off. I've finally relented and agreed that we'll all go to Granny and Grandpa Wilcox on Christmas Day and I'm hoping that Matthew will see this as a major concession. After all, he does have to put up with a great deal with Mum.

Meanwhile letters from Lola's school demand that little bit of extra effort since this is her last year there. Can I help with food and entertainment for the Christmas party/make an extra special hat/help with the costumes for the nativity play? HND, I am informed by Lola, has already made ten Xmas cakes for the teachers and her own mince pies. Thank God I get all those dry old cakes full of weevils baked for me by grateful patients. If I sprinkle a bit of icing sugar on them they'll be just fine for school.

Lola's now gone back to school and she keeps going on at me about some boots she wants that Clare has (probably designer, costing £150) and how most of her wardrobe 'sucks'. I've said if she really wants them she can have them for Christmas. She didn't like that, stormed off in a sulk.

It's cold and very dark on this side of our small planet. It's dark when I take Lola to school, dark when she comes home and pitch bloody black by the time I get back from the surgery. Every so often I look up the weather in Australia in the paper and think lucky bitch . . .

Love you madly, honestly, Suexxx

What About Me, Too?

Dear Diary,

I know that both Romeo and Juliet had short and tragic lives but neither of them had to take GCSEs. The thought of mocks after Christmas is killing me. Why don't they let us take them before Xmas so that at least we can relax along with the the rest of the world during the holidays? And the thing is that I know I have to get good grades in the science ones if I'm ever going to make it as a doctor, but what if I don't and what if I'm a crap doctor or when I get to medical school, if I ever get there, I discover that it's not really what I want to do and I want to be a film star instead? Mum's really pleased about the fact that I want to be a doctor and I really don't want to disappoint her but if she'd only just get off my back about revising, I mean I am TRYING. I've texted every single person I've ever known in an effort to avoid chemistry. And look, now I'm even writing in my diary, my ❤(LOVE) diary, so I don't have to work. I mean, what is the difference between a neutron and a proton and who cares anyway? I've read the sheet that's supposed to explain the whole thing for morons like me about ten times and I still don't understand it and that worries me because I ought to know. But if you can't actually see a person's atoms then you're never going to know what's wrong with them so it can't be that important if you want to be a doctor.

Chattie is grounded until the mocks are over so I can't even see him except for at Christmas when I can't see him anyway because we have to go to Granny and Grandpa

Wilcox. I'm sure if we could see each other we'd work harder, we could test each other. Saskia's grounded too, and under threat of being sent to a crammer if she doesn't get all As and A*s in her mocks. Ruby's useless at revising because she just wants to talk all the time and Fran isn't bothering to revise at all. She can't see the point when they're not the real thing.

GCSEs – PREDICTED GRADES BY TEACHERS
Triple science As and Bs hopefully
English A/B
History B/C
Geography B/C
Drama A/B
Maths E/F
French B

What About Me, Too?

Dear Diary,

Monday the 9th of December

It's all over. Everything's finished and it's all my fault. Mum and Dad were rowing about the fact that Dad had taken me to McDonald's yesterday so I went up to Frankie's room to talk to her but she told me to piss off because she was revising for her exams, when actually I could see that what she was doing was trying on all her clothes because they were lying all over the floor. So I took Dad's mobile to check up on Laura while they were arguing and that's when the trouble started and it's all my fault. The signs from his text messages were not good. The last one said, 'not long now, b patient' and her messages to him flatter him in this really sick way like she tells him he's sexy. DAD? SEXY? And how good he was in bed last night . . . eugh! Disgusting! So I was just texting back to say how terrible she was in bed last night and that 'I still love my wife' when Mum walked in the room and asked me what my score was. I could have lied. I should have lied, but at that moment I didn't want to. I couldn't keep it to myself any longer. It's like such a big, big thing to know. So I gave her the phone and she read through the messages and then World War Three broke out and it's all my fault.

They didn't just row in the house. They rowed in the street. They screamed at each other and Mum even got into the car and wanted to drive off somewhere only Dad wouldn't let her, so there was a lot of engine-revving and door-slamming and then I thought that maybe she was trying to stop him from leaving so then I was worried that she might run him over. It was so embarrassing. I just wanted them both to come back inside. But then when they did, they were still shouting and screaming at each other and it was so loud and angry I started screaming and punching myself in my room so that nobody could hear me. It's all my stupid STUPID **STUPID** fault. I HATE MYSELF. Frankie came up and gave me a hug. We sat on my bed for ages, waiting for them to calm down, which they did eventually. And now I'm in bed and I can't get to sleep and Dad hasn't been in to say goodnight to me, because of course he must blame me for ruining everything and Mum's been crying again, but at least she has been in to say goodnight and give me a hug. I must be such a bad person. If I wasn't here then maybe life would be easier for everybody else. But Dad hasn't left, so I don't know what's going on.

What About Me, Too?

Dear Diary,

Wensday the 11th of December

Dad's still living here, I think, because his things are here but he's been out a lot and nobody has said anything about what happened. We had a dress rehersel for the nativity play today. I'm a sheperd, Tanya's a wise man – how hilarious is that? She's so stupid she wouldn't even recognize the baby Jesus if she stepped on him – and Clare is Mary, which means that her mother has been in school most of the week making costoomes because it has to be the best nativity play ever. Mum put together a costoome for me last night with Dad's old cricket shirt, some brown tights and an old fake fur coat of hers hanging off my shoulders and she made me a hat out of a square bit of old sheet with a scarf twisted round my head to keep it in place. I thought it looked really good. But then when I put it on for the rehersel, Clare's mother said it wasn't nearly good enough and that she would have to make me something better over the weekend. How mean is that, when my Mum made it? I'm not going to tell her but what's she going to think when she comes to the play next week and sees me wearing something else? Clare's mum also kept asking me questions like, 'How are things at home?' and 'How're Mum and Dad?' and it was obvious that she knew because she would have heard everything but I didn't say anything. It's none of her busyness. And then when I went to the loo I could hear her talking about us to one of the other mothers. I heard her say, 'Their rows are terrible, the poor child.' Well I'm not that poor, not as poor as Camilla, or Clare who has a cow of a mother.

What About Me, Too?

From: Sue James
Sent: Saturday 14 December 23:10
To: Angela James
Subject: Why is it that everything happens at once at this time of y . . .

No, presents haven't arrived yet but I'm sure they will and if they don't, what the fuck! They are hardly deprived. Anyway, not sure what sort of Christmas we're going to have. Matthew has been bonking the tart again. I'm furious and we're on total no-speaks at the moment. I haven't kicked him out yet and he hasn't left so not sure quite what to make of it, but simply can't deal with anything until after Christmas. It's not fair on the kids, plus I'm sick with the flu, as is Frankie, it's the nativity play on Monday, Tom's first birthday on Thursday and Mum arrives on Friday . . . It's Matthew's birthday on Friday too but if he thinks he's going to get anything more than a black eye from me then he's deluded as well as devious.

Opened the front door this morning to the postman and found six dogs sitting at the bottom of the steps. Chloe's been lying around with her legs wide open, displaying bright red pudenda – on heat – great. Took her straight to the vet to see about having her spayed to wails of distraught complaint from the girls but he won't do it until she's been out of season for a month – great! So took her to the park and kept her on the lead. Within minutes, every dog in the neighbourhood was following us. Wouldn't it be just fab if the same thing happened

to human females? You could just turn around and pick the
male you liked the look of best AND be safe because you'd
definitely use contraception. Sadly, Mark's black Lab was not
one of the pack and nor was he. I gather from Mavis, his next-
door neighbour, that his wife left him last year (for another
woman!) and he now looks after their sons. What does that do
to male pride, I wonder?

So, if you don't hear from me again before you go to
Thailand, I'm either busy or dead. Ring us on Christmas Eve or
early on Christmas morning if you can from wherever you are.

Love, Scrooge

What About Me, Too?

Dear Diary,

Monday the 16th of December

Clare's mum dressed me up in this really horrible, itchy
costume for the play this afternoon and when I told her that
I wanted to wear what Mum had made she said that I
couldn't because the colours didn't go and she wanted all
the sheperds to look the same. Mum was right at the back
of the hall with Tom behind a wall of camcorders so I really
hope that she didn't notice that I wasn't wearing her
costume. She said she thought I did really well and that it
was the best play ever but she couldn't have seen much
because she missed the bit where I come to see the baby
Jesus because Tom was crying so much that she had to take
him out of the room. Dad never turned up. Mum saved a
seat for him but he never came. Mum said something must
have come up – yeah, like Laura probably. He'd rather be
with her than see my play. My head hurts and I've got a
sore throat and I really hope that I'm getting the flu too so
that I don't have to go to school tomorrow because my
Christmas hat is crap and Tanya's already teasing me about
it. I wish everything was happier, that Mum and Dad could
be nice to each other and love each other like they used to.
I wish I could have been strong enough and lied about the
text messages, then maybe everything would be all right.
They're not talking to each other at all and I'm not sure
whether this is better or worse than having them rowing. I
mean, is Dad going to be with us at Christmas? Are we still
going to Granny and Grandpa Wilcox or are we going to

have to stay here with just Granny? He was home this morning so he must have come in very late last night because he didn't come home before I went to bed. It doesn't feel very Christmassy here.

What About Me, Too?

Dear Diary,

Why does Christmas have to come at the end of the month when I've spent all my allowance? If it was on, say, the 5th of December, just after everyone got paid, there'd be no problem buying everyone nice stuff but all I've managed to get so far is a poxy key ring for Mum. There's only seven more shopping days left and I'm in bed, dying of some incurable disease and Dad doesn't even care enough to give me a loan. I just rang him from my death bed and all he could say was that I should have been saving since September, like I didn't already know that. Derrrrrr. I want to get Chattie something really nice, because he's still so hurt by what my horrible, hypocritical, dickhead father did, although he always denies that when I ask, just stares at me like a sad dog with those watery brown eyes. And then Ruby keeps going on about what an expensive present she's got me – hardly subtle.

Saskia is still grounded and says she's so bored at home she just wants to wrap her gob round everything from the Advocaat to the vodka in her parents drinks cabinet which kind of defeats the object of the punishment, only her stupid parents don't know that. She says they're like watching her the whole time and her mum keeps taking her shopping because she thinks that'll make up for her not being allowed out with her friends when actually she has so many clothes that she can't even be bothered to take them out of the bags. Hayley is completely lost without her. She keeps ringing me up to see if I'll go out with her and what are we doing and yesterday she even suggested to Saskia

*that she should sneak out – put a whole load of pillows
down the bed and come out drinking with us on Friday.
Mad. Her parents'll find out and then they'll pack her off to
some horrible private boarding school in the country where
she'd have to wear a brown uniform and sandals.*

*Mum may be a doctor but she hasn't been up to see me
once in my death bed since this morning. I know she's sick
too but she's not as sick as me. I think I'll go through all
the photographs and make Dad a collage of all the happier
family moments we used to have before he went bonking.
If I could find a picture of Laura I'd stick her in too and
gouge her eyes out. That'll teach him not to fuck up our
lives. What else does he expect anyway, if he won't lend me
any money.*

What About Me, Too?

Dear Diary,

Thursday the 19th of December

Tom is one today! Dad promised he'd come home early from work so that we could all sing happy birthday to him but he hasn't got here yet and I really need to see him to know that he forgives me for reading his phone. I haven't seen him since their big row and I really, really need a hug. Even though Mum was really sick, so sick that she couldn't go to work, which has never happened before, she looked really happy with Tom. She kissed and cuddled him the whole time. She gave him a knew truck with wooden bricks in it to help him walk round the house and he's already slammed it into my legs three times. But now she's gone back to bed for a bit because she's feeling so ill. Dad's still not home and the cake's sitting on the kitchen table with one candle in it. Poor Tom, not much of a party. But he is still too young to notice the diffrence between having a proper birthday and everyone being too ill and tired to make it special.

Dear Diary,

Friday the 20th of December

Granny arrived today, which means it's nearly Christmas!!! Mum gets in such a state whenever Granny comes which is stupid because it's me and Frankie who have to change things, not her. I've had to move ALL my stuff into Frankie's room which stinks, and I'm sleeping on a mattrus and the floor is disgusting because it's covered with snotty tissues because she can't be bothered to put them in the bin. Mum told her to tidy up her room but she just chucked all the stuff into one corner and then when I told her off for not doing it properly, she just laughed at me and said what did she care about it, and that it was her room and if I was staying in it I had to live with it. That's not a very nice way to treat someone who is like a guest there, like your own SISTER, so I've stolen her phone and I'm not going to give it back to her until she starts being nice to me again.

Dad's grumpy because it's his birthday today (he's ancient, forty-seven) and nobody's remembered to get him anything except me. I made him a card and painted a cardboard box for him to keep his things in when I was ill in bed. Mum didn't get him anything, not even a card. She says he doesn't deserve it. I know birthdays matter less when you're old but they still matter and he needs a cake so Toyah and I are going to make him one this afternoon. Maybe then he'll forgive me. Nobody has said one single thing about it – like are they going to split up again? – and I really need to know. The one really good thing about having Granny here is that everyone has to be nicer to each other, except Frankie, of course, who's had a really bad row with Chattie which means she thinks she can be really horrible to everyone, and me in particular since I'm in her room and can't get away from her. They're probably going to break up and I completely understand why because if I was Chattie I wouldn't want to go out with anybody as horrible as her. Granny sits in the same chair in the sitting room all day long, waiting for people to come and talk to her or bring her cups of tea, which I'm very good at. She says I'm clever to use proper tea and not bags and that she's going to knit me my very own tea cosy to keep the pot warm. We had a nice chat too about how, when she was a little girl, her dad used to dress up as Father Christmas on Christmas Eve and drift up and down the hallway after she had gone to bed to make her all excited. I like having Granny here because at least she's normal, even if she does drive Mum mad.

Much later in bed. Dad still hasn't come home and his cake is sitting on the kitchen table with forty-seven unlit candles on it. I know because I stuck them all in and it took me ages.

Dear Diary,

I don't understand what I have to do to make Chattie happy. He's like really possessive and jealous but he never actually comes out and says he loves me in a way that I believe him, so how am I like to really know if he loves me as much as I love him? I bet Romeo and Juliet never had this problem, and that was true love. Ruby says he wouldn't be jealous if he didn't love me but that doesn't feel like love to me. Loving someone means that you want what's best for them and that doesn't mean holding onto them so tightly that you squeeze all the life out of them. Fran and Serena think I spend more time with Chattie than I do with them and they say that I ought to be putting my friends first because no boy is THAT worth it. They're right but Chattie doesn't see it that way. He's mad at me just because he lied to his mother last night just to be with me (she doesn't want him going out until after the mocks are over so he told her it was a school Christmas event) and we went to this bar where they're really cool about ID and I drank too much of course, but just how do you stop vodka and Coke sliding down your throat when it makes you feel so good? He says I was flirting with this boy when all I thought I was actually doing was talking to him and Chattie dragged me outside and got really mad with me, told me to stop being so selfish and to think of him and I got mad back and told him that I could talk to whoever I liked. We had this really bad fight about it and he stormed off into the night and now I can't sleep and I've texted him to say sorry but he hasn't texted back

*and until he does I don't think I'll ever be able to sleep
again. And we're going to Granny and Grandpa Wilcox
tomorrow and I really, really want to see him and know
that everything's OK again before we go.*

Dear Diary, 🖉

It's Christmas Eve!!! We're going to Granny and Grandpa
Wilcox tonight and Mum and Dad have been arguing about
how to get everything into the car for ages. At least that
means they're talking to each other again and we're all
going, so maybe Laura is dead or something. The fact is our
car is too small for all of us plus presents, plus bags, plus
Tom's travel cot but Mum keeps insisting that it will all go
in, it just has to be packed right, and keeps taking
everything out and piling it up on the pavement while Dad
shouts at her and tells her she's mad and why are women so
bad at spachial awareness. What's that about? She's
determined it will work and hasn't shouted back at him but
it's only a question of time before she does. What does it
matter to him anyway, when he's going up on his
motorbike with all his stuff in his side panniers? Mum's
driving, Granny'll go in the front and me, Frankie and Tom
will be stuffed into the back, worst luck, for about 100
hours, with Frankie texting madly on her phone. Tom'll cry
because he's bored and Mum'll ask me to play with him
and keep him happy – ME, not Frankie because she's too
busy talking to her friends AND we won't be able to have
the radio on because of Granny. Then of course we'll have
to have the whole breakdown on the M1 on Christmas Day
story all over again, how we waited three hours for the AA
because they were short-staffed because it was Christmas
Day and we didn't have any food or water with us except
Frankie's giant chocolate stocking that Clare's mum had
given her, and how Dad's parents were more worried about

the turkey drying out than our welfare. We've heard that story so many times we can't ever hope to forget it, when I would have thought it was something that was best forgotten. Why don't adults just learn how to move on?

Dear Diary,

Santa is pretty mean in Yorkshire. That's because Granny
and Grandpa Wilcox said they'd do it instead of Mum. I
got kids' stuff like animal rubbers and felt-pens. They must
think I'm still a baby. Frankie didn't do much better. She
got some pretty tissues, a gyroscope (which is still in a box
and she'll never use) and some deodorant, which for some
reason really offended her when I would have thought it
would be really useful. Tom, on the other hand, got loads
of toys. Mum was nice about it though. She came up to see
us in the attic where Frankie and I are sleeping on camp
beds and said that she was sorry and that she should never
have let them do it and that she'd make it up to us when we
got home with a shopping trip – just the three of us girls.
We hardly ever stay here and now I think I know why. Do
you know that Granny Wilcox made Chloe sleep in the
car??? It's freezing out there – how mean is that? Me and
Frankie went down very early this morning after we'd
opened our stockings and sneaked her up to our bedroom
so that she could warm up in bed. I don't care if they find
out and get cross. She's part of the family now, OUR
family.

Mum took Granny to church after breakfast and seemed
really keen to go just so that she could get out of the house
and then we opened the presents under the tree. Mum and
Dad gave me this amazing karaoke set for the computer
which means I can record my own songs, which I really,
really like and a whole load of clothes which I hate. I tried
to look pleased with them but Mum could tell I didn't like

them and then I felt bad. I got loads of money, though, from both the grannies which means I can go and buy my own stuff and Mum said we could change the things she'd bought me when we went shopping. Everyone made such a fuss over Tom, I mean I love him but anyone would think that from the way Dad and Granny and Grandpa Wilcox went on, there'd never been such a perfect baby born before. Granny and Grandpa gave him a full Brio train set and then they all got really upset when he wasn't interested in it. Dad spent ages setting the whole thing up all over the living-room floor and then when Tom fell over it and mucked it up Dad got cross, which is so totally stupid because he will play with it, lots probably, when he's older and when he wants to. They also gave him one of those chocolate stocking sets which made Mum furious as he isn't allowed chocolate because he's too young and Mum says it's bad for babies, but Granny Wilcox says a little chocolate can't do him any harm. So then Dad had to side with his parents because we're in their house and Mum picked up Tom and took him and Chloe out for a walk, instead of helping with the lunch.

Just as I suspected, this has been one of the worst Christmas Days ever and I can't wait to get home.

Dear Diary,

I'M SO **BORED**. I love Chattie, I LOVE CHATTIE. TEXT
ME, CHATTIE, PLEASE . . .
    I'm SOOOOO BORED HERE.
    Give me slums over suburbia any day.

What About Me, Too?

From: Sue James
Sent: Friday 27 December 16:21
To: Angela James
Subject: I think it really is all over this time

Ange darling, dearest Ange,

How I wish you were here with me right now. You're probably still in Thailand, can't remember when you're due back and we missed your call which is a real piss-off because Matthew arranged with his parents that we would be there on Christmas Eve as well as Christmas night without consulting me and there was no arguing with him. In fact, I knew that we would probably have THE ROW TO END ALL ROWS if I so much as opened my mouth because it meant packing up everything earlier, including Mum and all the Christmas presents, with Matthew of course not doing anything to really help, other than reminding me in that horrible bullying way of his that we should have left London by now and that the traffic was going to be terrible.

The traffic WAS terrible, with Mum wittering on banally about traffic signs and contraflows along the M1 because she was so overexcited at seeing anything of the world outside North Butting, and Frankie chattering constantly into her mobile about equally trivial things with the odd intermittent shriek of laughter. After about six hours of this we finally arrived at the in-laws. Matthew had got there hours before on his motorbike, looked smug and relaxed but at least had the decency to unpack the car.

That is, however, about where his, or indeed their, decency stops. They made Chloe sleep in the car, which we all found really upsetting (except Matthew of course, who defended their actions with 'in Yorkshire dogs sleep in kennels outdoors, she was lucky to have the car'). They seem to think Santa shops at Poundstretcher and they made no secret of the fact that Tom is their favourite grandchild, which is just SO rude it rendered me speechless. When I tried to discuss this with Matthew in the hope that he would talk to them and persuade them to tone it down a bit, he just told me to stop being paranoid and that grandparents were allowed to have favourites and that Tom was just a baby and babies needed to be spoilt. They fussed over him the whole time, seemed captivated by his every charming movement or word and even laughed when he chucked his lunch all over the floor, which they never would have done with Frank or Lola. Frank is old enough now not to care, but Lola has only just stopped being the baby and needs to be spoilt too. Matthew, because he was on his own patch, also spent the whole time putting me down in front of his parents with a smugness that made me want to hit him. You name it, I was it – bossy, nosey, untidy, so disorganized it was a wonder that Tom ever had clean clothes. So I hit back with, 'At least I'm faithful to this family,' which shut them all up (game, set and match). Then yesterday when we got home we had the motherfucker of all rows and I told him to leave, so he has. Packed a bag late last night.

At the moment I couldn't be happier about it because it's just such a relief and so peaceful here without this tempest of a man around the place. I haven't forgotten Tom once now that there's one less person to have to remember. Julie, bless her, has been round and says I'm lucky in that at least I know – lots of other men have affairs and their wives never even notice anything odd because they're so good at lying. I can't help feeling that I would be luckier if he wasn't having an affair at all and just got on with family life and his share of the work. Both the girls are subdued but OK. They have been here before, but we need to talk and that's hard with Mum and Tom around.

Mum's actually managing to be quite funny about Matthew's parents. She slags them off continually because she doesn't quite dare slag off Matthew yet in case he should come back. But she's also trying to keep the subject open in case I should want to talk to her about it, which is quite sweet. Their kitchen has 'horrid formica units, SO common darling'. Their cooking is dreary: 'Fancy serving pork on Christmas Day, what with Jesus being a Jew, and without any apple sauce.' Grandpa Wilcox is 'about as dull as a lamp post AND I can never understand anything he says, not like Dad, of course, who always had such charm with the ladies,' and their presents were, of course, not a patch on hers. 'I don't think it was very sensitive of them to give you oven gloves when you never do any cooking anyway' (subtext – 'because you're too busy at work all the time'). Mum gave me some new checked pyjamas – I asked for them. Shame it wasn't a silk negligee really, given that I am now, most definitely, up for grabs once more. I really should see if I can get Mum going on HND. She could be dynamite!

She's hollering at the moment for something so I'd better go and see what she needs and then I promised Lola that we'd play scrabble on the kitchen table with Mum before supper.

Hope you had a great time, masses of love and speak soon.

Sx

Dear Diary,

Sunday the 29th of December

We've been home since Thursday but Dad hasn't, and he hasn't phoned either. I don't know where he is and Mum won't say anything. I wanted to talk to Mum today but we were having such a nice time playing with Tom, hiding his favourite rabbit behind cushions, that I didn't want to spoil things and make her sad. I miss Dad and everything feels really weird here without him and lots of his shirts have gone, so I guess he's moved out again. It's really quiet without him, which is good in some ways because at least it means they're not arguing all the time and I don't have to worry any more about his phone going and whether or not I should tell Mum because, thanks to me, she now knows everything. But he's not there when I expect him to be. He's not in the kitchen in the morning making toast when I wake up. He's not nuzzling Chloe's fur with the back of his foot as he has a nap on the sofa. He's not boasting about how quickly he managed to jog round the common as he runs a bath. He's not even teasing me about my watery tea. But what I really, really miss is hugging him. I just need to hug him and the fact that I can't makes me cry inside all the time, only I don't show anybody.

So I try and help Mum as much as I can because she looks so tired. I unloaded the dishwasher this morning and only broke one plate. I have to pull myself up onto the counter to reach the cupboard where they live and I knocked the top one off but Mum didn't mind and Granny helped me clear it up. It's nice having Granny here, although of course she doesn't make up for Dad. She's been telling me stories about when she was a little girl at night, when Mum puts Tom to bed. It's as though she knows that's when I'm going to miss Dad most because he used to do that. That was our time together. I didn't know that Granny was quite poor when she was a child and that they only ever had meat on Sundays. It was only when Grandpa's busyness was successful that they made any money and could have meat every day.

Dear Diary,

Haven't been home since we got home and Dad left. I've been staying at Fran's because Ruby's family are away, and it's kind of weird here because like even though I can do whatever I want and Fran's mum even let Chattie stay last night (he told his mum that he was staying with Daniel and that they were revising History together), it's kind of frightening not having anyone looking out for you. I feel bad about Mum, but I really don't wanna have to look after everyone now that Dad's gone, plus Granny drives me mad, criticizing everything I wear, say or do. Fran and I have been discussing our various dads and have come to the following conclusions:

- *Mine – adolescent, can't help himself, pathetic. 3/10*
- *Hers – the model divorce; she has her own room there, he pays her allowance, takes her away on glamorous holidays, has really famous, cool people to dinner so she likes being there, but when I asked her if she felt close to him like she did with her mum she said no. 6/10*
- *Ruby's dad – decent but boring. 5/10*
- *Saskia's dad – controlling, racist bigot. 0/10*
- *Serena's dad – dead. 0/10. Although she does use that a lot to make people feel sorry for her and it works, or it used to anyway with me. Whenever she wanted people to pay attention to her she'd like go on and on about how she couldn't even remember what he looked like.*

What About Me, Too?

- *Hayley's dad – grumpy but has been a lot happier since he's been off work with depression.* 5/10

So maybe mine's not that bad really.

Dear Diary, ✐

Mum is taking Granny back to her home today and she
wants me to go with her because Frankie is at Fran's house
and she says I can't stay here on my own. I can't go to
Clare's because they're in Italy and anyway her mum
probably wouldn't want me around even if they were here.
When I asked Mum if I could be with Dad, she said she had
no idea where he was and that I could try ringing him on
his mobile and if I got hold of him to tell him to afford her
the decency of knowing where he is. He didn't pick up so I
left a message on his voicemail saying that. Then I helped
Mum pack up Granny's stuff and gave Tom some lunch
and tried to be useful so that Mum wouldn't get too
stressed out. She only nearly lost it once, when Granny
refused to get into the car. She said she couldn't see why she
had to go back to North Butting when Matthew wasn't
here any more (ANY MORE? Does that mean he isn't ever
coming back?) and she could help look after Tom, which is
true because he absolutely loves her, but Mum just said that
wasn't possible and wouldn't explain why. Granny sat in
her chair and refused to move when it was time for us to
go. Mum tried to reason with her but Granny just gripped
hold of the arms and stared back fiercely, just like Tom
does when he doesn't want to do something and then Mum
got cross and told her to stop being so selfish and then
Granny snapped back that she didn't have any choice about
that because there was nobody else to think of but herself in
the home, so I said I'd make everyone a nice cup of tea so
that we could calm down and talk about this sensibly. In

the end they came to a deal. Granny agreed to go if Mum agreed to let her come back here if a room doesn't come up soon in this new, nicer home which is nearer to us. So now I'm sitting in the back of the car – writing a bit wiggly in my diary – Tom is asleep beside me and Mum and Granny haven't said a word to each other since we left London. I can feel how cross Mum is about this. The one good thing about Granny going is that I'll be able to move back into my room tonight. But what if Granny comes back to live with us? Where will I sleep then? I absolutely refuse to even consider sleeping in Frank's stink pit unless of course she moves out, which might be the answer since her room is bigger than mine.

From: Sue James
Sent: Tuesday 31 December 12:49
To: Matthew Wilcox
Subject: Re: What business is it of yours?

EVERY business of yours is mine, sunshine, because I'm the mother of your three children and THEY need to know where you are. I couldn't care less, but don't you think I'm at least owed the courtesy of knowing where you are? And no – why should I fucking well ring you on your mobile, and why should Frank or Lola have to either, for that matter, when you're their dad and the grown-up and they need **YOU** to make the effort to contact them, not the other way around.

What About Me, Too?

From: Sue James
Sent: Tuesday 31 December 15:32
To: Matthew Wilcox
Subject: Re: Re: What business is it of yours?

ME SELFISH? You're the one who couldn't think further than your dick. You're the one who fucked a bimbo and left me when I was pregnant with your son and had the audacity to accuse me of being unfaithful when you knew perfectly well that wasn't the case. Christmas was just hell with your parents, not just for me but for both Frank and Lola, because YOU refused to ever put our needs before yours and your pathetic, puerile need to impress your parents and still be Mummy's little boy. I've had enough of it, Matthew, enough of your selfish, childish solipsism, your selfish midlife crisis, your selfish refusal ever since Tom arrived to even ask us what we would like, and if that means me being selfish for a change, then so be it.

Put it this way, it would be kind of you to talk to F and L, to tell them where you are, that you're all right, that you love them (if you do) and to make an arrangement to see them. That's if you can fit them in between work and screwing the bimbo.

You're a shit.

Sue

From: Sue James
Sent: Tuesday 31 December 18:40
To: Matthew Wilcox
Subject: Re: Re: Re: What business is it of yours?

Just because she's a legal secretary and got a brain, doesn't mean she isn't a bimbo and a marriage-breaker and you're not a shit. How does she feel, I wonder, knowing that you can be unfaithful to a marriage with kids? Trust you, does she? And ARE you playing the field or putting all your eggs into one bastard? You weren't like that before and what I can't even begin to work out is why you've grown so bitter, so angry with the world and with me just because you've grown older. All I've ever done is work hard and try and keep home life happy, putting my needs last. Why on earth are you not grown up enough to do the same?

It may interest you to know that since you've been gone, Frankie has been home for just one night, preferring to spend her time with Fran and Saskia, and Lola has been crying herself to sleep at night.

Oh, and by the way – Happy New Year.

What About Me, Too?

Dear Diary,

Friday the 3rd of January

Dad rang yesterday and said he was renting a flat near his office and that he would come round on Saturday and take me to see it. But he's just rung to say that he has to go away for the weekend so he won't be able to take me, but he will make it up to me next weekend. Mum says he's working very hard and that he's probably got a big case on but ALL WEEKEND, without even an hour for me? I cried so much my head hurts and Chloe jumped onto the bed and buried her nose between my hands and my face to lick away the tears. She makes it all better somehow. Mum's going to take me and Camilla to Legoland instead but that's on Sunday, ages away. All I'm left with is this empty feeling because he would rather go away with Laura than be with me.

After a while my head hurt from all the crying so I asked Mum if we could take Chloe out for a walk. She said, 'What a good idea' but then Tom was sick and she thought he might have a temprature so Mum said I could take Chloe out for a short walk on my own. 'You're such a big girl now you can do it, but don't go too far and definitely not on the common.' I guess that now Dad's gone Mum has to let me do more, because otherwise nobody would walk the dog if she can't. So I put on her lead and my coat, kissed Tom on the top of his head and felt really grown up as I walked out the door. Chloe pulled me along the high street, thinking she was going to the common. But I wanted to go

to the cemetery. It's so beautiful in there and doing
something daring would help me forget about not seeing
Dad, I decided. It was a bit scary at first, windy and the
branches of the trees clacked together above our heads, but
Chloe seemed happy to be able to run around and I felt safe
with her. I walked along whistling, thinking about how
happy I was to be going to Frankie's secondary school
because Clare and Tanya wouldn't be there and every now
and then I tossed a stick into the undergrowth and stopped
to read a tombstone while Chloe retrieved it. For every
name I could imagine a person coming alive to play with
me on the path. Silly fantasy games, I know, but it was fun.

When we got to the Lion's Tomb there was a boy sitting
astride his back, tossing stones high into a bird's nest.

'I like your dog,' he mumbled when he noticed that I
was watching him.

'Thanks,' I said, wondering if he was the person who
was actually living in the tomb but not wanting to ask. It
seemed rude somehow because nobody would like to have
to admit that they lived there. He was about the same age
as Frankie so maybe he had been kicked out of home like
Toyah said. So I asked him if he'd managed to get any of
the stones into the nest and he said, 'No, still that's better
than yesterday's score,' and we laughed.

And then I didn't know what to say, so I picked up a
stick and chucked it for Chloe.

'Did she find you or have you had her since she was a
puppy?' he asked as he watched her nosing about looking
for the exact same stick.

'She found us, on the common.'

'Thought so. A dog that smart would never be alone for long.' He said it wistfully, like he'd like a dog for company too.

'Are you from round here?' I asked, trying not to sound too nosey.

'Today I am, as for tomorrow, who knows.' He swung his leg over the lion's head and jumped down into the brambles. If they scratched him, he didn't let on. And then he was gone, just like that. He disappeared down one of the many twisting paths between the gravestones and I wished he hadn't. He was fassinating and I wanted to know more. I hadn't even asked him his name.

When I got home, Tom was crying constantly and Mum was walking up and down the kitchen rocking him, trying to calm him down. He's not well at all. Gr8.

From: Sue James
Sent: Friday 3 January 12:14
To: Matthew Wilcox
Subject: How could you?

How could you do that to Lola? Have you any idea how disappointed she is? What could possibly be more important than Lola at a time like this? Frankie is so furious with you at the moment for leaving that you're probably best kept apart and Tom's too young to understand and calls every man he meets dada but Lola, sweet, kind, adorable Lola, needs to see you.

And we need a phone number and address for this flat, Matthew – why are you being so fucking secretive? Do you think I might come round with a knife and stab her? Presumably the she-devil is living there with you. Don't worry, duckie – I wouldn't waste the time.

What About Me, Too?

From: Sue James
Sent: Friday 3 January 15:22
To: Matthew Wilcox
Subject: Re: How could you?

So now you're a lying shit. What client needs you to be away
ALL weekend?

Thanks for the contact details, good of you.

Let me know when you can find time for your children and
I'll consult their social secretaries and see if they can fit you in.

Sue

Dear Diary,

Sunday night. Do you think there's something wrong with our relationship because I haven't had an orgasm, at least I don't think I have and it is says in Cosmo Girl *that if you don't know, you haven't. And do you think that means there is something wrong with our relationship because Chattie doesn't give me one, or am I physically disabled in some way and won't ever have one? They sound like so amaaaazing, better than drink or drugs, and natural and healthy, so I really don't wanna miss out on anything. It says in* Cosmo *that I should show him what I like but I don't really know what that is and I CAN'T talk about this with Ruby or Fran or the others because it would be just so embarrassing, and even though we talk about everything, this just seems like so private. Chattie asks me if I've come and I say yes because I want him to feel good and then tonight, when I said I hadn't, he got tired and fell asleep.*

The one good thing about Dad being gone is that Chattie can be here. But I'm not sure whether it's gonna be OK for him to stay. Mum hasn't said anything and I don't wanna ask in case she says no. I don't THINK she's gonna dare ask him to go when she knows how much it matters to me – like the nurse in Romeo and Juliet, *all she really wants is for me to be happy, which means she's a good mum even though she still can't cook and her dress sense stinks.*

What About Me, Too?

Dear Diary,

Sunday the 5th of January 🖎

We had an AMAAAZING time at Legoland. The one bum thing was that Frankie and Ruby came too, even though they were supposed to be spending the day revising for their mocks which start tomorrow. They said it was only English and you can't revise for that and they would do better in the exam if they'd had some fun, and Frankie made such a scene about being left out that Mum finally agreed. That meant it was a bit of a squash in the back because Frankie's so fat. There weren't enough seat belts so Mum told us to duck if we saw a police car. The other bum thing was that we had Chloe in the back with us as well, farting away because we couldn't leave her at home alone all day and they have kennels at Legoland. She wasn't pleased about that even though we took her for a walk first and then gave her a large bone thingy. I wanted to leave her in the car because she knows the car but Mum said she'd be fine and that she was just a dog. I don't know how she can say that about Chloe, she's like a sister to me, not just a dog, and she looked so sad in her eyes like she was crying when we left and I want her to be able to have puppies only Mum won't let her because she's so mean.

Anyway, Legoland was SUCH FUN. I can't believe we've never been there before. Tom just went mad in this giant room full of Duplo and didn't ever want to leave so Mum let us go off on our own to ~~kew~~ ~~cue~~ queue (had to look that up in the dictionary. Cool to have a book with all those words in the same place). We decided on the cars where you drive round miniature roads and then they give you this really cool driving licence. It was such fun, and then we went off to ~~kew~~ queue again for this massive ride that plunged almost vertically down through water and we all got so wet that Mum got a bit cross because we didn't have any spare clothes with us and it's the middle of winter. I've never seen Camilla laugh so much, she was so happy. I think I'm going to ask Dad to take me there again soon, just me and him.

From: Sue James
Sent: Sunday 5 January 23:10
To: Angela James
Subject: Re: Happy New Year!

Glad yours was good. Mine was pretty solitary with Frankie out at a party and the others asleep, but at least it was peaceful.

Latest report on family members goes as follows:

Mum – a nightmare. She's rung at least sixteen times since I took her back to NB last Monday and seems to think that now Matthew isn't here, I have every available minute to devote to her needs. I suppose it's coming from the generation that put the man first. The kids can take care of themselves. Mrs Leach has rung twice from North Butting. Mum's refusing to eat again and has been abusive to the staff (racist or homophobic comments, I suspect, although she wouldn't elaborate as to what), so I'm going to chase Clarice's tomorrow and beg for a place.

Matthew – being a complete bastard and we're locked into email contact only. I'm so angry I can't bear the thought of talking to him. I know I kicked him out but he was happy to go and it's up to him to make an effort with the kids. I don't think I've ever felt this angry with anyone. I would have thought his first priority would have been the girls, but apparently not. He promised to take Lola out this weekend and then failed to keep his promise.

Frankie – I'm really worried about her. She's very stroppy when she's here, which isn't often at the moment. I have no idea where she is half the time, or what she's up to and when I ask I just get a grunt which sounds a little like 'Ruby's' but could easily be 'groovies'. It's not even been a year yet since all that trouble we had with her, so it's not an ideal time for us to be separating, but then when is? She could easily go off the rails again so I'm trying to keep a close eye and stay on the same side, but it's hard sometimes. Mocks start tomorrow and of course nobody has ever had it so bad. She stomps around the house screaming things like, 'I'm so stressed and nobody even cares' and then when you try and be sympathetic or ask what you can do to help, she shouts, 'Fuck off and leave me alone.' Imagine what she's going to be like when it's the real thing in June? Nothing suits her – my cooking since Toyah's been off, the state of her room which she maintains should be cleared up by Lola since she messed it up – so unfair it's laughable – and it's all my fault, apparently, that Matthew's left. Had a massive row about it last night when she accused me of not thinking enough about their needs, and that I should have done more to make him want to stay. 'What about US?' she screamed at me. Well, what about them? Why is it all my fault and not his when I am the one who has always bent over backwards to put their needs first? I haven't run off and had an affair.

Lola – quiet and a bit clingy, wants to know where I am the whole time, as if she's frightened I might disappear as well, but basically OK, I think. We've done everything together this week while I've been off work and I think that's helped. She doesn't say anything when I try and talk about it, just listens and looks sad. Julie took Lola out last week and tried to talk to her about it but she didn't say much apparently, other than she thought Matthew would move back soon because he had done so before, when Tom was born. My feeling is that the marriage is over and that we should probably divorce, which makes me feel more sad, lonely and washed up than I can say. Took them all to Legoland yesterday. F threw a tantrum as we were about to leave and said it wasn't fair to leave her behind, even though she had Ruby with her, so my little treat with Lola and Tom was not to be. I had to take them both. But we also had Lola's friend Camilla. Frank and Ruby succeeded in losing them, when I had given her explicit instructions for them all to stay together all the time. I know the chances of them being abducted by a paedophile are very slim (although ten-year-old blonde girls are apparently most at risk), but I still panic whenever Lola's out somewhere on her own, plus being responsible for Camilla and her prosthetic leg quadrupled the anxiety, and I was about to contact the Lego authorities (what are they made of, I wonder?) when I found them by the water shoot. They had been brave enough to go down on their own but had got soaking wet in the process, so I was allowed to vent my spleen on that instead of the fact that they had been lost because, of course, they didn't think they were lost at all. When Frank's with Ruby they go into this symbiotic blinkered state, talking and giggling with each other so they probably didn't even notice the girls wandering off in the crowd. It took nearly an hour to find them. Frank swears she couldn't hear me ringing and only noticed when she saw fifteen missed calls on her phone and called me back, but actually, I know she was making merry, looning about in the adventure playground and probably intimidating all the toddlers. They were blindfolding each other with Ruby's scarf at the top of the climbing frame in a rather dangerous way.

Not bad, Legoland, as those places go. I think I could even brave it one more time with you and the boys next time you're here if you fancy it. London looks like a Christmas tree graveyard at the moment. There are forlorn Norwegian pines on every street corner, huddled together for warmth with the odd pathetic bit of tinsel dangling down. I even saw one yesterday with a crumpled fairy on the top. What ARE they waiting for I wonder, a bus?

Much love,
Sxxxxxxxxxxxxxxxxxxxxxxxxxxxxxxxxxxxxxxxxxxxxxxxxxx

What About Me, Too?

Dear Diary,

Tuesday the 7th of January

I really miss Dad not being here when I'm at home and then when I go to school, all I can think about is how Clare isn't like my best friend any more. When I talked to Mum about it she said there were lots of other children to play with and I should just find some new friends, but that's really hard when Tanya spends every break and every lunchtime trying to wind me up by telling me that Clare doesn't like me any more. Clare got more stuff for Christmas than the entire class got put together. Her dad gave her this thick bracelet made out of real gold, which she wears to school which is just showing off because you don't actually need a real gold bracelet when you're only ten. When I told her that we'd taken Camilla to Legoland, she just said she'd been to Legoland loads of times and that it wasn't nearly as cool as Disneyland in Florida.

Dear Diary,

Thursday the 9th of January

Dad rang and is going to come and pick me up at ten on Saturday morning. I'm really excited about it because he has to come for me this time. I've gone through all my clothes and I can't decide what to wear. If I had my ears pierced then I'd look more grown up for him and I'd be able to join Clare and Tanya's club. I'm going to get up early on Saturday and do a really good job cleaning up the kitchen for Mum so that it's nice for her while I'm away. With Frankie in this sort of a strop (she has mocks and has been in a really bad mood all week), she's worse than useless round the house. I have to go up to her room and bring down about 10,000 mugs and put them in the dishwasher. Mum's been running round her like she's some sort of princess – making her cups of tea when she hasn't even asked for them and buying her special bath stuff to relax her. If that stupid sister of mine had bothered to do the work in the first place instead of going out all the time and drinking vodka and having SEX with Chattie, then these exams would be easy. If she gets pregnant or fails it's her own fault. And these aren't even the real exams – they're just fakes. What are Mum and Frankie gonna be like then?

What About Me, Too?

From: Sue James
Sent: Friday 10 January 06:23
To: Matthew Wilcox
Subject: Tomorrow

I would appreciate it if you could in future consult me when you want to see the children, rather than making individual arrangements. Lola is free tomorrow but she could easily not have been and wouldn't remember if there was something else planned. I sincerely hope that she is not mistaken and that you really are coming to pick her up this time. What time are you coming and is this just Lola or Tom too?

Dear Diary,

Saturday the 11th of January

Dad came today like I knew he would and it was kind of
fun, I suppose – well, that was what I told Mum anyway. I
don't want her to think that I have more fun with him than
I do with her. He took me back to the shop where Mum
bought my disgusting Christmas clothes so I could change
them and he let me try on whatever I wanted, which was
real good because Mum wouldn't have. I got this amazing
shimmery party dress and some fishnet tights, a crop top
and some thongs and a few sexy, strappy vests for the
summer. I kept coming out of the changing room to ask
Dad what he thought and he SAID he liked everything, but
actually I think he hardly noticed because he spent most of
the time reading the newspaper and talking into his phone,
presumably to HER.

Then we went out for some pasta and then we went to
the motorbike shop and I was kind of hoping that he might
be about to buy me a helmet so that I could go on the back
like Frankie does, but he didn't. He spent about sixteen
hours looking at leather trousers and gloves and bike bits
and bikes and talking to the men there and I got so bored I
practically fell asleep, but it was good to be with him. Then
he took me back to his flat, which is tiny with only one
bedroom in it so I won't be able to stay there. He says I can
sleep on the sofa there whenever I like, which I think I will
do sometimes if Mum lets me, and it's got the sweetest little
kitchen which only one person can stand in at a time. I hate

the carpet though. Green. Yuk. And it sort of smells funny.
Dad says this is only a temprary place to stay which I hope
means that he'll be coming home soon, when he's sorted
things out with Mum. The only bad thing about today was
that I met HER. She walked in – WITH A KEY – after we'd
only been there for about ten minutes, and I was hoping to
have the whole day alone with Dad. Then she started
talking to me in this sickly-sweet voice like I was only three
or something and I felt like kicking her. She went on and on
about how pleased she was to meet me and how much she'd
heard about me. Yeah? Well I wasn't at all pleased to meet
her and she's really ugly, with black hair like a witch and
long red fingernails. So last century.

From: Sue James
Sent: Sunday 12 January 21:16
To: Angela James
Subject: Single motherhood

The full horror dawned yesterday morning and boy, was it gruesome. Matthew arrived to collect Lola and was instantly smothered with hugs and kisses on the doorstep. The dog squealed and jumped around with excitement, Tom pulled at his trouser leg, wanting to be picked up, while I just sort of stood there with my arms folded leaning against the doorframe, trying to look indifferent and sexy in my prehistoric, shabby dressing gown. He looked fresh as a daisy after a good night's sleep, and ten years younger – the jogging and sex with a minor must be beginning to pay off, or it could just have been that he was wearing a rather chic new lilac shirt. He looked relieved too – he hardly looked at me and seemed clear-headed and happy – BASTARD. There was none of that confusion and being torn in different directions that we had last time, he just seemed relieved. BASTARD. Didn't even want to come in, just claimed his little girl and together they walked down the path laughing and talking, leaving me to deal with Tom's first proper tantrum because he knew he had been left behind. Last year Matthew seemed so uncertain about what he wanted: he wanted to row with me, was looking for answers or reassurance or some sort of connection, sometimes I even thought he needed me to decide for him, to prove somehow that I loved and needed him, but that's all gone now and I'm just left feeling really betrayed. It's such a cliché, Ange, to be left on the scrapheap in menopausal middle age for somebody twenty years younger with a tight vagina.

So I spent yesterday trying to make myself feel better, venting my aggression by playing soldiers with my SAS son. And what a fantastic snogger he is too – gives me great long, wet smackers whenever we cuddle. Then I rang Julie and arranged to meet her for lunch, put on some make-up and my best clothes and went up to town with Tom on the Tube to Sheekeys fish restaurant and had a heart-warming, nourishing feast, as well as several puddings. Julie's such a good friend; we laughed a lot over a bottle of expensive red wine, and she's so sane and wise which just makes me feel insane and unbalanced beside her. Tom, amazingly, loves scallops and behaved well, didn't throw his food around once. You've got boys, Ange, what do I have to do to make sure that HE never falls in love with anyone else, at least not until after I'm dead anyway??? There is also the dog. Such devotion, I never knew that dogs were capable of such unconditional love. She wiggles the whole back half of her body with excitement when I walk in through the door and looks at me adoringly with those deep watery eyes because I feed her. I've moved her basket up to my bedroom because it feels cosier with us all snoring away on the top two floors.

Frankie got up at the astonishingly early hour of eleven and spent the whole day doing revision. When Lola returned triumphant and happy, although she rather sweetly pretended that she'd only had an OK time and buried her head into my arms and said she'd missed me, we got some takeout pizza.

I felt blissful again with both my girls beside me on the sofa as we watched crap Saturday night TV and discussed who was and wasn't fit/funny/talented/going out with whom etc. We had such fun that I didn't even rise to the bait offered by HND when she knocked on the door at 10 p.m., expressed her surprise (thinly veiled disapproval) at Lola still being up and then asked me if I could stop Chloe from going out into the garden late at night because her barking wakes up Clare who needs every minute of sleep at the moment because of her entrance exams. (Just rub it in, won't you, bitch – she's going to be bought a better education than Lola. Must make a point of letting Chloe out after midnight from now on.) And THEN, before I had even a moment to think of a cutting but polite reply, she starts going on about the amount of litter in the street and could I write to the council complaining. I looked out at the street, expecting to see paper billowing about in the wind but it looked perfectly fine to me. So I said, 'What litter?' and then wished I hadn't because she practically listed it. If ever there was a woman who needed a job, it's her.

I think the money side is going to be tough, and sooner or later Matthew and I are going to have to bite the bullet and talk to the children, as well as about the future. Not looking forward to that much.

I'll check Mum out next weekend if I've got time. Clarice's have been very unforthcoming so no news there, sadly.

Love, Suexxxx

What About Me, Too?

From: Sue James
Sent: Sunday 12 January 21:25
To: Matthew Wilcox
Subject: Lola

You seem to think she's a sixteen-year-old prostitute judging by the clothes you allowed her to buy yesterday but then again, since you've become a middle-age sex maniac and child molester I suppose that's not so surprising. Although I would have thought that even you would have liked to keep your daughter looking like a little girl for just a little while longer. Lola thinks you're taking her away next weekend. Where to? And how fucking dare you even SUGGEST such a thing without asking me first.

We need to talk, Matthew.

From: Sue James
Sent: Sunday 12 January 21:35
To: Matthew Wilcox
Subject: Re: Talk to my lawyer

What do you mean 'MY' lawyer? Martin has been laywer to both of us up until this point, so why is he now yours? I take it by this rather glib comment that you want permanent separation. Well, that's sad, Matthew, and what's even sadder is that after all these years together you haven't got the balls to even have a conversation with me about us. If you mean talk to my lawyer about access to the kids, then that stinks even more. All you have to do is pick up the phone and ask if they're free and I have no intention of talking to anybody about that. It's for YOU to ask ME if YOU can see them because YOU DON'T LIVE HERE ANY MORE – not the other way around. As it happens, Lola hasn't got plans next weekend but then neither has Tom. But I don't suppose you want him, do you? Too much like hard work.

As for the clothes, Lola may have said she wanted them but I would have persuaded her out of them because they're just not suitable. Funny how you go ballistic when Frank (who is nearly of age) has safe sex with a boy she rather likes, but don't even notice the fact that Lola, who is only just eleven, walks out of a shop looking like she's gagging for it. But then maybe you just thought she looked 'nice'.

What About Me, Too?

Dear Diary,

Wednesday the 15th of January ✏

Even though I like really really miss him, I feel sort of happier just knowing where Dad is. I can imagine him in that little flat at night. The only trouble is that SHE also comes into those thoughts sometimes and then I just want to think about something else. Also, Mum has been really nice to me, she's come home early from work every night this week and watches TV with me and we've been talking about the summer holidays and all the exiting places we could go to together. The only sad thing is that she probably means together without Dad, but what I'd really secretly like is for all of us to go on holiday, if they could only find a way of making up. I've told Frankie about HER and how hideous she is but she didn't seem all that interested, just said Dad was really insensitive to let her be there the same time as me, but I suppose I had to meet her sometime. What would be really cool would be to find a way of getting rid of her. I could tell her how he's a bad loser and cheats at football but maybe she wouldn't care about that. She WOULD care, though, if I told her that Dad has dozens of girlfriends and that she is just the latest one. 'He'll soon get bored of you,' I'll say casually when she's feeling really secure in their relationship.

I've decided to fight this. I can make things difficult for the marriage-breaker bitch (Mum's new name for her). She's gonna really have to work to make me even begin to like her.

Dear Diary,

At 9.30 p.m. yesterday, on Wednesday the 15th of January, I met Chattie at the smoking bench outside the house and kissed him for the last time EVER and I'm desperate, DESPERATE to put back the clock. It's breaking my heart. I told him that I needed space, and suggested that we saw less of each other and he took it the wrong way, got really, really angry with me and said that I had to accept him for the way he was or not at all and stormed off into the night. I ran after him and pleaded with him to stay and talk but he just walked on, pushed me away like he hated me and said I'd never been or could be as committed as he was and that he was sick of arguing with me. I haven't stopped crying or smoking since. My throat feels raw and I haven't slept. I think maybe my problem is that I've met the right boy too young. Ruby (who's never had a boyfriend but is, of course, an expert on the subject) says that I'm lucky to have found someone so committed when boys usually just want sex rather than a relationship, only I just think that's what they say in books and magazines. I don't think most boys are really like that. They want someone to love them just like everybody else.

I put everything he has ever given me into a special box and cried over them for most of the night.

There's the pebble we found on Brighton beach which has a white streak in the shape of a C.
A burned CD with all my favourite songs on it.
Six postcards from his holiday in Sri Lanka.

What About Me, Too?

A gold necklace with a locket that I've never dared wear
but now I think I just might, all the time, with his
picture in it.
A Shakespeare sonnet which he didn't write but it's how
I feel about him now that it's all over and I've blown
it quite so badly:

> *Being your slave, what should I do but tend*
> *Upon the hours and times of your desire?*

It ends with:

> *So true a fool is love that in your will,*
> *Though you do any thing, he thinks no ill.*

I've hurt him badly, I know I have and that makes me feel
even worse, the responsibility for his pain. Films and TV are
full of stories about how bad it is to be rejected by someone
you love, but not about how really, really ugly you feel
when you have to hurt someone you love. I can't think
about anything but him and the emptiness that's left now
that he's gone. If loving someone hurts this much when it's
over, then maybe it's better not to love anyone at all. Why
am I so bad at relationships?

Dear Diary,

Friday the 17th of January

Anyone would think from the way Frankie is behaving that
somebody had just died or something. Chattie dumped her
the night before last and I can't say I blame her, although
she says she dumped him. But if that's the case, why is she
walking around the house crying all the time and saying
she's going to kill herself and definitely fail her GCSEs now?
Either she wants to be with him or she doesn't. She's really
taken him for granted. First she came in from school, threw
herself sobbing onto the sofa and said she'd been
~~hoomiliated~~ ~~Humilleated~~ hoomilliated in front of all her
friends because he dumped her in the playground and he
doesn't love her enough to be with her. Then I hear her
talking on the phone to Ruby about how he was so
possessive that she couldn't take it any more. Well, he can't
be both things. If he's possessive, surely that's because he
cares about her? Then she stormed around the house,
shouting and swearing that she hated him and refused to eat
any supper and now she's writing him a letter, probably a
really yucky love letter, crying AND she's put a lock of her
manky hair inside the envelope – disgusting! And all the
time Mum and Toyah have been fussing over her with cups
of hot chocolate and Mum ran her a bath full of her most
expensive oils and lit candles to soothe her like she's been in
a car accident or something and broken both her legs. If it
makes her this unhappy not being with Chattie, then why
doesn't she just ring him up and get back together with him

again? Mum has split up with Dad and Frankie has split up
with Chattie, so now it's only me and Tom who luckily
don't have anyone to split up with. It'll be a relief to go
away tomorrow to Kent with Dad for the night just to get
away from her, although I'm really worried that Laura
might be coming with us too and haven't felt brave enough
to ask.

From: Sue James
Sent: Sunday 19 January 08:46
To: Angela James
Subject: Heartache

Dearest Ange,

It's funny but I haven't felt this alone or hurt at being left since I was seventeen and Billy boy died. All of the other broken hearts between then and now don't matter, never did. When William died I felt that love could never be completely trusted – we were so together, rarely apart, and then he just wasn't there any more and I couldn't get used to that. Every time the phone rang I remember thinking it would be him and then remembering that it couldn't be. And now I feel like that bereaved teenager again. The end of a marriage is so much worse than the end of an affair, even though we shouldn't expect it to last for ever now, I suppose – I mean, how many people actually get to their silver wedding anniversary these days? Somehow, because you invest everything on building a life and bringing up kids together, you do sort of hope, deep in your heart, that it will. How else can you live as a family? Always looking over your shoulder for possible exits and asking yourself is this it? Always worrying about speaking your mind or farting in bed in case that becomes enough to provoke them to leave? When I fell in love with Matthew it was heaven. We felt so right together. It was so easy to commit everything to building a life together because I couldn't ever imagine it ending, and now it has and I feel as if I've failed him and the kids, failed to make something that was once good, stay good at a stage in my life when I probably need him more than ever. Who on earth is going to want me now? An overweight, middle-aged woman constantly on the verge of a nervous breakdown with an SAS commander of a small son, a teenage tyrant and a tween with dubious fashion sense, as well as a waiting room full of patients who foolishly believe that I can cope. I suppose there's always Bryson if I get really desperate. I think word must have got round even though I haven't told anyone at work, because he's behaving very oddly. One minute he's handing me research papers and trying to engage me in argument in the corridors, and the next he's trying to get me to go out with him for a drink. Perhaps the arguing is his way of flirting. Weird.

But it also has to be said that there are definite advantages to being single again. I can play the Jackson Five at top volume and sing along: 'OOOO rock a robin . . . rock . . . rock' (Matthew hated them and tried to throw my LPs out several times early in our marriage). I never need buy margarine for his heart, Yakult for his guts or Andrex wet-wipes for his hairy arsehole ever again. Presumably they're on the marriage-breaker bitch's shopping list now. And who has time for sex these days anyway? There's always something better on the telly. I may even decide to start partying again and it'll be Frankie saying to me, 'I want you back by midnight.'

Frankie's heartbroken because she's split up with Chattie and it's the end of the world because she's never been here before. So we've both been moping around, eating chocolates and watching endless videos of *Friends* and sweet Lola can't understand what all the fuss is about. She looks at us pitifully as if to say, why don't you just get on with something else? She's away for the night in Kent with Matthew. Bastard was supposed to pick her up at two yesterday and didn't arrive until four so that put her in an anxious mood, worrying about whether or not he was coming at all. Once again, Tom wasn't invited, wonder why?! Poor Frankie. It has been a bit of a blow. Her face was red and puffy from crying last night and she's refused to go out, even to Ruby's, so it must be serious. Still that WAS very nice for ME – with Tom asleep and Lola away, we curled up in front of the telly together and made chocolate milkshakes. Haven't quite worked out WHY they've split up yet, don't really want to push her on it.

It's cold, dark and wintery here and at some point soon I'm going to have to face the weather, wrestle Tom into his buggy and take Chloe up to the park for a walk. You never know my luck, I might bump into Mark with the black Labrador, but haven't seen him in weeks, I hope he hasn't moved or died or something.

Night Night, sleep tight. Love, Suexx

Dear Diary,

Sunday night ✐

We went to a place called Rye. The good news is that it's
near the sea and Clare's never been there. Dad and I went for
a really blustery walk along the beach alone because SHE
didn't want to come. Silly wimp thought it was too cold.
Dad wrapped me up in his coat to keep warm as we watched
the waves and raced me along the beach. The wind was so
strong that you could actually lean into it, well, I could
anyway. When Dad tried, the wind dropped and he fell
over!! The bad news is that we were staying in Laura's
sister's house, that Dad has been there before, which Mum
DEFINITELY doesn't know and I can't tell her, and that
Laura's sister has a really irritating, ugly, smelly little boy
who they expected me to play with. I'm eleven and he's only
six. He wanted me to play Cowboys and Indians and still
thinks that Thomas the Tank Engine is cool. They made us
eat together, kid's tea while they had proper food at an adult
candlelit dinner, and then I had to go to BED!!! And
READ!!! What do they think kids do these days, study
Shakespeare in their spare time? They didn't EVEN have a
DVD player. So I played on my Game Boy and refused to
talk to anyone exept Dad and whenever they tried to talk to
me I pretended to be deaf. I don't care what they think of me.
I really love being with Dad but it just feels so odd having all
those other people around too, like why SHOULD I have to
share him with anyone when I have him so little, and then I
can't even talk about it with him because I'm not sure what

I should or shouldn't say. He asked me how things are at home and I didn't want to talk about it because that's not fair on Mum. So I said she was sad (because then maybe he'll feel sorry for her and want to come back), but I didn't say that I've heard her crying nearly every night and that makes me sad, and that last night I got into bed with her to cheer her up. If Dad doesn't come back soon then I will tell him how sad she is. And I told him that Tom was fine, but I didn't say that he smashed a plate and threw his juice across the kitchen floor last week and that Mum lost it and had to lock herself in the bathroom for half an hour to calm down while I cleared it up. I did have one major victory over the marriage-breaker bitch, though, on the way home. I wanted to listen to the Top Twenty. She said she couldn't stand that. Dad said he didn't mind and that he was driving. She said it was her car and that she did mind. I said it was the one thing that stopped me feeling carsick and I'd hate to puke up all over her black leather seats. No contest, babe. And then I sang along. She couldn't believe I knew all the words to every song. Mum wanted me to tell her all about it, wanted to know what Dad had been saying. It was hard enough just saying goodbye to him when I'm not sure when I'm going to see him again. So I told her that he'd asked how she was (I didn't say that I'd said she was sad, obviously) and I told her we went to the beach, but what else could I say?? I don't want to upset her even more so I ran up to my room and told her that I had some homework to do. It's hard knowing what to say when no one tells you what's really going on. But maybe if I'm really clever about it I can say just enough to bring them back together again.

What About Me, Too?

Dear Diary,

Monday. Chattie avoids me. He won't answer my texts. He won't talk to me when I try to talk to him in the playground. He won't even look at me. If only he would just stop for one minute and listen to me, understand how much I miss him, that I made a mistake, that he's the best thing that ever happened to me, that I need him, that I love him – yes, I really, really do because to feel this much hurt inside when you're not with someone means I must love him – then maybe he would give me a second chance. I can't think about anything else but him. I can't sleep properly and I can't concentrate in lessons. Everywhere I go I'm looking for him, hoping to bump into him, hoping to catch his eye. I'm practically killing myself, walking into cars and lamp posts, looking the other way or checking my phone for texts. If this goes on for much longer then I really am gonna fail my GCSEs and end up washed up on the dustbin of life, waitressing or serving hamburgers at McDonald's.

Dear Diary,

Thursday 🖎

Clare and Tanya have started wearing the same clothes.
Like they're in some sort of club or something. Short skirts,
fishnets tights and lots and lots of beady bangles up their
arms that click and clatter in class, and they both wear
these huge gold, hoopy earrings. I WISH Mum would let
me have my ears pierced. She thinks it's barbaric in children
but she let Frankie do it when she went to secondary school
AND she gave her a mobile phone, so why can't I do it now
when I'm nearly the same age? Miss Jennings always makes
them take their earrings out when we have PE because she
says it's dangerous. They always make such a fuss about
that, like they're going to miss them for a whole hour, or
their holes are going to close up or something, but when I
said that to them today Tanya just turned on me and said
'Mind your own busyness, busty.' Kieran heard her and
laughed and said, 'Since you're SO mature now why don't
you get down on your knees and suck my dick?' so I kicked
him hard and went to Miss Jennings and said I wasn't
feeling well and could I go and lie down for a bit in the
office. I hate having to change for PE now because there is
nowhere private to change and I have to hide everything
with my arms.

Mum took Chloe to the vet today for an operashon so
she won't have puppies. Mum says she'll be a bit sore for a
while. So I curled up beside her in her basket while Mum
cooked supper and put Tom to bed, because I didn't want

her to feel too alone or too sad about missing out on something so important in life as babies. I told her that I felt sad about things too, how much I missed Dad and how I couldn't really tell Mum that, and it would be just our secret.

From: Sue James
Sent: Thursday 23 January 22:10
To: Matthew Wilcox
Subject: Re: Frankie

She doesn't want to see you. I asked her this evening. She's miserable about Chattie and about her mocks, convinced she's going to get Ds and Fs and no amount of reassuring will persuade her that she might have got Cs. She's not eating much and I wouldn't be surprised if she was smoking again, in spite of my promise of a ton of money if she stays off the fags until she's sixteen. As for dope, I'm not sure, given the amount you consume, whether I'd be being responsible letting her see you even if she wanted to when she's this low. So you see, Matthew, you picked a great time in her life to add to her problems by being a crap dad.

I'm sorry that you miss the kids but you should have thought about that before you followed your dick. You can have Tom for exactly three hours on Sunday – collect him at two. Bring him back at five. Lola needs new school shoes.

Sue

What About Me, Too?

From: Sue James
Sent: Friday 24 January 07:35
To: Matthew Wilcox
Subject: Re: Re: Frankie

Hit a nerve, have I? Yes, I am suggesting that you could sit down and smoke a joint with her. That's exactly what adolescent/middle-aged parents who find it hard to accept their age DO with their teenage kids. And why is that such an outrageous suggestion, when you think it's OK to dress up your eleven-year-old like a tart, wear tight shirts and abandon all of your parental responsibilities because you want to fuck your secretary? I bet you're not even up now. Getting a good night's sleep? I've been up since six, building Lego towers and making everybody porridge. So the least you can fucking do is be here when you say you're going to be here and get Lola some new shoes. Make sure you take her somewhere where she can have her feet measured, and Lola is absolutely not allowed a heel higher than an inch at school. If you buy anything tarty, or patent for that matter, I will personally come round and shove them up your miserably mean backside AND I'll tell the school that her father bought them for her.

From: Dr James
Sent: Friday 24 January 13:42
To: Matthew Wilcox
Subject: THE JOINT ACCOUNT

Why have you stopped the standing order????? Are you now expecting me to support your three children 100 per cent financially as well as bring them up on my own????

I don't think it's on for a lawyer to do this sort of thing, is it? What would the partners say, I wonder. We're supposed to be civilized people, Matthew, not celebrities wrangling over the ownership of our kids in the tabloid press. So be reasonable and talk to me.

No Pay, No Kids, I say. They're all now very busy on Sunday.

What About Me, Too?

Dear Diary,

Saturday the 25th of January ✏️

Mum and Dad had a massive row on the phone. Mum didn't think I could hear because I was watching Saturday morning TV, but how was I gonna concentrate on that when I could hear that they were arguing about me? She was shouting at him about money and I heard her telling him that I was busy today, which isn't true because Dad promised to take me out to lunch and then maybe we would go bowling, so why would I make any other plans? Mum knew that. I really want to see Dad even though I saw him last weekend when we went to Kent but Mum just kept saying, 'Over my dead body,' and 'How can you even consider that sort of disruption when they haven't even got used to the idea of your going?' and then she slammed down the phone and stomped round the house in such a bad mood that I didn't dare ask her anything, like am I actually gonna see my Dad today? So I made her a cup of tea and took Tom into my room to play with my babies so that she didn't have to worry about him and he didn't have to hear her stomping and shouting.

Dad never came to collect me. I looked out of the window most of the morning, hoping he'd be early, waiting for him, but he never came. Mum didn't ever tell me why, just kept trying to suggest that we invited Clare over now that her exams were finished or went out somewhere but I didn't wanna do that just in case Dad came. I really miss him, really miss the feel of him hugging me, the sounds he makes when he's home but I couldn't tell Mum that, don't want her to know how sad I am about it in case that makes her even sadder, like she might think I love him more or want to be with him more. I couldn't stop crying about it, crying as I looked out of the window waiting for him to come, and then when I thought I couldn't hide the tears and the sadness from Mum any longer, I grabbed Chloe's lead, shouted to Mum that I was taking her for a walk and ran out of the house before she could stop me. I ran up the high street to the cemetery, sobbing. I couldn't stop sobbing. Everything's gone so so wrong and it's all my fault. If they didn't have me to row about then maybe they would still be together and happy. I was sobbing so hard I couldn't really see where I was going, I just ran like I wanted to run away from my whole life and then I felt somebody grab my arm.

'Are you all right?'

I wiped my eyes and tried to calm down and get my breath back. It was the boy who had been riding the lion. I nodded but couldn't stop crying and shivering. I had forgotten to put on my coat when I ran out of the door.

'No you're not, you're freezing,' he said as he put his arm around me. 'Come on, let's get you somewhere warm.' He led me along a path to the Lion's Tomb and down the same stone steps I had walked with Toyah. Chloe followed. He sat me down on an old sofa cushion in front of a small wood fire and put a blanket around my shoulders. Chloe settled down beside me and stared into the flames. After a while I stopped sobbing and shivering but I felt weak from all the crying. The boy handed me a chipped mug of hot tomato soup, which he had warmed up on a Calor gas stove and sat down beside me. He didn't try and make me talk or explain anything. He just sat beside me on the sofa cushion and stared into the flames, like he knew.

'I shouldn't be drinking this, this is your food,' I said guiltily when I had finished the mug. 'But it was delicious, thank you.'

'More? There is more if you want it.' He took the mug from my hand and got up to refill it but I stopped him. I really wasn't hungry.

'Have you been living here long? You've made it very cosy.'

The boy laughed, but he didn't answer my question, just stared into the flames and stroked Chloe behind her ears. He didn't need to know anything about my life but he wasn't about to tell me anything about his, either.

'Do you live here by yourself?' I asked, trying again.

The boy nodded.

'Isn't that really scary?'

'Sometimes. But there's a fox that comes by most nights and likes to keep me company. Particularly if I've got bacon. He loves bacon!'

'Mum says there's a fox that goes through our dustbins most nights. He eats everything, not just the bacon.'

The boy laughed again. 'They're a bit like dogs, foxes. Your dog's dad was probably a fox, he looks a bit like one.'

'He's a she, she's called Chloe.'

'That's a human's name. Dogs need names like Spot or Digger.'

'They do not!'

The boy laughed again. For a boy who lived all by

himself in a tomb he managed to do an awful lot of laughing and he had such a nice laugh, a giggly chuckle almost like a girl's. Then we started listing all of the dogs' names we had ever heard of and then HE made ME laugh when he told me about two dogs he had met on the common who were called Flip and Flop so when their owner called them he just shouted 'Flip Flop!' and everyone thought he was mad. And then I felt better. And then I remembered that I really ought to go home before Mum got worried. So I told him I'd come and see him again soon and bring him something good to eat. The boy didn't say anything, just stared into the fire and I knew he didn't believe me. I didn't really want to go and leave him there all on his own, but I had to get back to Mum and Tom. With Frankie out all the time, they need me.

'Thank you for cheering me up,' I said as I kissed him quickly on the cheek. 'I really will be back to see you soon but my Mum really needs me at the moment.' I stood up and he looked up at me and smiled.

'Take care of yourself,' he said kindly.

'I will. And you too.'

It was kind of weird and amazing all at the same time, meeting such a nice boy just like that when I was feeling so so sad.

What About Me, Too?

From: Sue James
Sent: Sunday 26 January 23:04
To: Angela James
Subject: Matthew and Mum as opposed to Matthew and son . . .

Matthew wants US to move and to sell the house and has this fantasy that we could live happily as neighbours on opposite sides of the street somewhere smaller nearby so that the kids can move between us. What WE might want doesn't seem to enter his thinking. Everything is about him, not us. And why should the kids have to go through the double disruption of moving as well as separation, which he clearly considers to be a permanent way of life although hasn't had the guts to say as much? I'm so angry I could set fire to all his belongings in the garden, only that's rather violent and not good for the kids either.

And bloody Mum has been misbehaving as well. North Butting have been on the phone and they have asked her to leave. I tried to convince Matron several times to give her another chance but she won't hear of it, so I will have to go down there tomorrow, DAMN IT, to pick her up. She's been spreading more lies about food poisoning, refused to go to bed when Matron decided it was lights out and sent a new gal hysterical by telling her that the staff put bugs in all the rooms and sedatives in their Ovaltine. Haven't told Frank and Lola yet, thought I'd break it to them over breakfast before they go to school. She'll have to sleep on the sofabed in the living room until I can work out what to do with her next. I need this like I need a hole in the head. Ironic that it should be Mum who gets expelled, not Frankie. I could kill her, Mum that is, not Frankie. I'm really worried about Frankie – she's showing all the signs of a teenager in distress AGAIN – she's out a lot, and I found her sobbing into Toyah's shoulder on Friday morning. I tried to comfort her but she just shrugged me off, told me to go away and that I wouldn't understand, which was hurtful. I'd be lying if I said I didn't mind. I know I should be grateful that Toyah is there for her and she can talk to her. I know, logically, that what matters is that she has someone sensible and adult enough to trust, and Toyah is fantastic in that respect, but it's like being stabbed in the gut, rejected, not needed. Of course she deserves privacy, I can be spared the details. But I am still her mum and just need to be able to feel that I can hug her when she's down. She was at Ruby's last night and has hidden herself away in her room tonight. Said she wanted an early night. Hmmmm. It must be Matthew leaving that's doing this – she doesn't want to see him. Surely it can't be Chattie? I know teenage rejection hurts, but this much? When she said she'd had enough of him anyway??

Sxx

What About Me, Too?

Dear Diary,

Chattie is still pretending that I don't exist and won't talk to me. He had to sit next to me in history on Friday because there wasn't another seat and I swear he must have heard my heart beating it was so loud. But he still wouldn't look at me or say anything. It's become like THE big gossip going round school because we were always so together and all anybody is interested in is who chucked whom, when it isn't like that. Love, true love, is much more complicated than that. If I'm to be really honest though, I have much more fun with my friends, even with Saskia (who seriously needs help but refuses to accept that she has a problem with food), than I did with Chattie in the last few weeks of our relationship. I can just be myself, let rip and drink too much and think about me, not him. Mum is not worth talking to about it because when I tried to tell her how I felt she actually had the nerve to call this Puppy Love and said that my first fling was bound to be short because of my age, which is just so insulting and patronizing and exactly what Juliet's parents felt about her and Romeo – and look what happened to that pair of star-crossed lovers! But if Juliet had stopped to think for just one minute about the advantages of being single, rather than acting so rashly and stabbing herself in the tomb over Romeo's body, if she'd just pulled herself together a bit and got back with her friends, she'd probably have got over it, like I will one day. Only you don't think that you'll ever get over it because the pain goes so deep. I know how she felt.

Went with Hayley, Fran and Ruby to another raze last

night, and without Chattie there it was more relaxing because I didn't have to worry about him being happy. It's kind of cool being with so many older people, it makes you feel older somehow, and not just a poxy schoolgirl. And there was so much to drink it was hard to say no, I didn't wanna say no. We passed a bottle of vodka round and each slug burned less so you wanted another. We just had a laugh and when you laugh and drink you forget all your troubles and I completely forgot about missing Chattie until I got so drunk that I couldn't stop thinking about him and Dad and how shit my life is right now and how piss-poor I am at relating to men, and then I started sobbing and couldn't stop. Ruby says I couldn't stop wailing and calling Chattie's name and saying 'Why me, why me?' which is like just so embarrassing and I don't remember that at all. They took it in turns, apparently, to rub my back and walked me up and down the street outside while I threw up the entire inside of my body. Why does getting drunk make you sob like that? Weird. My throat's really sore this morning. Ruby also says I begged them not to take me to hospital. Too right. Mum'd kill me and she's got enough to deal with at the moment without me as well.

What About Me, Too?

Dear Diary,

Wednesday the 29th of January

Granny's back. Mum says she was being naughty and got kicked out. How hilarious is that???!!! It's quite nice having her here because at least there's someone to talk to. Tom was really pleased to see her and sat on her lap for ages, clapping his hands together and giving her those big wet kisses that he's so good at. Funny how they're quite similar even though theirs eighty years between them. Tom points to Chloe and says DOG about 8,000 times just because he can, and Granny never seems to get tired of listening or agreeing with him that Chloe is indeed a dog, because she's so happy to be away from the old people's dump and here with her family instead. She'll put up with anything, even Mum in a strop, which she is most days.

Dad rang last night and it was kind of embarassssing because I didn't know what to say. It was also kind of weird hearing his voice on the phone because usually when he phones it's because he's away on busyness and he just wants to say 'I love you' and 'Sleep tight,' but this time it was like he wanted news and stuff and I didn't know what else to say other than that Granny was back, which he already knew because she answered the phone, pretended we didn't live here any more and put the phone down so that he had to ring back.

Toyah and I took Chloe for a walk in the cemetery on our way back from school today. I told her about the boy and she was really interested. But he wasn't there. The tomb was really neat. He'd made his bed and there were lots of tins and some fruit piled up in the corner by the Calor gas stove. We left him a packet of chocolate digestives and a bunch of daffodils, to remind him of spring.

What About Me, Too?

Dear Diary,

Friday. All Mum ever does is moan on at me about not clearing up or cooking when she's never even TAUGHT me how to do things like use the washing machine or roast a chicken. So how can I? Anyway, Toyah's a brilliant cook and now Granny's here, why can't she help? I know she's just stressed out again because Dad's left AGAIN and Granny's here AGAIN, but doesn't she realize that I'm gutted about Chattie and that when you live with this level of rejection it's hard to even concentrate on anything other than yourself, let alone GCSEs? Men are so selfish. Dad's selfish because he thinks he has a greater right to happiness than me, even when doing what he wants makes everybody else in this family unhappy. And Chattie's selfish because he only wants things done HIS way. There's no room for compromise. With these two examples of manhood around I think even Ruby would forgive me for becoming a lesbian. Although the idea of doing anything other than pulling is totally disgusting. I HAVE to focus on GCSEs, not the cleaning, or Granny, or Dad, or even Chattie. And Mum needs to understand that. I haven't dared tell her that I got a U for maths when I was predicted to get a C and that Mr Poland wants me to do some extra work over half-term to catch up. I don't know what happened. He says I didn't read the question properly and got them in the wrong order or something, when if I got some of the answers right I think it's really unfair to give me a U. I got As for all the sciences though, so maybe that means I can be a doctor. Mum was pleased about that. Chattie and I have been apart for sixteen days. I feel like half of me is missing, like I'm not whole or even real without him. We had such a special thing together, I felt protected from all the badness and loneliness in the world because he was with me. I can't stop thinking about him the whole time, wondering what he's doing, who he's with and whether he's missing me as much as I'm missing him. My star sign says, 'Nothing's over until it's over,' which is promising, but then his says, under love 'Don't get bogged down with old news – look around for fresh pastures,' which isn't what I want him to think at all but Ruby says he probably doesn't read Heat. *I'm thinking of getting a tattoo on my bum but Hayley says they really hurt and swell up and then I wouldn't be able to sit down for a week. But if I had a heart there, with a 'C' in the middle, maybe then he'd believe that I really, really love him?*

What About Me, Too?

Dear Diary,

Saturday the 1st day of February

I wish I could think of some way to make Mum happy. I clear up as much as I can whenever Toyah's not here and I look after Tom and I make tea for Granny, but she's in such a bad mood all the time and complains about how tired she is. So I think that all of us (Frankie Tom and me) should go away somewhere with Dad for the weekend so that she can get some rest. I've calculated that there are twenty-eight days and therefore 672 hours in February. Fifteen of those days we will be at school, but we won't be at half-term or at the weekend, so that means that there are twelve days (not counting today which is almost gone) when we could see Dad, so we should be with him at least six days or 144 hours to be really fair. But then when you look at 144 hours out of 672 it doesn't seem fair at all.

Dear Diary,

Tuesday the 4th of February ✏

Hours with Mum since Saturday: 36
Hours with Dad since Saturday: 0

Had a MASSIVE fight with Frankie over the computer. I was playing a real cool game and she just pushed me off because she said she had homework to do and GCSEs were much more important than playing. Well, excuse me. She didn't even ask me, so I kicked her and she hit me and then she hit me really hard and called me a 'bitch' and then Mum came home from work and heard us fighting and went absolutely mad with me, which is so unfair because it wasn't my fault in the first place. Frankie shouted at Mum that if we lived in a half-decent house with more than one computer it wouldn't be a problem, and why didn't anybody understand how much work she had to do with her exams coming and then stormed up to her room crying. What a baby. While Toyah was trying to calm everybody down, Tom climbed up onto the kitchen table and pushed over a vase of dead flowers and Granny did nothing to help the situation or clear up. She just asked when supper was going to be ready.

But Granny was really, really nice to me after school today. I had a big fight with Clare and Tanya about the boy in the graveyard. I stupidly told them because I thought they'd be interested and like me more but they just ran off laughing and told everybody that I was making up stories about ghosts just to get friends, which is just so unfair. I ran into the loos so that nobody could see me cry. Granny could see I was upset about something when I came home. So she said it was time she taught me how to make mirangs. We had to whisk the eggs for so long my arm hurt, but they tasted delicious. Frankie ate them all and didn't even leave one for Mum, which was probably another reason why I hated her so much I kicked her. She thinks she's the only one with problems. She never ever thinks of anybody but herself. She should be grateful that she has Mum and doesn't have to live in a tomb like the boy does. I must remember to find out what his name is. We spent all that time talking about dogs names and I never asked him his.

From: Dr James
Sent: Wednesday 5 February 13:40
To: Angela James
Subject: Mum

A quick one from work while it's quiet. Clarice's say they won't have room until at least April but have promised to give me top priority, I think just to get me off the phone. I've been ringing them daily. I've made a note to try them on Monday again and I may just have to go and camp on their doorstep and refuse to leave until they give us a place. The thought of Mum in my sitting room until April makes me feel ever so slightly sick. There are ten canvases stacked against the walls by the sofabed, all equally hideous – her technique hasn't improved – she talks all the time, an endless stream of consciousness that borders on the batty at times with the odd racist comment chucked in. She fusses endlessly about whether we're going to be late for school/work, etc. when she doesn't have to be anywhere at all. She complains about the state of the kitchen, the mess in the hall, the fact that dinner isn't ready and the noise of the traffic outside. In just three days she has managed to burn enough cheese on toast to set off the smoke alarm, forgotten she's run a bath so that it's overflowed through the living-room ceiling AGAIN and she's taught Tom to say 'Mummy witch', which he now repeats all day long, and which makes me seethe. I can't help but feel profoundly irritated by her presence, like why should I have to put up with her at all when I've got Tom and

What About Me, Too?

Lola and Frankie about to dive off into the deep end, if Frankie hasn't already (I'm almost positive she's drinking again). Then I just feel guilty, because of course you're not supposed to feel that way about your own mother, EVER. I'm not sure how much of her interfering guilt-tripping about working motherhood I can take and may have to adopt the traditional Chinese habit of pushing your ageing mother to the top of a mountain and leaving her there to be pecked to death by buzzards. I feel guilty about Toyah, too – it's more than she bargained for, having Mum during the day as well (although she says she doesn't mind) AND she's stayed on longer than she said she would because she cares and knows we need her. She's a total darling but we can't depend on her too much, it's just not fair. Complete silence from Matthew although he has rung Lola. It's half-term on the 17th – if Matthew could take Tom and Lola for a few days I could give Toyah some time off but then if I ask him he'll just say no to spite me, and I've already painted myself into a corner by saying that he can't see the kids because he's stopped his standing order into the joint account. Ring Mum, will you? And if there's a strapping Australian lass there who wants to come and live with us for a while and help out Toyah, let me know. The house is now heaving with people anyway. She could sleep in a cupboard.

Much love, Sxxxx

From: Dr James
Sent: Thursday 6 February 13:04
To: Matthew Wilcox
Subject: Half-term 17–23 Feb

I know Lola and Tom would love to see you at some point
during the holiday.
   When do you want them?

What About Me, Too?

From: Dr James
Sent: Thursday 6 February 13:56
To: Matthew Wilcox
Subject: Re: Half-term 17–23 Feb

You're not alone; we all have to work. You can have them both that last weekend provided you take them on Friday too (which means taking the day off, Matthew, not the week) so that I can give Toyah the day off. She needs a break.

Dear Diary,

Friday the 7th of February 🖉

Hours with Mum: 102
Hours with Dad: 0

The worst thing about Dad not being here is that I never
know when I'm going to see him next. It's the not knowing
that makes me imagine all sorts of things that Toyah says
will never happen, but what if they did? What if she's
wrong? Like, he could move to Scotland with Laura and
have some more children and forget all about us. Mum says
Tom and I are going to stay with him during half-term, but
what if he doesn't pay her enough and she stops us from
going, or what if he just forgets or Laura makes plans to do
something else and we can't come? And then what happens
if Dad never pays Mum any more money and we have to
move to another house and I have to go to another school??
Toyah says it's just the not knowing that makes me imagine
the worst. Actually, I wouldn't mind moving because I'm
going to have to go to a new school soon anyway and Clare
is still being a bitch. At last break she started saying really
horrible things about Mum and Dad. She said it was no
wonder that he had left us when Mum looks so scruffy and
doesn't do anything to make herself look good, like wear
make-up, and probably wears a grey bra. Which must be
what her mum says about my mum because why would
Clare even bother to think about her otherwise? Anyway,
most of her bras are black. 'She doesn't even shave under

her arms, how disgusting,' she said to Tanya at the top of
her voice so that everybody could hear and then they ran
off laughing. Granny could see I wasn't happy about it
when I came home from school. I don't want to talk to her
about what's going on with Mum and Dad because it feels
so disloyal so I just said that Clare and Tanya were being
horrible again but I didn't tell her what they said obviously.
So Granny said it was time I learned how to make a
fruitcake to go with all those 'lovely pots of tea'. She took
me down to the corner shop and we bought boxes of raisins
and sultanas and some eggs. It took ages to make. 'I bet
Clare doesn't know how to make fruitcake,' Granny said as
we took it out of the oven. 'Why don't we go over and offer
her a slice tomorrow when it's cooled down?' Well, she can.
I'm not going to.

Dear Diary,

Saturday morning 📝

Hours with Mum: 122
Hours with Dad: 0

Why does Frankie think she is the centre of the universe and that nothing else matters but her? She used up all the milk at breakfast, wasted it even, because she was on the phone while she was pouring it into a bowl and then turned to look at something on the TV and poured it all over the table. She cleared it up but then refused to go out and buy any more when I told her to. She's accused Mum of being mean yesterday because she said she wouldn't buy her a pink mini iPod or pay for her to have a haircut at this new cool salon she's read about in *Vogue*, and even though Mum didn't say anything I could see that she was hurt and cross because she went into the living room and had a row with Granny instead. SHE'S been smoking in bed. Says that if she can't smoke now at eighty, when can she? And Frankie just thinks that's hilarious and has taken sides with Granny when she KNOWS how much Mum hates it because she's a doctor. And now she says we're DEPRIVED because we've never been skiing and Saskia and Serena are going in half-term, and the boys there are really fit. Mum got so sick of hearing her go on and on about how much fun it would be, how we all needed a holiday with Dad leaving and how as a doctor Mum ought to be more concerned about taking us on active healthy holidays, that in the end she shouted, 'If it matters that much, ask your father and the marriage-breaker bitch and with any luck they'll break both their legs,' and then slammed the kitchen door behind her. I don't know how Frankie could be so selfish. How could we even think we could go skiing with Granny here and Tom not even two yet?

Granny took two pieces of my fruitcake next door to Clare's house and made me go with her. Clare's mum opened the door and was incredibly grateful and took the plate but wouldn't let us in. But she did then start questioning Granny in this really nosey way about whether she had noticed anything odd going on in our cellar, because she was convinced we had mice. She saw one scuttling into our cellar from her cellar through a hole in the wall when she went down to get a bottle of wine. Well, why does that mean we have the mice and not her? Granny was very polite about it and said, 'Oh dear, dear me,' while I just scowled behind her. Granny said she would mention it to Mum. And she also said to make sure that Clare got a piece of my cake because I had made it for her, which was really sweet of her. Mum just laughed when Granny told her about the mice. She said, 'There's just one large rat in this street and she's next door.'

From: Dr James
Sent: Friday 14 February 13:46
To: Angela James
Subject: Valentine's

Incredible though it may seem, got one this morning and haven't a clue who from. It's handmade with just one big pink heart on the front with a question mark inside and it was posted in Liverpool! So that rules out the kids because they don't even know where Liverpool is. Frank's furious that she didn't get one, thinks Chattie should have sent her one and threw an extraordinarily melodramatic scene over breakfast, worthy of an Oscar. But as Lola pointed out — she chucked him so why should he send her one?

For one brief excitable moment I wondered whether it might be Mark with the black Lab, then for one rather worried moment it occurred to me that it could be Bryson, but actually I suspect it's Richard, a patient who makes an appointment to see me every week with a different bogus ailment. The sterner I get with him, the more he seems to like me. His wife died last year and he's lost without her but definitely not my type — seventy-two and smelly. Rather nice though, ay?! Put a bit of spring into my step this morning.

Did Spike shower you with flowers?

Sxx

What About Me, Too?

Dear Diary,

Chattie looks terrible, miserable with dark rings around his eyes. I'm worried he might do something really stupid. I sent him ten Valentine cards, all signed so that he would know they were from me but he hasn't sent one back. He did see me wearing his locket today, though, at lunchtime. It's such a burden being in love with someone who is so sensitive and possessive. It's like if I don't give up my whole life for him, he doesn't want me at all, which Fran says is really stupid because nobody can actually own anybody else but I think it's actually secretly kind of romantic, like he wants to devour me. I'm worried that he could do something really, REALLY stupid like kill himself, like Romeo did. If he can't have me, he doesn't want anybody else and he might just well end it all now. People kill themselves because they're bullied or because they're worried about their GCSEs but this is much more serious. And then I'd be so grief-stricken and damaged by the trauma that I'd never be able to love anybody again – widowed before I was even wed. But he CAN have me. If this goes on for much longer I'll have to agree to everything he says because I won't be able to bear us being apart for any longer. Which is what Fran says he's trying to do.

From: Sue James
Sent: Sunday 16 February 20:19
To: Matthew James
Subject: The D word and the kids

My feeling is that IF this is the end of the road for us (your choice, never mine), then we should divorce and tell the kids ASAP so that they know where they stand. It hurts, Matthew, to have to be the one to make the running on this when all I've ever done is/was to love you, but it hurts all of us, and particularly the kids, to live with this terrible uncertainty. Could you please clarify that this is the case and then we can decide how next to proceed, but our first priority has to be the welfare of the kids.

Sue

What About Me, Too?

From: Sue James
Sent: Sunday 16 February 20:25
To: Angela James
Subject: Re: Living in Kew Gardens

Darling,

In hospitals they take the flowers OUT of the bedrooms at night because of the carbon monoxide poisoning. Now they need the beds so badly that they leave them in. Are you sure he isn't in fact trying to get rid of you by smothering you with love ... literally?? Beware the Bluebeard factor.

I've been totally brave with my wayward Bluebeard and broached the subject of Divorce. My secret curse of a slow, painful, debilitating disease doesn't seem to be working, so if I can't just eliminate him, we have to divorce. It's just not fair on the kids. What's really, really unfair is that I am the one who has to cope with emotional fallout, I'm the one doing everything I possibly can to support them while he simply walks away. I know Lola's suffering, she spends hours writing in her diary in her bedroom and rather than asking me the big question of whether or not Matthew is coming back she asks about other things, like are we going to have to move and even offered yesterday to sell her Sylvanian collection on eBay if we needed the money which just about broke my heart. That, and Frankie who has been unbelievably stroppy and got too drunk at a party last night. BUT she did come home and wasn't afraid to let me

233

see her in that state which is something, I suppose. We sat up until three at the kitchen table talking. I toasted about half a loaf of bread, trying to sober her up, and listened to her babbling on about Chattie and how much she missed him. I need to keep a close eye on her; OK, not read her diary or anything, I know, I know what the parenting handbooks say about that – she needs her privacy – but where is the borderline exactly between respecting her privacy and knowing what she's up to so that I can keep her safe? I trust her, sort of, but then the books also say that divorce can hit teenagers harder than it does small children, so all this might just be a reaction to Matthew leaving AGAIN. The one thing I don't have to worry about now is early sexual onset which I gather from one book is possibly triggered by divorce, because she's already done that. But Matthew leaving was certainly the trigger for all that trouble last year, although he still won't accept it. So I need to watch her, maybe take her shopping when Tom and Lola are with Matthew.

Mum, on the other hand, has never seemed better. Complains about the food we have got as well as the food we haven't got but eats like a horse. Never stops going on about how the house is a mess and how Frankie dresses like a prostitute and that it's all my fault if she never makes anything of her life because I work. And when she's not castigating me for earning an honest living, she's telling me how to look after Tom – reminding me to change his nappy about ten times an hour so he doesn't get nappy rash, telling me to change his clothes the moment they're dirty, like I have the time for that. Then yesterday, when I let Lola go off to the toyshop up the road on her own, she couldn't stop going on about how I shouldn't let her do that (she doesn't even have to cross a road to get there), that she was too young (she goes to secondary school in September, on her own) and that it was raining and she'd get wet. So in the end I went out to bring her home just to shut Mum up and couldn't find her which sent me into a blind panic and then, when I finally came home forty minutes later, soaking wet and about to ring the police, there was Lola curled up on the sofa with Chloe writing in her diary! She'd decided not to go to the toyshop after all because it was raining and had been reading in her room! If Mum could just stop telling us all how to live our lives and let us be, life here would be a great deal calmer.

But she has done me a great favour with HND who has been rapping hysterically on the door almost every evening about the mice she claims have taken up residence in our cellar. Mum rang Rentokil while I was at work. They've laid traps all over the basement but say that it is rats, not mice, and they are nesting in her cellar, not ours!! The filthy whore! They've just been visiting us to collect up nesting material and food (nice of them to help clean up the place). But it's her lovely, overheated, squeaky-clean house they want more than this dump. Too right. Just imagining her lying awake at night listening out for rodents makes me feel better. She probably spends most of her days standing on a chair screaming, which is why she hasn't been round much to bother us. I told Lola to make a point of telling Clare that rats can climb walls . . . they're out there . . . waiting to pounce . . . 'There's a rat in the kitchen, what am I gonna do . . .' Great song. Think I'll go and put it on now at full volume and have a good dance.

Much Love, Sxxxxxxxxxxxxxxxxxxxxxxxxxxxxxxxxxx

Dear Diary,

The trouble with Mum is she thinks that Dad leaving is the only thing that matters. It doesn't help but actually I have far more important things to think about, like my own love life. But what REALLY doesn't help is her going on all the time about the pros and cons of the Dutch cap or the coil and giving me statistics about the high rates of sexually transmitted diseases amongst the young who won't use condoms, and do I want her to make me an appointment with the family planning person at the surgery? And how she worries about the pill and the links with breast cancer, and how I would tell her if I got pregnant, wouldn't I? Pregnant! I know that as a doctor she can't help but think of everything as a potential health issue rather than an emotional one but I wish she'd just lay off me for ONE minute and get it into her stupid fat head that I'm not having sex with anybody at the moment, which is the main problem of my life. No one WANTS to have sex with me. That Dad doesn't want to have sex with her is understandable, but I'm only fifteen and much too young to feel washed up. If I could find someone else who was prepared to even touch my body then maybe that would break this awful cycle of not knowing. Chattie would either get so jealous that he would rush to defend my honour like the hero that he is, or he wouldn't and then I'd know that he really doesn't love me any more and that I'm washed up on the sexual dustbin of life, destined to spend the rest of my fertile life with pervs. The thing is, though, I am beginning to really freak out because I can't remember when my last period was and I didn't write it down in my diary like Mum said I should so that I could count the days, and now I really AM worried that I could be pregnant but I can't go asking her because she'll go mad, absolutely MAD. You don't think I could be pregnant, do you? What I also want to be able to ask her is whether it is possible to just die from unrequited love, but she'll just laugh because that's an emotion, NOT a disease. Mum doesn't think emotions matter when actually NOTHING matters more. If you're really, really sick but FEEL OK about it then surely that's better than NOT feeling OK? But to be THIS lovesick and feel THIS bad . . . nothing could be worse. When you love someone this badly and they don't love you back, how can you possibly go on with the future stretching ahead of you like some vast empty void? I don't think I'll ever love anyone as much as I've loved him.

Dear Diary,

Friday the 21st of February 🖉

Hours with Dad: 7

Dad picked me and Tom up this morning and took us to his tiny flat. I felt really bad about leaving Mum all on her own because Frankie is so pathetikally lovesick that she's not much use to anybody. Honestly, if falling in love is this much trouble then I think I'm going to stay single for ever and ever. But I have spent 225 hours with Mum and not even one single minute with Dad so I told her to get lots of rest and that I'd look after Tom. She has got Chloe, but I'm not sure who's going to look after Granny without me there.

Laura was of course acting as if I was some sort of three-year-old deaf parapleejic. She never stopped asking me if I wanted a drink in this sickly-sweet babyish voice and then when I said yes to try and shut her up she gave me one in a plastic beaker! She really hasn't got a clue how to look after kids and she looks at Tom like he's got some terrifying disease. Can't wait to see how she manages with his nappy, which no doubt Dad'll make her do before the weekend's out, or so Mum said anyway.

Dad took us out for lunch and then to a toyshop where he let us have whatever we wanted. Tom chose a giant bear which he won't let go off and I couldn't decide between a magic ~~cunjurors~~ cundgerers set and this adorable make-up and matching handbag set, so Dad let me have both and he

let me buy a set of miniture rubbers for Camilla because
she's started a collection. Laura was clearly bored by the
whole thing and kept saying, 'Can we go now?' like she was
six or something. We're now on our way to Kent again,
worse luck, with Dad driving and complaining about the
traffic and Laura saying if we hadn't spent so long in the
toyshop we'd have missed the traffic. Tom's been crying the
whole way which doesn't bother Dad or me because we're
used to it, but Laura seems to mind and keeps trying to
distract him with stupid stuff about what's outside the
window, like cows and the moon, which he can't even see
because it's dark. And then when she couldn't take it any
more she said angrily, 'Haven't you got a dummy or
something to shut the brat up?' which is just such a
horrible, mean thing to say to such a small innocent child
that I might just prod Tom the whole weekend so he cries,
and I'll say it's because he's missing his REAL mother and
let him make a horrible mess so that she runs screaming
into the waves to drown herself and dies a really horrible
death so that we never see her again, and then Dad will
have to move back in with Mum because, as Mum says,
he can't manage without a woman.

Dear Diary,

Sunday the 23rd of February

Hours with Dad: 41
Hours with Mum: 225

Tom has been clinging to Dad the whole time because he's only a baby and he doesn't know where he is or why Mum's not here but Laura doesn't even understand that simple fact because she's so stupid. Every time she tries to pick him up he cries really loud and hits her so Dad is having to carry him round the whole time to keep him quiet and now they're rowing about it. She says it isn't normal for a child to be this clingy and how he should put him down and let him cry and Dad says that Tom has hardly seen him since Christmas so she ought to be a bit more understanding and maybe help a bit more, so she stormed off angrily into the kitchen to make some cauliflower cheese for lunch with her sister and I can hear them talking about it, with Laura's sister trying to explain how hard it is on the kids when the parents are rowing. Too right, but what doesn't help is her sister on the scene as well, trying to steal him away. Laura really doesn't understand children. She thinks I'm old enough to do all the washing up so that she doesn't have to do it but thinks I'm too young to understand what she's saying unless she talks to me in this silly high squeaky voice. She also has no idea how to play at anything. We were playing scrabble this morning and she just couldn't be bothered to make any sort of score at all and then got cross because I beat her when I'm only eleven. Then, to make things even worse, Leo, who is the marriage-breaker's horrible nephew and who of course can't do anything wrong, has been bugging me all weekend to play Cowboys and Indians, so I chased him out into the garden hollering and pushed him over into a pile of nettles because those Indians had to resort to some really dirty tactics to stop the white man from taking over their country. I told him to quit bugging me otherwise I was gonna have to hang him up from the apple tree and light a fire beneath the soles of his bare feet, which was what the Indians did before they scalped cowboys. That shut him up. Then I went back to help Dad with Tom, now that Laura was out of the way, and the three of us had a really nice time together, playing and singing songs like we used to do. I really love being with Dad, love the feel of him there, the sound of his voice, the smell of him when he kisses me goodnight but I just wish I could have him all to myself. I don't see why I have to share the precious few hours I have with him with the marriage-breaker bitch. Why can't he just see her when I'm with Mum?

I couldn't sleep last night because it's like really creepy here and so, so dark, and went into see Dad for a cuddle and found them snogging. It was disgusting. I felt sick and ran out of the room screaming and jumped back into bed. Dad came in and gave me a cuddle and told me to go to sleep but it wasn't the same, it felt like I couldn't go back in there, even if I was ill or had a headache because they might be totally naked and doing more than just snogging, which is bad enough in front of a child. And then when I tried to go back to sleep all I could see was him kissing the marriage-breaker bitch like he really loved her. So I squeezed my eyes tight shut and imajined her lying dead on the kitchen floor with 100 stab wounds in her chest and imajined Dad kissing Mum instead.

The really, really bad thing, though, is that I've left Panda either in Laura's car or worse still, in Kent and I can't go to sleep without him. And I don't wanna go downstairs and tell Mum because that'll just give her something else to argue with Dad about because she'll blame him for not remembering to pack up all my stuff and she's already slagged him off about ten times for forgetting to bring back my toothbrush. So I'm hugging a doll but it's not the same thing. She's a bit hard.

What About Me, Too?

From: Sue James
Sent: Sunday 23 February 22:35
To: Angela James
Subject: Shipwrecked with Mum and a tyrannical teen

Dearest Ange, Angela Pangela (remember Great Uncle Sharon??!! Do you think she ever KNEW why we called her that? It was a pretty strong moustache even for an, old woman)

Agreed to a date with Ian Bryson on Friday because it felt so sad spending the entire weekend just with Frank moping about Chattie, Mum wittering on about nothing and the dog. (Matthew had Tom and Lola for the weekend.) But it was a mistake – it's better to be single than THAT desperate. Firstly he wears slacks and slip-ons as casual wear when every man I have ever been out with wears jeans. Then he chose to take me to one of those places where they play romantic muzak in the background AND I ABSOLUTELY HATE RESTAURANTS THAT PLAY MUSIC, LET ALONE MUZAK, WHEN YOU'RE TRYING TO CONCENTRATE ON SOMETHING AS IMPORTANT AS FOOD. Then he made suggestions as to what I should eat (he must date ants) and THEN he spent the entire time talking about patients. It's bad enough having to examine them during the day, the last thing I want to do is talk about them at night, plus it's indiscreet. He was even ruder about some of them than I am (which is saying something) but whenever I tried to change the subject he looked bored. I don't think he has any interests other than tropical fish. He has a tank at home and they all have names. And I really don't fancy him. He may be good-looking but he has hairy hands, which means he's probably got a hairy back as well. It was a relief to get back to Frankie, even though she was dying her hair again, (black this time), and Mum, who had set up her easel in the kitchen with a giant canvas to paint a bowl of fruit, which we then tripped over for the rest of the weekend, AND we couldn't eat the fruit because of course it couldn't be moved.

Tom's come back with nappy rash AND a cold and even though he's way off the scale weight-wise for his age because he's such a greedy pig, he looks malnourished. Plus he's definitely showing signs of separation anxiety. He won't look at me, as if I was somehow to blame for dumping him into the care of the marriage-breaker, and has gone to bed grumpily with a bottle, failing to respond to any of our normal bedtime songs. I'm furious with Matthew. I can't put Tom through this every other weekend. It's just not fair when he's this small. Do you think I could make some sort of deal with Matthew that he sees Tom here and has Lola there? And then the idea that that woman has even been touching my children makes me feel sick. Do you think I could get away with stipulating that SHE can't see them? Only him? I don't see why she has a right to spoil them or influence them against me. To be honest, I'd happily ban him from seeing any of his children ever again but then he'd probably join Fathers 4 Justice and start swinging his dick from the top of Big Ben in a batman suit as a publicity stunt, PLUS I couldn't do that to the kids, he is their Dad after all. But when he's THIS bad at looking after them AND he's not paying a bean towards their needs but spends a fortune on their wants (they came back weighed down with presents) it's really, really hard to put my anger on the back-burner and put their needs first.

Also there's the sordid question of money. Having Mum here is a total pain in the arse but at least we're saving money on not paying for her to be at North Butting. But until he is committed to regular maintenance I have no idea how well off or poor we are and have to be careful. I'm pretty sure that he's not the sort of man who's just going to disappear for ever and abandon his kids, but then I didn't think he was the sort of man who would have an affair again and leave. He's coming round here on Wednesday night – we're going to break the news to the kids together – so hopefully we can sort out some kind or arrangement from then on.

Left Mum on her own here with Frankie to go to work on Friday and came back to find the house reeking of smoke, which means Frankie is at it again. Told her the deal was off and she wasn't getting the £500 I promised at sixteen and she went ballistic, screaming that after what she had been through she deserved nothing less than a motorbike at sixteen! After what SHE has been through! The girl hasn't lived yet. Anyway, I counted to ten and tried to remain calm like the parenting handbooks advise, which is easy to say, bloody hard to do. What usually happens is a gradual build-up of mutual resentment. She comes home late from school and complains there's nothing to eat, that she has no money and is going to fail all of her GCSEs and I'm sweetly sympathetic like mothers are supposed to be. Then she spends sixty-five hours on the phone instead of doing any coursework – I button my lip and urge every cell in my body not to say anything. Then over supper she talks about nothing other than someone else's parents who are 'so cool, they . . .' let their daughter go to Glastonbury/take them to film premieres and parties where there are pop stars/talk about really interesting stuff over candlelit dinners/buy them decent clothes and take them skiing, and I feel reduced to the size of a pea, and just as boring. Or she preaches on about animal welfare and the health benefits of not eating meat as I'm tucking into a much looked forward to fillet steak, while she slaps enough petrochemicals on her face to give the dog cancer and refuses to accept that there are health downers to lipstick, make-up, deodorant and mobile phones because of course she likes them, but I can't like steak. Pointing out these inconsistencies will only lead to a row so I don't. Then she has a full-blown row with Lola, whom she says has been taking clothes from her room – so I make a point of taking Frank's side and tell Lola that she has to respect her sister's privacy, when actually I want to beat them both senseless. Then she floods the bathroom again and I have to shut myself in the airing cupboard and count to a 1,000 to stop myself from screaming. I keep it all together, stay calm, stay the grown up, stay in charge like the books say and then at 7.45, when everyone is at their most rushed and grumpy because we're all trying to get up, find homework, school shoes and get out of the house, I discover that she's taken the last of my tampons and totally lose it, setting relations back months over a piece of compacted cotton wool with a string on the end. Ridiculous. But it's really, REALLY hard to just laugh it all off and pretend that it all doesn't matter when every reasonable emotional cell in my body says she is the one who is being

What About Me, Too?

SELFISH, UNFAIR, INCONSIDERATE, NOT LISTENING TO
COMMON SENSE AND, MOST IMPORTANTLY, ME – HER
MOTHER.

I feel so angry that I could smash up the kitchen. I
practically burst my spleen keeping it all in tonight but I
managed it and let Mum have it instead for corrupting a minor
with cigarettes. She gave Frank the money to go and buy
them. If it's this hard not reacting over smoking, how on earth
am I going to manage it in the months ahead when she's
plucking her eyebrows instead of revising? And then no doubt
it'll be all my fault if she ends up as a waitress because she
hasn't got good enough grades to get into medical school. I
know, I know, it's her responsibility, they're her exams and
she has to do the work, but I can't help feeling that it is I who
will have failed her as her mother if she doesn't get those As.
We've given up hoping for any A*s.

Anyway, have a good week, sweet sister, kiss darling Stan
and Ollie for me and remind them that they have a Great Uncle
Sue here in England who will take them in when they just can't
stand you any more. I'm off to kiss my own cherub on his
sleeping head and then to bed with Lola and Chloe. Lola now
permanently in my bed, says it stops her feeling sad as she goes
to sleep. She's growing so quickly, mushrooming in front of my
eyes and soon my lithe little Lola will be too big to hug with my
whole body, you know, the way you can envelop a child and
become one. I can't do that with Frankie any more so I have to
admit that I'm loving every night that Lola's with me, and
neglecting to encourage her back into her own bed. Chloe
snores louder than Matthew and makes the bedroom stink, but
ho hum, I'm so lucky not to be alone. I think I can understand

247

now how single mothers start using their kids as emotional
props – must remember NOT to do that.

Much love,
Suexx

What About Me, Too?

Dear Diary,

Sunday the something of February. Whatever the date is, it doesn't matter, nothing really matters any more. Hayley's parents were away so she had a gathering last night which turned into a party. I didn't really wanna go because Chattie's been talking to this bitch from year 10 in the playground and I really didn't wanna have to face them together but it was worse than that, MUCH worse. I found him and Ruby alone together in one of the bedrooms and even though Ruby swears they weren't kissing, they were so close that even if they weren't, they were about to AND they both looked really guilty. I screamed 'bitch' and then ran away and sat on the smoking bench outside my house for about three hours in the freezing cold, trying to figure out what was really going on and wishing that I'd stayed long enough to have it out with her and punch her lights out. Ruby KNOWS how I feel about Chattie, how COULD she, she's like my best friend in the whole world and you just don't DO that. She called me like fifteen times last night but I didn't wanna speak to her, I never want to even see her again. And now she's texting me – 'All he wants to tlk about is u'; 'It's not how it looks. Call me' – and Fran's called me about six times to say that Chattie asked Ruby to go somewhere quiet so that he could talk to her about me and that I'd dumped him weeks ago so I really didn't have a right to question who he saw, but what business is that of hers anyway and I don't believe Chattie wouldn't wanna get with Ruby just to get at me. Ruby's never had a boyfriend and wants one desperately. She was always so jealous of him and me that I wouldn't put it past her to do anything just to see what he's like, what IT'S like. I should have found someone to snog in front of them, that's what Saskia would have done, or smacked her in the face which is what Hayley would've done, but instead I just ran like a stupid idiot and now I have to face them all at school tomorrow. And I still haven't had my period and feel really sick and bloated and now I can't even talk to Ruby about it. I can't be pregnant, I just can't.

What About Me, Too?

Dear Diary,

Wednesday the 26th day of February

I think today has been the worst day of my life. Mum
came home early and then Dad came home earlier than he
has ever been and for a moment I thought that maybe he
was coming home for good because he sat down at the
kitchen table like he'd never been away but then they told
us that they were going to get divorced. Dad did most of
the talking. He said that he loved us all very much and
that we could go and see him or ring him whenever we
liked, but if he loved us that much why doesn't he stay
here and be a proper Dad??? And then he tried to make it
all seem all right by talking about all the other children we
must know whose parents are separated and they're fine
but I don't care about any of them. I only know that it
doesn't feel right here without him and that neither of
them asked US whether WE wanted them to get divorced.
We haven't had any say, they haven't even asked us how
we feel about it and yet we're the ones who have to live
with the conseqwences. Frankie started shouting at him
about how selfish he was, how this was her GCSE year,
how she was supposed to be the one leaving him, not the
other way around and Tom started crying because he
could feel the tension but couldn't understand what was
going on and Mum just held him and rocked him and
buried her head into his little shoulder and didn't say
anything. With Frankie screaming and Tom crying, there
wasn't much point in me saying anything but there was

this large black hole where my stomach used to be and I didn't want Mum or Dad to see me cry so I ran out of the house and sat on the doorstep. I thought about going to see Clare. Maybe if I asked her for help and told her what was happening she'd be nice to me. But maybe she wouldn't. So I went to the cemetery, even though I didn't have Chloe and it was dark.

The gates were locked but there was a hole in the railings big enough to squeeze through. It was really, really dark once I got inside and so, so scary. Half of me wanted to go home, but the other half told me to stop being a baby and to follow the path. I could feel things brushing past me, the wind or maybe even ghosts, and I could hear things rustling in the bushes and brambles but I just kept focusing on the path in front of me. It was a bit of a relief having to consentrate on something else. When I got to the Lion's Tomb, the side door was open and there was a light coming from a lantern at the bottom of the stairs. There was a small fire smouldering. My daffodils I'd bought were dry and crinkled in a jar by the bed. There was a plastic plate lying on the floor that had been eaten off recently, but the boy wasn't there. I sat down in front of the fire and looked at all his belongings. It was sweet how he had tried to make it homely even though it couldn't have been less like a real home. He had hung a jumper up on a nail and propped up a picture of a woman beside his bed. She was pretty. I went over to have a look at it and was peering at it, trying to work out who she might be when he frightened me. 'Put that down,' he said. He was standing right behind me. I hadn't even heard him coming down the steps. I put it back quickly.

'I'm sorry, it's just that she looks so beautiful.'

The boy didn't say anything as he put some broken branches onto the fire.

'I'm sorry I haven't brought you anything but I sort of ran out in a hurry. But did you like the biscuits?'

'Yes. Thanks.' The boy sat down by the fire and stared deep into its embers, blowing occasionally to encourage the wood to catch. 'So what happened at home?'

I didn't want to say. I didn't really want to even have to remember what had just happened. It was so nice to forget about it. But then I thought there was probably no harm in telling him since he didn't even know who I was.

'They told us today that they're getting divorced.' I sat down beside him in front of the fire. The boy kept blowing until a flame flickered up and the branch caught fire.

'At least they told you.'

'Yeah, big of them, when what *we* might want doesn't even seem to matter. They just decide and we don't have any say when it affects us more than either of them.'

'But they care enough to talk to you. One of them could just have left and never come back, or worse, they could have asked you to leave.'

'Is that what happened to you?'

The boy poked at the fire with a stick. He looked uncomfortable, as if he were about to say something but couldn't because it would make him upset.

'Let's just say you're lucky, shall we?'

I wanted to tell him that I didn't feel very lucky but that sounded spoilt, given that he had to live all by himself in a graveyard and that's not very lucky. That's the sort of thing that Clare would say when she didn't get just what she wanted.

'What's your favourite food?' I asked, changing the subject once the fire was really going.

'Roast chicken . . . All that crispy skin!' he laughed. 'But you don't want to worry about bringing me anything because I'm fine here, look at that corner! Stuffed with food. Are you hungry?'

I shook my head. 'But I probably ought to be getting back. See if they've stopped shouting at each other. I'll come by tomorrow.'

He poked at the fire as I left and I felt really bad about leaving him all on his own but I shouldn't have been there in the first place and ran home quickly before I could change my mind.

When I got back home, Dad was still there arguing with Frankie, trying to get her to understand that he had a right to happiness just as she did, particularly now when he only had a few years left. Crap, if you ask me because he isn't really any happier now than he was when he lived here and as the grown-up he ought to think about our happiness first because we have no choice now but to be unhappy. Frankie didn't say anything that obvious, she just screamed at him that she hated him and ran up to her room in tears. So I made everyone another cup of tea and took Tom to Granny who had been listening, of course, to every single word from the crack in the kitchen door and put on *The Jungle*

What About Me, Too?

Book so that Mum and Dad could have some time to talk
and work things out properly. I'm going to get Toyah to
take me shopping after school tomorrow and we'll drop a
bag off at the Lion's Tomb on the way home. I think you
can buy ready roast chickens in Sainsbury's.

Dear Diary,

Thursday the 27th day of February

Woke up feeling really glum this morning. Like there's no hope left. I thought he'd come back again like he did last time, because he loves Mum and he loves us. But this feels so definite, like the end of everything. I thought maybe that me, Tom and Frankie mattered enough to bring them back together but we don't. Mum took me to school this morning and squeezed me so so tightly when the bell went, tighter than she ever has before. She wanted to make me feel better, like it's all going to be all right, but it felt like it was all over, like I might never see her again, which I know isn't true but it felt like that. And then I couldn't really consintrate on anything at school because I kept thinking about how I might lose my dad for ever because lots of them don't bother to keep in contact with their children, that's what Camilla says anyway. And then when I think about how it's all gone so wrong I want to cry but if anyone sees me doing that I'll be in trouble so I try and keep the tears inside, only that's hard sometimes.

Dear Diary,

Saturday the 1st of March ✏️

I told Clare and Tanya that Mum and Dad were divorcing, thinking that they would feel sorry for me and be nicer to me, but they just ran off laughing and said I was making it up. Only Camilla seems to understand. Mum's obviously had a word with Miss Jennings who is being extra specially nice to me, which only makes Tanya nastier so I wish she wasn't.

I got a letter from Dad this morning, my first ever letter from Dad. He said that this was the last thing he had ever expected or wanted to happen (so why did he let it, then?) and that he had wanted to stay married to Mum but that she was the one who had asked him to leave and wanted the divorce. When I talked to Mum about it at bedtime last night she said that Dad was the one who had gone off and had an affair and that he's been leaving us ever since she got pregnant with Tom while she had always loved just Dad. So now I don't know who to believe.

Mum got a letter too this morning about schools. I didn't get into Frankie's school which means I'm going to the bigger school up the road where most of my friends will be going so I don't really mind, although it is a bit disappointing because it means maybe I'm not as clever as Frankie, or maybe they just don't want me. Clare's mum has already been round to tell us that Clare has been offered places at two of the best private schools in London and now she doesn't know which one to choose. She stayed for ages, wanting to talk about how difficult a decishon it was going to be and how they might even have to pay the deposits on both schools if they couldn't decide before she even asked, 'And how did Lola do?' I could see that Mum was furious. 'What a shame,' she added as Mum showed her to the door, 'I'm sure she'll get in eventually.'

Mum practically smashed the glass in the front door as she slammed it.

What About Me, Too?

Dear Diary,

Sunday. Dad's a complete weirdo and a wanker. If he thinks I'm ever gonna come and see him in that flat with that weirdo girlfriend of his, other than when he offers some totally irresistible thing like a motorbike, he's totally stupid as well. I hate him. And I hate Ruby too for betraying me, when everyone knows that your friends come before boys even when they're as nice as Chattie. He smiled at me at school on Friday and asked how I was. I said I was fine when actually all I wanted to do was pull him into my arms and kiss him there in front of everybody. Ruby's now decided that I'm overreacting, jealous and possessive but she never actually says that to my face, she calls or texts me like the whole time. But what really pisses me off is how two-faced all the others are being. When I say that I think Ruby has done like the worst thing you could ever do to a friend they all agree with me, but I know that when they're with Ruby they're agreeing with her about how possessive and jealous I am as a person. Girls are so duplicitous (bet Saskia doesn't know what THAT means even though she is it). It was Juliet who faked her death with poison while Romeo just killed himself when he found her 'dead' because he was too thick to realize that it might be a trick. Saskia is of course winding the whole thing up, telling me what Ruby's saying behind my back, because she just loves it when Ruby and I fall out. Saskia is just THE MOST IRRITATING PERSON IN THE WHOLE WORLD. She has to be the centre of attention the whole time, like 'I'm so great because I've been spotted by a modelling agency' (although they have yet to give her any paid work, which of course she doesn't like being pointed out). In lessons she's always putting her hand up like some little Miss Know It All, and you can see the teachers sighing at the prospect that they might have to ask her because she's so smug, and then even if she gets the answer wrong she's not put off, I mean has she no shame? And then she's always telling the teachers uninteresting little facts about herself, like her parents met in Paris when we're talking about Paris in French. So? Like, do we even want to know? No! And then at lunchtime, because she's gotta stay slim she takes hardly anything to eat from the dinner ladies but snatches at everything we choose when we sit down, which is just SOOOOO irritating I want to hit her, particularly when you know that everything she's eating is gonna be puked up in the bogs ten minutes later. Still no sign of my period. I bought a pregnancy-testing kit on the way home. They are so fucking expensive that it's no wonder that most teenagers never bother to use them.

What About Me, Too?

From: Dr James
Sent: Tuesday 4 March 13:23
To: Matthew Wilcox
Subject: Re: Arrangements

Frank adamant that she doesn't want to see you. I have not poisoned her mind against you, as you suggest, she's old enough now to see you for who you are and I'm not going into battle over this on your account when I have enough to deal with already, just keeping all her other needs together. You've got to find a way to reach her and sort it, and without bribery, please.

Lola wants to see you this Sunday if you're going to be in London. She doesn't want to go to Kent. There's a TV series she's passionate about on at around 5.30 and she doesn't want to miss it.

I'm not happy letting Tom come for the night anywhere at the moment. He's too young to be apart from me for more than a day plus, Matthew, he came back with terrible nappy rash last time and I'm not prepared to risk that again. You can have both Tom and Lola for the day on Sunday but please pick them up promptly at ten and return them either by five thirty for Lola's programme or afterwards and fed, please. Still no sign of that standing order you promised to pay. I now think that we should shut the joint account and agree monthly maintenance through mediation. Why give lawyers any more money than they actually need, when they only spend it on tarts and marriage-breakers anyway? I'm trying to set up a meeting and will email you with likely dates.

Oh, and by the way, Lola didn't get into Frankie's school. She's on the waiting list but if she doesn't get in by September will have to go to the Massive, Drug-taking Comprehensive on the High Road where she will get a place because nobody else wants to go there. Could you perhaps investigate whether there's a better secondary school in your flat's catchment area and see if you can get her onto the waiting list, given that you have only just moved there and would have been too late to apply? We might as well exploit the one potential advantage to your decision to end this marriage.

Sue

What About Me, Too?

From: Dr James
Sent: Tuesday 4 March 16:53
To: Matthew Wilcox
Subject: Re: Re: Arrangements

I have not changed my tune in anyway, Matthew. I did not ask
you repeatedly to take Tom, I merely questioned why it was
that you didn't want him, only Lola. I am perfectly happy for
you to have him for the afternoon, even the day, just not
overnight because it upsets his routine. I find it hard to believe
that Tom's needs can be met in your makeshift one-bedroom
flat. Have you got a cot, toys, nappies, bottles and the right
foods? How can I be sure that he'll be safe there when I haven't
even seen it? And why is money such an issue with me?????
What an extraordinary question, Matthew. Because three
children cost, Matthew, and GPs are not paid as handsomely as
lawyers, Matthew, and because you have a responsibility for
their welfare, Matthew.

Sue

Dear Diary,

Tuesday the 4th of March

The thing about divorce is that the kids never get to have a say about what they want and then, as Camilla says, when they do, they get dragged into a large courtroom and asked who they want to live with by this old man they've never met before wearing a silly wig. I mean, how could you possibly say anything there? How could you possibly know? I hope that never happens to me. I think if anyone made me choose between the two people I love most in the world I'd become deaf and dumb or I'd say that unless they could work it out so that we could all live together in the same house I wouldn't live with either of them. Some nights, when I can't get to sleep because I'm upset and missing Dad, and the feeling's so strong I can't think of anything else, I imagine him coming to rescue me from my bedroom. I think of all the ways I could escape from here and Mum's bad moods and Tom crying, and I lie in bed thinking of what the boy might be doing. I don't like to think of him being lonely. So usually the fox is with him.

I've been back to see him twice since we left him the roast chicken. Toyah says he will need lots of carvomydrates to keep warm so we've taken him some fresh bread and muffins. I think he's beginning to trust me because he has been telling me a bit more about his life, which is just so, so sad. The woman in the picture by his bed was his mother, only she died and his dad married somebody else who hated him, but he didn't want to tell me any more. He loves Chloe though, and she seems to like him. They play tug of war with a stick and she always wins.

From: Dr James
Sent: Wednesday 5 March 09:01
To: Matthew Wilcox
Subject: Your answerphone message last night

Lola heard it. She was the one who pressed play when she saw
the light flashing and heard you ranting away like that. That you
should slag me off and call me names doesn't surprise me,
nothing you could do now would surprise me. But how do you
think Lola felt, listening to you calling her mother a 'liar' and a
'manipulative bitch'? She loved it so much she ran upstairs
sobbing before you'd even finished shouting into the phone. I
am not suggesting that you are incapable of looking after your
children properly, but I fail to see how a small bachelor flat is
suitable for three children with an age range of one to fifteen.
You are being unrealistic. I have no idea what a clean break
settlement means but I am not prepared to discuss anything
with you now other than through the mediator. We can argue
until the cows come home about who left whom, and who is
ultimately to blame but I don't think that is going to get us
anywhere. However, there is one thing that I am absolutely
certain about, so don't even think it. I will never accept shared
care. They live with me. This is and always has been their home.
Why should they have to live with split lives because of your
selfishness?

What About Me, Too?

From: Dr James
Sent: Wednesday 5 March 17:10
To: Matthew Wilcox
Subject: Re: Arrangements

I DO NOT AND HAVE NEVER PUT MY OWN EMOTIONAL NEEDS BEFORE THEIRS. HOW **DARE** YOU ACCUSE ME OF THAT AFTER WHAT YOU HAVE PUT US ALL THROUGH IN THE PAST EIGHTEEN MONTHS.

IF YOU EVEN SUGGEST THIS TO THEM AS AN OPTION I WILL SCREW U FOR EVERY FUCKING PENNY U HAVE. WE HAVE TO COME TO AN AGREEMENT AND THEN CONSULT THEM. YOU CANNOT ASK CHILDREN TO ARBITRATE ON THIS WHEN THEY HAVE THEIR OWN EMOTIONS TO DEAL WITH AS A RESULT OF YOUR ACTIONS.

Lola going to a better school near your flat, if indeed there is one, which I doubt, is not tantamount to a suggestion that she should live with you in term time, or half the time or even any time. You're clearly much more stupid than I ever realized.

Sue

From: Sue James
Sent: Sunday 9 March 15:17
To: Angela James
Subject: Thanks for the cheque . . .

Much appreciated. That's a sweet thought even if it does make me feel a little like I'm running an old age people's home myself (can you imagine *me* doing *that*?!), but will take you up on your offer until we've settled Mum somewhere, anywhere. When she's not criticizing or interfering, she's tugging on the guilt strings by saying that she hates being a burden which just makes me feel so bad, because of course she is a burden. I resent the fact that the moment I have two minutes to myself because Tom is asleep or with Matthew (like he is now) she expects me to devote myself to her (which is why I'm escaping on email to you). I resent that fact that I now feel torn in all directions, caring for everybody else except myself. And then I spread myself so thinly that I don't seem to be able to have any fun with the kids any more or spend real quality time with them. I just rush about all the time and say, 'Not now, Lola.' And financially I'm completely screwed, paying for everything and everyone until I know exactly what I'm going to get regularly from Matthew. I sat down and listed all our outgoings this morning as soon as the kids had left and they're way over my income so I'm consciously cutting out all of the non-essentials, which usually means anything to do with me or my pleasure. Deliberately didn't go to the garden centre this morning even though it's a lovely sunny, crisp spring day and a perfect time for planting and redoing the window boxes because I know I'm always so tempted by the sight of tender little orphan plants I spend £100 just to give them a home. And then I feel guilty about being such a moaning minny when actually I ought to be grateful that all three children are healthy, that Mum is still alive and that we're not poverty stricken, malnourished and depressed like half the people in my waiting room.

Frankie trashed her room last night in a fit of rage and then stormed out of the house, not telling me where she was going or when she was coming back. I was incredibly worried about her and couldn't get to sleep until about 4 a.m. when she finally answered her phone and shouted at me. She had definitely been drinking. The damage to her room is mainly surface, given that most of the stuff in there should have been chucked out years ago but it did sound frightening while it was going on. Lola was quite scared by the crashing and shouting but instead of saying she was frightened, sweetly ran to Tom and distracted him with games so that he wouldn't be. I just stood there, listening to her let rip and letting her do it, I mean the girl needs to get some sort of release somewhere with all this going on and I'd rather she did that than take drugs, shoplift or screw someone with the clap on the common. Mum, of course, was very disapproving. Muttered on and on about how I'd spoiled her when she was a baby because she was my firstborn and then dumped her with a nanny who didn't care about her when I went back to work and that now I was being punished for that decision, which is just so mad it's laughable because that was thirteen years ago and Philippa adored Frankie and was much more patient with her as a toddler than I was. I know, I know, it's just how Mum sees things but it's bloody irritating when you've got a teenager needing sedation, a toddler chucking Duplo at the china and a dog that hasn't been exercised, barking and leaping around the house. I mean, what you really need at that point is Mum moralizing and she doesn't just say it once, but over and over again until you just want to scream and trash the room yourself (only grown-ups aren't supposed to do that). I suppose what really gets to me is the thought that she might be right. I mean, does everybody have this sort of trouble or is it something I've done that's gone deep into her DNA to cause this sort of disruption? Is it because we're divorcing? Is it the school? GCSEs? Chattie? Or maybe all of these things, or none of them but something else I'm not even aware of? With Lola everything is still pretty black and white but with Frankie it's a technicolour medley of confusion.

Took Chloe for a long walk on the common this morning after Matthew took the kids to clear my head. It's a curious thought being single – it really is just me now. If I'm being realistic it's probably me, myself, I for the rest of my life and I'll turn into one of those eccentric middle-aged women who don't care about their appearance, who children imagine to be witches, or worse, an old sheep dressed as lamb who spends all her spare money on male escorts. Mind you, Bryson is being pretty persistent. Asks me regularly if I fancy a drink, and when faced with the choice I know I'd rather be single. I use the kids as an excuse – 'They need me to be around as much as possible at the moment' – but what is it with him? I'm much too old for him, emotionally absent bottle-feeding mother perhaps?? Touch of Norman Bates?

What About Me, Too?

Must off to Sainsbury's before the kids get back, the cupboard is bare.

Masses of love,
Suexxxxxxxxxxxxxxxxxxxxxxxxxxxx

Dear Diary,

*Sunday night and still single. Will ANYBODY EVER fancy
me again? Went with Fran and Saskia to a party in Clapham.
No idea whose house it was and Chattie wasn't there which
was a bit disappointing but the music was good and there
was so much to drink it was hard not to drink it. It's such a
weird feeling when you drink so much that you can't walk
straight but I do now know that I can handle four WMDs,
but five make me wanna puke and lie down and die. At least
with vodka and Coke it feels kind of clean drunk, like you're
not being poisoned. Pregnancy test came up negative but I
STILL haven't had a period so maybe I've got ovarian
cancer. I mean, if I'm not pregnant, why haven't I had a
period? Ruby away for the weekend so I didn't have to deal
with her which was a relief but there was this REALLY FIT
GUY who goes to the sixth form college in Clapham. When I
tried to talk to him, he just put me down so badly by asking
me how old I was, like that matters, and then called me
'jailbait' when I told him I was fifteen and walked away!
Fran says I should have lied and said I was sixteen since I
am nearly, but 'jailbait'! That's SO RUDE! Texted Chattie
again to tell him that I miss him and love him still but
understand if he never wants to see me again but he didn't
answer, he hasn't answered a single text I've sent, which
means he's either still so hurt he won't talk to me or he
hates me or, as Fran says, he's trying to wind me up so much
that I actually get down on my knees in the playground and
beg him in front of the whole school to go out with me
again.*

What About Me, Too?

Got home to find my room in such a total state that I had to shove a whole lot of rubbish onto the floor just to be able to lie down on the bed. Mum said she would help me clear it up but she still hasn't even though Tom's now finally in bed. But at least she hasn't had a go at me for staying out last night, or about coursework, so maybe she's finally learning something. Do you think she'd let me go to the sixth form college instead of staying on at school? At least then I'd get away from Ruby the Boyfriend-stealer and Saskia. Might ask her when she's helping me with my room. I'm SOOOOOO BORED OF MY LIFE I JUST WANT TO SCREAM . . .

Dear Diary,

Sunday the 9th of March. In bed ✏

Dad took us to Kew Gardens which is like the first time he's ever done anything fun with us since he left at Christmas. There's this amazing playground with ~~inflatables~~ ~~inphlatibles~~ inphlatables that look like flowers and Tom ran around like the mad boy he is until he got so tired he started winjing, and then of course Laura didn't know want to do. She just shouted ssshh all the time, so loudly that all the other real mothers looked round at her like she was some sort of child-abuser, it was soooo embarrassing. I would have thought that THE most important aspect of any stepmother was kindness but she just isn't the maternal type.

I felt really bad about leaving Mum this morning because she looked soooo sad as she waved goodbye from the doorstep, and Frankie completely destroyed her room last night and I just know that Mum was upset about it. I also felt bad about leaving her alone with Granny, and there being no one to make her a cup of tea and make her sit down when it's all getting too much. She was so pleased to see us when we got back it was like OBVIOUS that she and Granny had had a fight about something but she wouldn't tell me what. And now I feel bad about telling Dad that Frankie is turning into a violent psychopath because he got really angry about it and started slagging Mum off for being irresponsible, which is just so unfair because Mum didn't do it, Frankie did. So now I feel sort of disloyal to Mum because I shouldn't have told him but it's really hard knowing what I can say and what I can't say when like my whole life is wrapped up with just them and school, only they never understand anything about that.

The one thing about all this going on is that Tanya and Clare seem so pathetic, I mean like if they think what they're doing really matters. Camilla says they're bullying me and that I should talk to Miss Jennings about it but if I do that and she tells them off then it'll only make things worse.

It's Mum's birthday next Friday the 21st and I want to get her a realllyyyy good present to make her happy again. I've got £15 pocket money saved up but Toyah says she's gonna help me make something. Time to sleep now. School tomorrow, worst luck.

From: Dr James
Sent: Monday 10 March 13:23
To: Matthew Wilcox
Subject: Re: Frankie

I don't know what Lola told you but that is a gross distortion of the truth. Frankie did indeed chuck stuff around her room on Saturday night but that's hardly an act of vandalism worthy of the courts. Anyway, as all the handbooks say, it's her room.

Mediation date fixed for the 21st at two (see attached letter for address plus my bullet points for discussion) – yes, my birthday. Don't forget the present.

Sue

What About Me, Too?

From: Dr James
Sent: Tuesday 11 March 08:50
To: Matthew Wilcox
Subject: Re: Re: Frankie

Me? Too Liberal? You're the one who smokes dope. You're the one with the loose moral values who left his children. She's NOT off the rails, Matthew, just stressed out understandably because she's got GCSEs, you've left and Chattie's dumped her.

2 is when she can do, I've taken the afternoon off work so that we can start to sort this out so cancel whatever it is and be there.

From: Dr James
Sent: Tuesday 11 March 12:47
To: Matthew Wilcox
Subject: Re: Re: Re: Frankie

That's the most ridiculous thing I've ever heard. Don't you think I'd rather be doing anything, ANYTHING else on my birthday rather than sitting in a room with a total stranger trying not to argue with you? But it's the only date she can do before April and I really want to start resolving things so that we can both just get on with the rest of our lives. Why should my birthday give me any sort of advantage this year when it never has before? You completely forgot about it last year, and in previous years the best you've ever managed is a present that YOU wanted and some takeaway. And you're wrong about money too – I'm not an extravagant gold-digger, and that you could get that so wrong after so many years of marriage is incredibly hurtful. It means you've never really known me at all. I hate money, actually. It's just that I have three children, your children, who cost. But how much exactly, Matthew, do you spend on the marriage-breaker? Something tells me she's not the sort of woman who splits the bill.

I've looked up the meaning of clean break settlements and I'm told that's not even legal when there are kids so you must be a really crap lawyer. Big of you to offer me half the house when I kind of considered the whole thing, roof and all, my home. Our home. The children's home.

What About Me, Too?

Dear Diary,

15th March and it's about eleven weeks until GCSEs. I made a revision timetable last night and if I stick to it I can cover everything, only I've already failed it because I was supposed to do two hours' biology last night and I spent most of the evening watching TV with Granny. She's not bad as grannies go really. She gives me fags and when Lola said, 'What's masturbation?' because someone said the word on the telly Granny told her to go next door and ask Clare's mum!!! Lola actually got up to go, only I stopped her and whispered an explanation in her ear. I just wish Granny would stop going on about my clothes and what I wear, which is so none of her business and I wish Mum would stop nagging me about revising and just trust me to get on with it. I mean, I KNOW what I have to do and the last thing I need is her banging on all the time about how there's only a few weeks left because I KNOW that. Whenever there's like a minute's slack she's on my back with 'Do you want me to help you with some science?' and she's always trying to get me off the phone or away from the TV when I NEED both just to wind down and stay sane. She's a doctor and ought to know that the best work is done after a good rest.

There's a glimmer of hope, though, with Chattie. Toby was being really heavy with me in the playground yesterday. Toby is like THE most disgusting boy in the whole school – spotty, smelly, really rank and I can't believe I ever pulled him, but he thinks he's like really cool for some reason best known to himself and he was coming onto me yesterday. Asked me if I wanted to go out with him. I said no, never in a million years would I ever go out with him so he started chasing me round the playground, chucked water at me and then cornered me by the boys' bogs and pressed his disgusting body against me and it was Chattie, sweet, adorable, kind Chattie, who pulled him off me and ended up having a fight with Toby, which Mr Hamilton had to separate and both of them got dragged up to see the deputy head. I went too, told him it was all my fault and that I could explain what happened. Mr Short (he's tall actually) told Toby that if he ever heard of him harassing a girl like that again he would suspend him and told Chattie off for trying to sort it himself rather than getting a teacher. Toby stormed off down one corridor and Chattie walked off the other way with me running after him. He said he wasn't hurt but he was limping slightly and then he disappeared into the boys' bogs. I waited for him outside and he smiled when he came out, asked me if I was OK and said that if Toby ever came near me again he'd beat him to a pulp, which is just so sexy it's like lit up my whole weekend because now I can believe that there's hope. I really must love him. I think I can even forgive Ruby now for what she did, although she still swears she didn't. I texted her this morning to see if she wants to go shopping and she texted back immediately to say yes so we're meeting at two o'clock which is like only two hours away so I'd better get up and get ready AND my period came in the night so now nothing seems wrong any more and I'm gonna buy myself that really nice dress in Topshop as a reward.

What About Me, Too?

Dear Diary,

Wednesday the 19th of March

Toyah AND GRANNY picked me up from school today
and then we went off in a taxi to visit all Granny's things in
storage, which is a secret. Mum musn't know.

It was like walking into one of those ancient Egyptian
tombs where the pharows kept all their favourite
possessions. Granny was so exited when she saw all her
things again that she couldn't stop talking. She told me
where every bit of furniture came from. How they had
been given this large wooden wardrobe when Grandpa's
parents died and how it was the ugliest thing that had
ever been made but they couldn't sell it because it was the
only thing he had to remind him of them now. Granny
said that it took up most of their bedroom but Grandpa
would never let it go and my mum and Auntie Angela
grew up pretending it was the wardrobe from *The Lion,
the Witch and the Wardrobe*. They used to hide in there
when they were sad or had had a fight so actually it was a
magic wardrobe after all. When she came across a dark,
wooden table she told me how she and Grandpa had
carried this table all the way up the hill to their house
from a market only to find that it was so big that it
wouldn't go through the door and then they had to take
it back down the hill again and find someone who would
buy it off them. Only nobody did, so they carried it back
up the hill again, sawed off the legs and then had to pay
someone a fortune to put them back on again so that the

table wouldn't wobble. She laughed at the story but I could see there were also tears in her eyes as she remembered her life with Grandpa. I don't really remember him much because I was only five when he died. She has so many lovely things – lamps and old books and pictures and a tea chest full of letters and photograph albums and pictures that Mum and Auntie Angela did when they were small. We spent ages going through everything while Toyah and Tom played games up and down the corridor. I found a recorder which she says I can have, which is really cool. And she showed me pictures of when Mum was a little girl – playing on a beach – and told me how she was scared of the sea when she was a baby and used to cling to her leg and there's this really sweet picture of her hugging Auntie Angela, cheek to cheek, and they're both laughing. Mum was such a sweet little girl, much prettier than Auntie Angela, which is funny because now that they're grown up it's Auntie Angela who is prettier. Maybe I will be prettier than Frankie when I'm her age. Granny says I will be because I'm a good girl. We stuffed letters and photographs and Mum's pictures into two large carrier bags to take home with us. Granny and I are going to make something very special for Mum's birthday to make her happy again. Granny stopped and looked hard at all her things before we locked the door. I could see she was thinking that she might never see this huge part of her life again so I squeezed her hand. 'We could come back here next week and you could tell me more stories Granny,' I said, to make her think that this wasn't the end of everything.

'I'd like that' she said. 'It's funny paying a visit to things rather than people.'

'Like stepping back into the past,' I said.

'Precisely. Now it's time to find a taxi home for tea.'

Granny says no one makes a better pot of tea than I do.

From: Sue James
Sent: Saturday 22 March 12:46
To: Angela James
Subject: Re: HAPPY BIRTHDAY!!!XXXXXXXXXXX

Thank you, sweetie sweet. Yes, had a really lovely day in spite of Matthew who gave me a pair of handcuffs wrapped up in pretty paper in front of the mediator. Ha ha, very funny. Actually, I'd like to handcuff him to the outside of a high-speed train going through Eurotunnel. He dominated the entire hour, interrupted me whenever I tried to speak, put me down the whole time and then when I said I had never wanted it to come to divorce he just laughed and said the whole thing was my idea. So it wasn't a good start, although the woman has clearly seen all this before. She let him let off steam and then outlined how we might progress from stalemate. We did at least agree at this meeting to each pay half her bill, which I suppose I must interpret as 'a good start'.

Felt pretty glum about my birthday on Thursday night, expected little more than a crumpled card from Frankie and a handmade one from Lola, if they remembered because everyone's been completely silent on the subject. Plus the full reality of being single AND forty-five hit home – on the downhill slope to fifty now – but woke up yesterday to Tom leading a procession of my wonderful family. Mum got him up before he could wake me, and dressed him like a prince with a golden crown and a purple velvet cape. He carried this enormous card into my bedroom. Lola followed, carrying a tray of tea and cups, Frankie followed, carrying a plate of *pain au chocolat* with a lit candle in each one and then there was Mum with a massive bunch of the most heavenly spring flowers. They sang 'Happy Birthday' and then settled down on my bed for breakfast and we looked at this incredible card. I don't know how they managed it without me noticing. It's a collage of photographs cut together to make a silly bigger picture so there's, for instance, a black and white one of me as a little girl, pouring a watering can seemingly over Tom's head, and they've even found a picture that I haven't seen since we were kids. Do you remember that one where you're sitting on a potty, looking very grumpy and I'm bringing you the bog roll? Well, it was in the chest. Toyah took them to the storage place after school and they brought back bags of stuff. Mum's even kept drawings that I did as a little girl. There's one of all four of us as stick people, but I've drawn myself about twice as big as I have you and I'm wearing proper clothes while you look like a faint, wispy anorexic with no hair. We had such a laugh over that. I can't think why I've never seen it before. Anyway, everyone was late for school but who cares? It was just so moving that they had all made such an effort to make things nice for me on my birthday. In fact, it's probably been the happiest, least complicated one in years.

It was also the most beautiful day so I took Mum and Tom up to the common with the dog to look at the daffodils. The common is at its best in springtime, there's so much pink blossom and narcissi as well as thousands of the more vulgar yellow daff but it's a wonderful sight, so much vivid colour in the sunshine after the gloom of winter. Mum loved it and

managed to walk quite a long way. Then I took them both out
for lunch at the brasserie round the corner and we talked,
really talked about Dad and you and how difficult it's been lately
being married to Matthew. I just felt so moved by the whole
thing, having Mum there, feeling how much she loved me and all
of us, and how, more than anything, she just wants us to be
happy. But SHE also seemed so much happier, really enjoying
being out and with me and Tom, tucking into some good food
and a glass of wine, really interested in everything going on
around her, the pictures on the walls, people at the other
tables and it's so sad and so awful that we have to put her into
another home where she simply doesn't get this kind of fun or
the sense of being really hooked into family life.

I know she drives me bonkers, I know she can't live here
permanently, but wouldn't it just be great if there was another
way for her to live her last years? If only there was some
compromise, some halfway measure between bunging her back
into a home and one of us giving up everything else for the
foreseeable future to look after her. And then it occurred to
me that maybe there IS another way. We could move, we
might have to anyway, and buy something further out with
more bedrooms so that Mum could live with us. Lola could get
into a better school than the drug dump down the road and
Frankie could move into a sixth form college. I didn't say
anything but it is a thought, particularly if Clarice's show no sign
of coming up with a place. And then, as we were drinking
cappuccino and I was beginning to feel sick at the prospect of
meeting Matthew at the mediator's, she handed me a long slim
box with the most beautiful Victorian beaded jet choker in it. It
was Granny's apparently, given to her by Grandpa on her

fortieth birthday, and I burst into tears, deep sobs that made everyone look round at us and made Tom cry too. I wore it to Julie and Tim's for dinner and everyone commented on it, so I felt like a real belle for once. It was a fun dinner, ten people, champagne, the most delicious salmon *en croûte* (I don't know how she's so good at making them) and a voucher to a spa for a day from Julie. They sat me next to a rather dull but quite good-looking man called Brian who works with Tim. Julie matchmaking again but I don't think it's to be.

Much love,
Suexxxxxxxxxx

Dear Diary,

Toby's been trying to wind me up all week. He calls me frigid and a nigger-lover, and taunts me with 'Where's your khun boyfriend now to protect you?' whenever he gets a chance to corner me in the corridors. I had to knee him in the balls yesterday to get out of his way. And then today I found this sticky white smear over the arm of my coat – the bastard's wanked over it in the bogs. Ruby says it's sexual harassment as well as racism and that I ought to report him to the head but actually I don't think I should believe a thing she says at the moment because it's obvious, so TOTALLY obvious that she still fancies Chattie and thinks she's in with a chance. Fran agrees and says that if I do go to the head it'll only rebound on Chattie and they'll beat him up. And Saskia doesn't understand why I'm making such a fuss, says that's just what boys are like. That's just stupid and made Fran so angry they had a massive row about feminism and abusive relationships in the cloakrooms. Fran accused her of being blinkered and spoilt and stupid and said her dad was a racist thug anyway, and Saskia burst into tears and went for her hair and Hayley had to separate them and then I got really furious because suddenly it was all about Saskia again. She'd managed to turn the whole conversation round so that we were talking about her and not me. Chattie's been keeping me at a distance. Spends every lunchtime in the library revising and when I asked him if he wanted to go out for a drink on Friday he said he had to stay in. He's promised his parents he will stay in and revise at the weekends from now on which just makes me feel bad because I haven't been doing any revision but then, as Fran says, who bothers until the last minute anyway. I suggested we could do some revision together but he just smiled and said that 'wasn't possible'. Surely anything is possible if you want it to be?

Dear Diary,

April Fool's Day ✐

Clare and Tanya seemed to think that they could be even nastier to everyone today just because of the date. They put a slug in Camilla's pencil case and made her cry. And they have decided to form the mobile phone club which you can only be in if you have a mobile phone, which they have dilibratly decided to do because they know that Camilla and I haven't got one. They're being even more horrible to Camilla than they are to me. They call her 'smelly' and diss her clothes and call her teacher's pet because Miss Jennings lets her do more than anyone else because of her false leg. It's like they set out to make her cry and that just makes me so angry that I want to make THEM cry but that isn't right either. Sometimes there are two or three girls crying their eyes out in the playground and they don't know why, and the boys just look at them like they were mad. Mum says that children pick on other weaker children in order to divert attention from themselves when they feel weak but all Clare and Tanya do is DRAW attention TO themselves because they are being so obviously horrible to someone who has less than they do – like a foot. Mum says that we've been with Camilla for so long now that no one remembers that she hasn't got a foot but I remember. How can you not when she limps into the classroom at the end of the line at every playtime and helps Miss Grant keep the score at every PE lesson because she can't keep up? I've decided that Clare and Tanya are not my friends any more.

What About Me, Too?

I don't care what they say or do from now on, they can't
hurt me if I decide I don't need their friendship. Clare is
such a boaster, too. She boasts about how much money
they have and she can't stop boasting about how she's
going to a much better school than everybody else which
just makes me want to punch her. School finishes next week
and I can't wait. I hate school and I hate Clare.

Dear Diary,

Saturday 5th April. Agreed to have lunch with Dad today on condition that he did not comment on any aspect of my appearance, ask questions about Chattie or GCSEs and that he took me to Bertorelli's. What I forgot to mention was that he should also leave his new girlfriend behind but I would have thought that was obvious at your first meeting with your eldest daughter after you have declared divorce. Not to him, apparently, because she came too. Firstly she looks young enough to be my friend, which is just disgusting. Secondly HER CLOTHES! Horrid polyester trouser suit over a polo-neck sweater, the sort of thing that forty-year-olds wear in the suburbs, with popsocks and flat suede Hush Puppies. So straight, soooo M&S, soooo squeaky clean, soooo unlike Mum. AND she had these really awful long red fingernails which she was clearly proud of because she kept rapping them against the table like some sort of stressed out weirdo, when actually I was the one finding this tense. Anyway, she didn't even try to be nice to me, just stared at me through her mascara like she was sizing me up. As you can imagine, the conversation didn't exactly FLOW. Dad kept clearing his throat like he does when he's nervous and asking stupid questions like 'How's school?' to which there's only one answer really – 'Shit.' So I ate my food and tried to keep calm about it and then she started asking really nosey questions like had I seen Chattie recently and where did I like to go on a Saturday night, like I'd tell HER?????? And Dad did nothing to try and shut her up and THEN SHE starts having a go at me about how I'm giving my parents a hard time and didn't I realize they were worried about me and how it wasn't good for me to drink so much alcohol at my age. I couldn't believe it. EXCUSE ME but does she know that Dad smokes dope? I've never even met the woman before, she's screwing my father, a married man, and she thinks SHE has a right to give ME a moral lecture about how I should live my life? So I said, 'And what fucking business is that of yours?' and then Dad told me off with, 'Don't be rude to Laura, she just cares about your welfare,' to which I could only say that I wasn't being rude, she was way out of line and then Dad felt torn between us. But instead of changing the conversation or trying to be nice to me with 'What do you want for pudding?' or 'Why don't we all go shopping?' he starts laying into me as well and asks me why I've been so difficult lately and is it GCSEs? At which point I just lost it, pushed away my plate, tipping over my Coca-cola as I did so all over Laura's lap, which was a pleasing scene worthy of a Hollywood movie, and stormed out of the restaurant saying, 'I KNEW this was a bad idea. Why don't you both just leave me alone, fuck off and die, BOTH OF YOU.' I ran out into the street and round into Paperchase in the Tottenham Court Road so that they couldn't find me. Or see me cry.

From: Dr James
Sent: Monday 7 April 13:49
To: Matthew Wilcox
Subject: Re: Our eldest daughter

She is not rude, inconsiderate, difficult or destined to become an alcoholic. She is just a teenager. How did you expect her to react when you brought the tart along with you? Not clever, Matthew, but then you're not. It's not up to Frankie, it's up to you to find a way of patching up your relationship because you're her father and YOU left HER, not the other way around. Which is why your latest set of demands is completely unworkable – Frankie doesn't want to see you at all and who can blame her, Tom is too young to be shlepped about and spend nights away from me, which leaves poor Lola in the middle bearing the brunt of all this mess. Don't you dare quiz her again about me or the others.

What About Me, Too?

Dear Diary,

Monday night ✏️

Mum's in a rage. Tom's screaming because Mum's in a rage. Toyah's been off sick so I haven't been able to talk to her. Granny's in pain with her arfritees and Frankie's on MSN Messenger. She's a useless sister. In fact, is she even my sister? I keep ringing Dad but he never answers. I've left loads of messages on his mobile phone but he hasn't rung me back. Maybe this is it. The beginning of the end. He's on a plane to America with Laura and they're off to start a new life. Or maybe they're in a restaurant celebrating the fact that she is pregnant with their child, a lovely baby daughter to replace me. It's raining and dark and late so I can't go out and see the boy. But I'd like to.

From: Dr James
Sent: Tuesday 8 April 18:35
To: Matthew Wilcox
Subject: Re: Re: Our eldest daughter

Wanker

I'm off home now to see your children and poison their minds against you

Then I'm going to stick pins into a wax model of you

Then I'm going to set fire to the rest of your possessions in the garden

Then I'm going to hire a private investigator to stalk your every move

Then I'm going to sell the house and move us all to live with my sister in Australia so that you never see any of your children ever again

WANKER WANKER WANKER

What About Me, Too?

From: Sue James
Sent: Saturday 12 April 11:34
To: Angela James
Subject: Sorry forgive me sorry forgive me sorry forgive me
sor ...

It's been an unbelievably busy, emotionally fraught time and I
simply haven't had time to ping you properly but basically, yes,
we're all fine. I'm on the phone to Frankie's school daily now,
trying to push Lola up the waiting list for a place. I'm on the
phone to Clarice's every other day, trying to push Mum up that
waiting list. Toyah's been off sick most of the week with
gastroenteritis so I've been dumping Tom on Barbara, a friend's
childminder, to get to the surgery. Then I dash back at 3.30 to
pick up Lola, pick up Tom and either take them back to work
with me if I'm doing an evening and let them play with the
stethoscopes and syringes (only joking, Ange) or dump them
with Frankie if I can track her down. As for Mum, I had no
choice other than to leave her with some ready-made meals to
heat up, my mobile number and strict instructions not to go
upstairs so that she didn't fall over and break both hips.
Actually she managed just fine AND has made friends with
HND who, if truth be told, has been very nice to Mum. She
invited her over for lunch, took her for a gentle walk in the
park and they've discovered a shared passion for bridge, so
HND (or Fuchsia – Mum now corrects me all the time) has
invited her to come over and play with them next Friday

because the wife of the couple they play bridge with every Friday (imagine doing that – every Friday – ugh!) is going to be away. I suppose I have to be pleased about their new friendship, because it makes Mum happy, even if it does mean that she is blabbing away about all our secrets.

Frankie was out yesterday so I left both Lola and Tom with Mum and there was mayhem when I got back at eight. Tom was heaving books off the shelves in the sitting room, having pulled out every single item of clothing that he could reach from Lola's cupboards, tipping over the chest of drawers in the process and smashing a photo frame (I think he must have been standing on the bottom drawer to reach something); Lola had given up trying to look after him because she couldn't cope and had buried her nose deep into her diary in my bed. And Mum, for some extraordinary reason known only to herself, was trying to clean the oven. Why? I think it would have been less worrying to have found her at the top of a stepladder cleaning the windows because at least there's a POINT to that. Who ever bothers with the oven if you can possibly help it when the door stays firmly shut most of the time and it gets so hot that every single germ gets killed anyway? Once a year I might get the hammer and chisel out, I suppose, when I'm totally desperate to vent my aggression on something ugly. Or in the old days when Matthew's beastly mother was coming to stay. But there was Mum on her knees, wearing yellow rubber gloves, rubbing away with a Brillo pad as if her life depended on it. When I tried to get her to stop she said she was determined to achieve something today and this was it. Bonkers when you're as frail as she is but there was no arguing with her.

Matthew is being such an unreasonable pig that he is keeping me awake at night. I toss and turn with my teeth clenched with anger but haven't quite yet got to the point where I'm reaching for the Valium or the Benylin. Mediator has forwarded me his list of demands, which include shared care, NO CHILD SUPPORT and half of the house. Might just as well have added an end to Third World poverty, because he's never going to get it. I think this is likely to turn very nasty indeed. Anyway, sorry once again for failing to respond to your emails – I've barely logged on and have got lots of virus warnings which is a bit scary. Someone at work was telling me how you can now get headphones, plug them into your computer and do something call skyping which means talking through your computer on broadband for free. Do you think we should consider it? Haven't got broadband (sounds like a low fat margarine, doesn't it?) but would consider it if you have and we could make this skyping thing work. Also desperate to see you. Any chance of you all coming over to stay for the summer? Or we could take a house by the sea? We'll all badly need a holiday once the GCSEs are over. Would love to be able to go somewhere for the Easter weekend so that we can all get away from this mess for just a night or two but feel I have probably left it too late

Masses of love,
Suexxxxxxxxxxxxxxxxxxxxxxxxxxxxxxxxxxxxxxxxxxxxxxxxxxx

Dear Diary,

Sometimes I feel so weyed down by worries that I just want to crawl under a blanket and close my eyes in the warm dark and never wake up again. It's like there's so much to think about now that I'm getting older. I go to school and hate it there because there's always something that makes me upset, usually Tanya telling lies about me. Then when I get home I remember that Dad isn't there and won't be there ever again to cuddle or kiss goodnight and the house doesn't smell of him any more now that all his motorbike stuff has gone from the hall and his aftershave has gone from the bathroom. He rings me every day when I get home from school to tell me that he loves me and then he tells me that he wants me to come and live with him and I never know what to say because even though I really, REALLY miss him and want to live with him, I could never leave Mum and Tom and even Frankie. How would they cope without me? He makes all these promises about how we could move to the country and I could go a really good school and learn how to ride and have a horse, but that would be even further away from Mum and Tom even though it all sounds lovely. He's going to Greece with Laura for Easter. I asked him if I could come too because I've never been to Greece but he said that sadly that wasn't possible. Mum says Laura wants to have Dad all to herself and they'll probably spend the whole time looking at ruins because that's what Dad likes to do and Laura doesn't want a child around to make life difficult for them at night. I suppose she means sex. Uggghhh! I hope she falls off a cliff.

If I imajine that hard enough then maybe she will. What I really, really want is for him to come back here so that I can live with both Mum and Dad and don't have to choose. But when I said that yesterday he said that wasn't possible either. But anything's possible if you want it to happen badly enough.

From: Sue James
Sent: Sunday 13 April 21:52
To: Angela James
Subject: Re: What about Uncle David?

Good idea, I'll give him a ring in the morning. Mum hasn't seen him in years, he never once went to visit her at North Butting and I rather long for the feel of crisp linen sheets.

Sxxxx

What About Me, Too?

Dear Diary,

Dad really, really wants me to go and live with him, he asks
me all the time and I never know what to say. I would like
to but that would just make Mum so unhappy and she
needs me. I did all the clearing up after supper tonight and I
helped look after Granny today. She wanted to wash her
hair and she can't really do it by herself. She needs me to
pour cups of water over her hair because she can't bend
over. And then how would Tom manage without me? I
asked Toyah what she thought today and she just looked
sad and said that I shouldn't have to make that decision. So
I took Chloe to the cemetery after I had dried and brushed
Granny's hair and asked the boy. He agreed with me. He
said that so long as you have a mum you're all right and if
I lived with Dad I'd have to live with Laura too and she
could hate me like his stepmother did. I hadn't thought of
that.

Dear Diary,

It's Good Friday and Mum is taking Granny, Lola and Tom to stay with Great Uncle David, who has the hairiest nostrils you've ever seen. You have to be really good there so I'm not going. Mum was so tired she couldn't summon up the energy to insist I go, plus she said it would be easier for Uncle David if they didn't take Chloe because they've got a horrible, molting, snappy little pug and the last thing she wants to do is to offend their horrid little lapdog with our beautiful lithe and beautifully glossy sheepdog. So I'm staying here, for Chattie. He's started replying to my texts so now there is hope in my miserably sad, single life and I even think I could concentrate on some history and revise an essay on the causes of the First World War. Everyone's away or revising so I can't even have a party when this is a free house and that's just such a waste. The only person around is Ruby but I'm NOT going to ring her up or even ever speak to her again because every time we talk she asks me really personal things about Chattie, like she's fishing for information so she can make out to him that she really knows him and is on the same wavelength. She flirted so outrageously with Chattie on the last day of term right in front of me and I could see he kind of liked it, kind of liked HER, which is even more infuriating so now I don't think I can ever really trust her completely again, which is crap when she used to be my best friend and really crap when there's no one else around to talk to but her.

What About Me, Too?

Dear Diary,

Sunday Morning and the Easter bunnies haven't laid a single egg in the garden but they dumped at least ten tons of chocolate next door. I'm really glad that Lola wasn't here to see Clare skipping round the garden with a wicker basket from the Conran Shop, squealing like an overspoilt piglet. Mum remembered, though. I found a flake egg wrapped up at the back of the fridge with a yellow sticky saying, 'Love you, Mum xx' on it. She left me some pizza and pasta in the fridge and figured it would take me till Sunday to get to the back but actually I found it last night and ate the whole thing in front of the telly.

I've been completely alone here now for forty-eight hours and it feels so weird, the house being this quiet when usually it's so noisy. It's really lovely having the whole place to myself. I put the radio on really loud and dance naked round the house. I can revise on the kitchen table without Mum looking nosily over my shoulder or Tom disturbing me by trying to get me to play with him or just screaming loudly until he gets what he wants. It's also kind of hard to miss Mum when she like rings me every three hours to check that I'm OK. I picked it up an hour ago thinking it was her and said, 'I'm FINE, MUM, REALLY' when it was Ruby so I had to talk to her, couldn't put the phone down, could I, and we watched MTV together and discussed each video in detail until my ear hurt and I remembered that actually this bitch was after my soulmate and the love of my life and I said I had to go and put the phone down. She thinks we could just about scrape a gathering together tonight but the hard bit is gonna be preventing Toby from coming. I don't think it's worth the risk, not now that Chattie's talking to me again. Although if I start getting so bored that I'm watching ten-year-old repeats of EastEnders . . .

What About Me, Too?

From: Sue James
Sent: Monday 21 April 12:13
To: Angela James
Subject: Uncle David's

Brilliant idea – Mum loved it and spent a great deal of time
sitting out in the spring sunshine in their beautiful garden talking
to David, who was genuinely pleased to see her, while I played
with Tom and Lola and went for walks and Mildred did all the
cooking. Perfect. Great platefuls of steaming roast beef and
Yorkshire pudding, fish pie, some really good red wine and as
much ice cream as the children could eat. And I slept better
than I have done in months in a large eiderdowned bed with a
view over rustling trees to the green Chiltern Hills and Tom
and Lola peacefully beside me, their cheeks rosy from fresh air,
exercise, hearty British cuisine and the central heating up too
high. I slept with the window open, listening to owls and foxes
and wondered whether this is the answer. Pack up Ledbury
Way and move the children way out of London and as far away
as possible from Matthew into a lovely village house with a big
garden and fields to explore and a village school and I could
work in a lovely little local practice. And then I remembered
how bored teenagers get in the country (Frankie refused to
come) and how there's nothing to do but take drugs, get pissed
and drive stolen cars round service stations and supermarket
car parks in the middle of the night and how there's no public
transport to get them anywhere so you end up driving them

everywhere and thought, Um . . . We did have a lovely time though – all of us came back in a much better mood – and I think Uncle David was pleased to have done something to help out, even if he was relieved to see the back of us so that he could go off and play golf today.

Got back to a house reeking of smoke and that clearly WASN'T Mum. Didn't question Frankie as to whether or not she had had a party because I couldn't face the row after forty-eight hours of peace, the house wasn't in too bad a state AND, more importantly, she was alive. She made a desultory attempt at cleaning up and looks very hungover. But there's nothing missing from the wine rack. If I can just keep her vaguely on the straight and narrow until after GCSEs then I'll have succeeded in part because at least that stress will be over. HND has of course left a furious note about the noise, which I found torn up in the sitting-room bin. I hope they partied loud late into the night.

The one thing that does piss me off though, is that Frankie failed completely to walk Chloe WHICH WAS THE ONLY THING I ASKED HER TO DO. The dog has crapped all over the lawn and is so manic she's certifiable. So took her for a long walk on the common this morning and bumped into Mark with the black Lab. YESSSSS!!!! We walked the whole way round together and fell into a really good conversation about teenagers and how difficult they could be and how hard it was to look out for them all the time when you were on your own and how his eldest son really missed his mother and was being disruptive at school, and the teachers were being really understanding but actually he was really worried because he was behind with his coursework and going out just a bit too much and I thought, boy, have I heard all this before. Tried to reassure him with how we went through all that last year with Frankie (although obviously didn't tell him the real nitty-gritty about the bunking off and the shop-lifting) and how she was still pretty volatile. It was good just to be able to talk to someone who is going through the exact same thing, with kids roughly the same age. Anyway, I really like him, Ange. He's just so easy to be with and talk to, a gentle person, not an alpha male like Matthew, battling with everyone in sight to guarantee his own victory. There was this sort of embarrassed silence as we parted with neither of us knowing what to say other than 'See yer,' so that means I'm going to have to spend every spare minute of the day (and they're hardly profuse) at the common like some sort of teenage stalker if I'm to stand a chance of seeing him again. Why didn't I just suggest a drink?

Anyway, time to go and take everyone out to Pizza Express for lunch. Mayhem on Easter Monday but Frankie and her friends have eaten everything out of the fridge so there's nothing for it but to dodge the flying dough balls, grab a high chair for Tom and some colouring pencils for Lola and at least take comfort from the fact that every other family in southwest London is here too, wrestling with the same familiar family life, even thought it means paying about £100 for cheese on toast.

Much love and kiss those darling boys of yours. I long to see them,
Suexxxxx

Dear Diary,

Friday the 25th day of April and the weather is HOT!

Dad came back from Greece yesterday and came straight round to see me. Mum was at work and I was playing with Tom in the garden. He's bought us loads of presents: some slippers for Tom and a little wooden train set; and this amazing ~~embroidered~~ ~~emberoyded~~ embaroided skirt for me, and a doll, and a giant tin of colouring pencils AND this really weird statue that Dad says is like a lucky charm to keep away evil spirits. Creepy. The presents were great but seeing him was even better. Tom climbed all over him and they played windmills. Dad spins him round and round and then he said why didn't we all go up to the common together and take Chloe for a walk. So we gave Toyah the rest of the day off, made Granny a large pot of tea and settled her down in front of *Gone with the Wind*, her favourite film, and then off we went, just like we used to do when he was here all the time. It was as if nothing had changed. We ran around and threw balls for Chloe and Dad pushed Tom on the swings and then we had an ice cream and then Dad took us back to his flat for some tea. Laura was there too, worst luck, but I've decided to ignore her and pretend that she's just a fly that buzzes round the room so that she doesn't get in the way of me and Dad. Tom was asleep by the time Dad took us home. The really hard bit though was kissing him goodbye. Mum whisked Tom out of Dad's arms up to bed, she didn't even say hello, just scowled and left Dad and me there hugging on the doorstep. He told me that he loved me and that he meant what he said about me coming to live with him and that he really missed me, that we could have such fun together and that I could see Mum whenever I wanted. And then I felt all sort of confused again, like I didn't know what to say or do, so I just squeezed him as hard as I could, so tightly that my eyes watered, and I told him that I loved him and then ran into the house to find Granny, just to check that she was OK.

Dear Diary,

Saturday the 26th of April and it's still HOT!

A really terrible thing happened to Chattie while we were with Dad last night. He got mugged by a group of boys from school on his way home from the Tube station at six o'clock when there were loads of people around and nobody helped him. Can you believe that!!!! They kicked him and punched him and kicked him and punched him and Frankie says they called him a khun creep, which is just so rude and I think they may have even stabbed him – yes STABBED him a hundred times, well, maybe not a hundred – but he is very lucky, Mum says, not to have been badly hurt. I think his mum took him to hospital but he was discharged this morning. Frankie is of course behaving as if he were dead or something, crying and wailing round the house like it's the worst thing that has ever happened, but it has given her the excuse to go round to his house with a large box of chocolates. But what really scares me is that if that's what happens when you're just on your way home from school then it could happen to me. What if someone punches me for my mobile phone that Dad says he'll give me???

I go back to school on Monday and I am NOT looking forward to it. Clare blanked me when I was in the garden with Tom yesterday and her mum has written another snotty letter to Mum, complaining about the noise from her music and Chloe barking and the fact that Tom's plastic slide in the garden is garish and could we move it closer to our house so that she can't see it from her windows. Mum just laughed and threw the letter into the bin. That's the fourth note we've had from her in a week. She hasn't dared knock on the door since the rat people came. I keep thinking about Dad and how he wants me to go and live with him. Because I do want to sort of. But I don't want to have to be the one to decide. I can't talk to Mum about it because she always looks so sad and tired and if I did she'd just get so mad with him, even madder than she already is. I can't talk to Dad honestly about how I'm not sure because he'll just try and persuade me. And Frankie's so up herself the whole time because NOTHING IS MORE IMPORTANT THAN CHATTIE AND GCSES – not even me. But I did ask Granny today who she would have picked if she had had to choose between living with either her mum or her dad. We were making mirangs. I've got quite good at them. She said that she wouldn't have had a choice because people didn't divorce when she was a child, they just killed each other. I think that was a joke. She said you stuck together as a family through everything. I wish I'd been a child when Granny was.

Dear Diary,

Chattie was really pleased to see me. I could tell by the way he looked at me. My heart was pounding so loudly as I walked back through his front door that I'm sure his mother could hear it. She was really pleased to see me too, and took me into the kitchen to go through every single detail of what had happened before she was gonna let me anywhere near his bedroom. I thought I was gonna die before I even climbed the stairs to get to see him she talked so much. She was really shocked and couldn't believe that the police were so uninterested in tracking down the muggers. Said they didn't even take a statement from him. I told her that the police couldn't care less what teenagers did to each other, that as far as they were concerned we all gave each other what we deserved. If Chattie had been twenty-five and more able to kick up a fuss then they might have done a bit more, but teenagers are just invisible and unimportant. She seemed shocked by that, so I gave her a hug and told her he'd be fine and ran up the stairs before she could say any more. He's got two really nasty bruises on his face (it was all I could do not to fall on them and cover them with kisses) and he says his stomach is really sore where they kicked him but he's had it X-rayed and they don't think there's any internal bleeding so he's very lucky indeed. I asked him if he knew who they were. He said that he didn't, but I kind of think that he does know and doesn't wanna tell anyone in case he gets into even more trouble. I then said was it Toby? He shook his head and said no, that he'd never seen them

*before and that he was most upset about the watch
because it had been given to him by his great grandpa in
India when he was little, and that to them it was just a
watch, but to him it was much, much more. If it WAS
Toby, I'm gonna kill him. Chattie says his mum won't let
him out of bed and keeps bringing him this really
disgusting herbal tea that her granny used to dole out in
India whenever anyone in the family had suffered a shock.
It's so disgusting he's been pouring it out of the window
so we had a good laugh about that. It's hot though, really
hot and stuffy in his bedroom and he says he wants to go
out but his mum won't let him until the shock has gone
because she thinks that he could get mugged again. So I
helped him hobble over to the window and we sat there
together looking out over the gardens at the blossom and I
held his hands between mine and kissed them. It's just
such a horrible thing to have happened. When he kissed
me back it was just the most romantic thing ever. We've
not been going out, not even touched each other, for over
three months and it's been the longest three months ever.
So when his tongue met mine, our mouths just exploded
and neither of us could stop and I felt so horny I just
wanted to jump all over him but whenever I so much as
touched his body he winced with pain. So it's gonna be a
while before we can do more than kiss, but oh what a kiss
that was!! I'm going round tomorrow with some books so
that we can revise together and test each other. I just feel
so much better about everything now that I know we're
back together. I'm never gonna make such a stupid
mistake again and he's gonna have to kill me first if he*

ever decides that he wants to leave me. From now on all that matters is him and me and GCSEs (that rhymes if you put it into rap).

Goodnight.

What About Me, Too?

Dear Diary,

Friday the 2nd of May and I HATE SCHOOL!!!!!!!!!

We've only been back four days and already Tanya has tried to make things totally difficult by telling Camilla that I said that she smelled and had nits and that I didn't want to be her friend any more, when I NEVER said that. I may have said that she had nits and smelled ages ago before we were friends but that was then, not now. I can't believe that she could be so horrible. Then yesterday when I was talking to Britney in the playground, she just barged in between us and took her off by the arm without me. Then she told Miss Jennings that I had copied from her and THEN she trashed my new special top that Dad bought me. She said it was cheap. So I kicked her really hard and would have kicked her again and again and again until she couldn't speak or walk no more, until she was so hurt that she'd never dare hurt me again, only Camilla pulled me away and told me to be careful because Mrs Brook was on playground duty and she always gave detentions for fighting so I stopped. I leave this school in two months' time and I can't wait to get away from that horrible bitch. I don't know what school I'm going to go to. It's hard not knowing where I'll be but one thing's for certain, at least I'll be away from Tanya.

I got a letter from Dad in the post this morning. He says that if I went to live with him he'd pay for me to go to a really good school like Clare's going to and that I could have riding lessons in London and get my ears pierced and have a mobile phone and that I could have whatever I wanted. He put twenty-five kisses at the bottom. I counted them all and kissed each one back and then I hid the letter in the chest of draws under my pants and socks. I don't want Mum to see it and get upset. I'd love to live with Dad and have him all to myself all the time. I think I'd cry less because I wouldn't miss him so much and I wouldn't lie here in bed at night dreaming of all the ways that we could be together again. But then I'd have to leave Mum and how can I leave Mum when he just has?

What About Me, Too?

Dear Diary,

*It's hard to believe that Chattie and I were ever apart
because we are like SOOOO connected at the moment,
which of course Ruby is finding hard but she'll just have to
live with that because he loves ME and not HER. He's not
back at school yet and the head gave everyone a really
serious talk in assembly this morning about behaviour
outside school and warned that anyone found bullying or
assaulting another pupil outside school would be expelled.
Too right. Hopefully that'll mean Toby'll be out of my hair
before too much longer. Now that my love life is back on
track and our star signs predict nothing but the most golden
years ahead of us, I have only my GCSEs to think about (as
well as what I'm going to wear to Fran's party the day they
are all over) and they are freaking me out because the first
exam is only FOUR WEEKS AWAY . . . history. I've been
going round to see Chattie after school and we've been like
testing each other but then we start kissing and who cares
about the Russian Revolution then, and I know it's not the
end of the world if I don't get good grades, but it feels like
it could be and I'd really like to stuff all Dad's outrageous
presumptions about me down his throat by getting nothing
but As and A*s. That'd teach him not to tell me I'm
wasting the best years of my life like he told me on the
phone last night, when how would he even know what I've
been through or how difficult it is to get good grades or
even understand the difference between a Bolshevik and a
Menshevik? I've asked Mum if I can go and see one of her
doctor friends about going on the pill, because as soon as*

*Chattie can bear to be touched without wincing he's gonna
get jumped and after that scare about being pregnant I
really DON'T wanna find that I am pregnant for real. Mum
said she would, provided I refused ever to have the three-
month injection because she says it's not good for young
women to have such a mega shot of hormones in one go
when I've only ever taken paracetamol and a litre of vodka
and that I'm hard enough work to deal with at the moment
as it is. Charming.*

What About Me, Too?

From: Dr James
Sent: Thursday 8 May 13:45
To: Matthew Wilcox
Subject: Yesterday's meeting with the mediator

Your conduct was culpable. I have never denied you access to the children. I simply think that you have to consider their needs before your own. Frankie does not want to see you at the moment and is stressing out over her GCSEs which are imminent. Lola is showing all the signs of a child distressed by uncertainty – over us, where she will live and where she will go to school – and Tom is too young to understand anything much. Your smooth pretence at wanting to be the caring, sharing Dad did not impress that poor mouse of a woman trying to make peace between us. She has seen it all before. If you want to bankrupt us both by dragging us through the courts then so be it. I will fight you to the death to stop you from winning shared residency with our children. Nothing could fuck them up more.

Sue

Dear Diary,

I wish I was still a small, small child who could curl up in
a ball and not know that any of this was happening. When
you're small, like three or four, you just play all day long
and escape into your imajinashon. You don't understand
how bad things can be like I do now. I don't want to grow
up. I don't want to have to make really important decisions
about who I live with because whatever I say, one of them
will be really upset. I'm not sure whether it is possible to
cry any more than I have been. And they're not the same
sort of tears as small child ones. When you're small and you
cry because your ice cream falls onto the ground it feels like
the end of the world, but your Mum and your Dad are
there and they wipe away your tears and buy you another
one. And everything gets better really quickly. But now
there's nobody to wipe my tears and make it all better. I
have to do this all by myself and I don't think I can. I don't
know how and that makes me feel so weak and lonely.

From: Dr James
Sent: Friday 9 May 08:57
To: Matthew Wilcox
Subject: Re: Yesterday's meeting with the mediator

Having Mum here and working in no way detracts from my ability to look after my children. And I will not ask Lola what she wants because she is not old enough or mature enough to be able to know, other than that she loves us both more than any other two people on this planet.

Sue

From: Dr James
Sent: Friday 9 May 13:12
To: Matthew Wilcox
Subject: Re: Re: Yesterday's meeting with the mediator

You must have such a bitter and twisted mind to even think that a child Lola's age would weigh up how much she loves someone in the way that you suggest. Of course she loves you, Matthew, you're her father, but if you carry on in this way she will turn against you as she grows older because hero-worship of the father tends to evaporate with adolescence and she will see you for the hypocrite you actually are.

Dear Diary,

Friday the 9th of May 🖉

Dad AND Toyah came to pick me up from school today.
I didn't know he was coming but he took me shopping for
some new shoes and then out for tea and I was really happy
just to be with him, and NOT at home with Frankie
stomping around the whole time, histereekal about her
GCSEs. You can't even speak to her like a normal person
any more because she just shouts at you and if there's any
music on or any noise even from Granny she says, 'That's
it! My concentration's ruined and now I'm going to fail my
exams.' Pathetic. Then when she's feeling really stressed, she
makes a point of telling every one that at least one teenager
every year KILLS themselves over their GCSEs. Well it
would be just my luck if this year it was her. So it was great
to be with Dad, just him and me skipping along beside him,
holding his hand, until I realized that Mum didn't know
where I was. She rang him on his mobile and got really
cross with him in the restaurant and he was shouting at her
down the phone so that everyone could hear and it was so
embarrassing I just wanted to crawl under the table and die.
He kept saying things like, 'She's fine' and 'I have an
absolute right to see Lola whenever I want to,' and it was as
if I wasn't there. As if what *I* wanted and who *I* wanted to
see or be with counted for nothing. He took me home then
but he was really cross about it and practically dragged me
there. And then they had another row on the doorstep so
now I feel it's all my fault because if I'd just gone home

with Toyah none of this would have happened and maybe they wouldn't be fighting quite so badly. I've been crying into Chloe's fur so that Mum can't hear me, I've let Chloe come into my bed and she's been licking me all over my face, cleaning up my tears like she understands. Sometimes I think that if I just wasn't here then things would be easier for everyone, they wouldn't have anything to fight about.

What About Me, Too?

From: Dr James
Sent: Monday 12 May 09:15
To: Matthew Wilcox
Subject: Your outrageous conduct

Toyah assumed I knew that you had Lola; you knew better, yet you deliberately decided NOT to tell me that you had picked her up from school. I spent an hour and a half frantically trying to track you down – your mobile was on constant voicemail until you answered it in the restaurant – without knowing where Lola was. If you ever, EVER do that to me again I will screw you for every fucking penny you have and refuse all access permanently. Lola was really upset by it – once again she has heard us rowing angrily over her like she is some sort of possession, rather than a human being with her own needs and feelings and that's just not healthy, Matthew, only you never think of her, do you? Only yourself.

Dear Diary, ✎

I wish I had a magic wand and could wave it over this family and make everything happy again like the fairy godmother in *Cinderella*. Fairy tales are so cosy because they always have happy endings. But they're just stories, not true – made up things like Father Christmas and the Tooth Fairy because grown-ups want everything to be happy for us all the time. I wish I still believed in the Tooth Fairy. Granny says she still believes in the Tooth Fairy and she brought her a lovely new set of false teeth when all her real ones fell out. That's the trouble with not being a child any more when you're only eleven. There's no magic left to make things better.

What About Me, Too?

From: Dr James
Sent: Tuesday 13 May 09:32
To: Matthew Wilcox
Subject: Re: Your outrageous conduct

I have a waiting room full of patients and am already late. Yes,
I do expect to be consulted first because I have primary
responsibility for her welfare now that you have buggered off.
And you used her, Matthew, you don't just 'forget' these sort
of things. And Frankie is not slacking or destined for the dole
queue, as you suggest. She is about to take GCSEs, she needs
sleep, good food and as much peace as possible to concentrate
and she is unlikely to find any of that chez vous. She does not
NEED you harassing her to spend time with her on the phone
each night when spare time is the one thing she doesn't have at
the moment. If you care so much about your children's welfare,
why didn't these concerns cross your pimple-like brain before
you resumed sex with a minor? It's such a cliché, Matthew, but
then you never were much of an original.

Dear Diary,

I can't believe this is happening to us. It feels like there's this big black hole inside of me and it doesn't matter how much I cry or how much I try and fill it with thoughts about all of the good things we have like Tom and Toyah, it never seems to go away. Not even when I'm sleeping. If I wasn't here for them to fight over everything would be better, I know it would. Toyah says they're fighting because they both love me so much, but when I said that to the boy he said that they loved me so much they were using me to get at each other.

From: Dr James
Sent: Thursday 15 May 10:59
To: Matthew Wilcox
Subject: Your letter

Lola has been subdued all week. She pretends everything is all right when I ask her, busies herself looking after everybody else but actually she's miserable. And now I know why. I found your letter in her chest of drawers this morning. I cannot believe that you could do such a stupid and insensitive thing. How could you put that type of pressure on her about living with you? You're tearing her apart, Matthew. You should be ashamed of yourself. I hate you.

Dear Diary,

Monday 🖉

I'm not sure what I'm going to do next but I ran away from school today. It's better this way. I packed a rucksack with some clothes and food this morning and ran away at lunchtime. It's kind of weird being on the streets when all the other children are at school, everyone looks at you in this odd way. So I went to the cemetery. I'm going to live with the boy in the Lion's Tomb and keep him company. All his stuff is here but he isn't. I'm writing in my diary so as not to get too scared by all the noises coming from outside. He'll be here soon. I know he will.

What About Me, Too?

Dear Diary,

Six o'clock. I've eaten all the fruit and biscuits I brought with me and tried to light a fire but it's not really catching. Still no sign of the boy and I wish he'd get here soon because it's getting cold and he's good at lighting them. Mum will probably have discovered that I've gone by now. I hope she's not too worried. I hope Dad gets there soon to reassure her. If they have to work together to find me maybe then they'll remember why they fell in love in the first place.

Dear Diary,

Mum and Dad are freaking out about Lola downstairs. She went missing from school at lunchtime with a rucksack and some clothes but nobody noticed that she had gone until Toyah went at 3.30 to pick her up and she wasn't there. The teachers thought she'd gone to the dentist's. Typical fuckwits. So now Mum and Dad are shouting at each other, blaming each other for her disappearance, when actually if they just stopped hating each other for one minute, they might actually realize that they're the ones who've probably driven her to do this in the first place but that's too heavy a thought for either of them which is why they're freaking out. Mum's so freaked she's even had a massive row with HND about Clare bullying Lola (which she does, but now is not the time to alienate the stupid bitch still further when she was only trying to help, and her stupid spoilt daughter might actually know where she is). Mum says Dad's been putting on too much pressure to make Lola go and live with him and Dad says Mum hasn't been paying enough attention to Lola's problems at school, to which she replies that she hasn't had the time because HE'S been sapping every ounce of her emotional energy, threatening her with court. So I'VE been the one ringing up Lola's friends and the police and telling my stupid parents to shut the fuck up, and I'M the one with a GCSE tomorrow afternoon (it's only DT but it's still a GCSE and I need to get some sleep to pass it). At least Granny's being quiet. She never stops talking or telling us what we should or shouldn't be doing but then when something totally disastrous actually happens round here she hasn't an idea in her head about what to do about it. I think Lola's probably hiding out in a friend's garage or Wendy house. I think one of her friends must know where she is but doesn't dare say anything. It's gone quiet down there now, so I think I can brave it again for round two. I think it's time we rang some hospitals. I know this sounds odd but I am actually beginning to get really, really worried about my little sister.

Dear Diary,

The boy came back at about ten, I think. I was asleep under
my coat on his mattress when I felt him cover me with a
blanket so I sat up and pretended I hadn't been asleep at all,
which of course he didn't believe. He told me to get right
into the bed and get some proper sleep but I couldn't do
that. It's his bed and I don't want to take it from him. He
hasn't asked me why I'm here or whether I'm staying for
long but he doesn't seem to mind me here. He's made a big
fire so it's lovely and warm and he came back with a whole
box of mangos which I think he must have stolen from a
market because if he had bought them why would you
bother to buy just mangos? Anyway, they're delicious and I
don't miss Mum so much now that he's here.

Dear Diary,

I finally fell asleep for a few hours at about two after Mum and Dad finally agreed to disagree with silence, but I kept dreaming about Lola, shivering and vomiting in some doorway, covered in cardboard boxes. She's so obsessed with homeless down and outs. She like talks about them whenever you pass someone begging on the pavement and how she wants to bring all these junkies home and let them sleep in our sitting room, so I suppose that's why I was dreaming about her joining them. Dad spent most of the night touring the streets on his motorbike while Mum sat by the phone checking in with the police and hospitals hourly. She looked terrible. I've never seen her look so worried. Then at seven this morning my mobile went and it was Chattie who said that he'd had a call from someone who had been to Camilla's house last night revising with her brother and that Camilla had been really twitchy about Lola and kept saying, 'She's safe, I know she's safe.' So I rang Camilla and basically threatened her over the phone and she told me where Lola was. Dad was still out touring south London on his bike, so I told Mum to stay by the phone and I would ring her the moment I found her if Camilla was right. She didn't like the idea until I pointed out that the longer we stood here arguing about it, the longer Lola was out there, potentially alone.

I took Chloe with me to the cemetery. It's really creepy in there on your own. I kept hearing rustling behind the tombstones, probably rats or mice – ugghhh – and I was glad I had Chloe with me. We looked all over the place for the Lion's Tomb and when I finally found it Lola wasn't there and I couldn't see how Camilla could have thought she would be out here in this creepy place all alone and all night. But Chloe kept scratching at the stone and sniffing and wagging her tail and wouldn't come when I called her. I couldn't see what she was so excited about but then I noticed a gap in one of the big stones just at the bottom of the lion and pulled it back. There were steps plunging down into the darkness and a strong smell of smoke. Chloe ran down the steps and found Lola, curled up asleep on an abandoned mattress, hugging her rucksack, beside a small pile of burnt twigs. She looked pale and scared but as Chloe licked her face, she woke and the colour rose to her cheeks. She was so pleased to see us. She hugged and kissed Chloe and even hugged me.

I helped her up out of the tomb into the sunshine and we sat down at the lion's feet and I put my arm around her. I told her that she was braver than I was, because I would never spend a night in such a damp, dark hole with nothing but the rats and the ghosts and then I rang Mum, who of course ran straight round to find us without leaving a note for Dad. Which of course provoked another row when we all got back home until I screamed at them to shut the fuck up or we would both run away for good this time and make sure they never found either of us again. That shut them up. I took Lola upstairs while Mum made us all a mega fry-up for breakfast. Lola and I had a bath together and talked about the divorce and how stupid Mum and Dad were at times, but that's it with grown-ups. The more dealings I have with adults the more I think that there isn't any such thing as a true grown-up, you just get older and learn more about life as you experience it and if you're lucky you get wiser; Mum and Dad haven't ever divorced before so it was bound to be difficult for them but that didn't stop them from loving us. It's because they love us that they're fighting. If we didn't exist they could just divide up the house and part as friends. I think that helped a bit. I can see it's kind of hard for Lola to understand all this when she's only eleven and she's only just beginning to understand how shit life can be as you get older. It's lucky she's got me.

Dear Diary,

Tuesday lunchtime

It's so good to be home and **SOOO, SOOOO** good to have Mum AND Dad here at the same time, now that they've stopped rowing. Frankie says I would probably have slept all morning if Chloe hadn't found me. Clever Chloe, and Mum says I would probably have suffixicated from the smoking fire if I had. First she burst into tears and hugged me so tightly I could hardly breathe anyway (Frank said it was the relief), then when we took her down into the tomb she kind of wailed with horror at the thought that I may have come so close to actual death. Which is mad because the boy sleeps here every night and hasn't died of suffixication. But he isn't here. There was no sign of him when I woke up. I think maybe he either ran away when he heard Frankie coming because he doesn't want to be found or he was out looking for food that he could steal before anybody was up. So I told Mum and Frankie about the boy and how he lived here all by himself and how we needed to help him and then I started to cry really loudly, I couldn't stop, like I was crying about my whole life and Mum pulled me onto her lap and rocked me and shushed me until I couldn't cry any more.

A really nice policewoman has been round to talk to me. She said I was very brave. And then when she asked me if I thought I might want to run away again I told her I wouldn't, but if they start rowing again, I just might.

What About Me, Too?

From: Sue James
Sent: Tuesday 20 May 14:20
To: Angela James
Subject: Sweet, darling, precious Lola

She's fine now, we've found her, she's home and fast asleep in her bed but what a nightmare twenty-four hours this has been. I never ever want to have to live through that again. She ran away at lunchtime yesterday and nobody noticed that she'd gone until Toyah went to pick her up from school and she wasn't there. I rang Matthew, presuming she was with him because he's pressurizing her heavily to live with him, but he didn't have her and of course exploded with rage and spent the entire phone call blaming me for being irresponsible.

The police said she'd probably turn up when it got cold and dark and took her details. Then we just sat there with a thousand different horrific permutations running through our minds and waited. Waited for her to come home, only she didn't. When a child is ill, really ill you worry endlessly about them but they are there and you can devote yourself entirely to helping them, willing them to get better. But when you have no idea whether your child is safe or snatched you just feel so helpless, so utterly desperate and helpless. It's agony.

We rang every single child in her class but nobody seemed to know where she could have gone. Matthew walked the streets searching for her with Chloe, which was better than having him pacing the floor at home, because of course we were both so insanely anxious that we couldn't stop rowing until Frankie put us in our place, bless her. Frank and Toyah trawled the Internet, looking for sites that help with missing children. It's utterly appalling, Ange, the number of young teenagers who simply go missing from home, but they're older, they're running away from abusive, unloving parents, they're the ones you see sleeping in doorways and begging for money or cigarettes. I couldn't believe that Lola would do that, she's too young to understand. I couldn't believe that she would wilfully run away from Tom, from Chloe, from me and for what? But I also couldn't bear to think of something terrible happening to her like being snatched by a stranger.

We sat up all night, praying for her to come back. Mum was unbelievably supportive, kept telling me not to worry, that Lola was safe and hiding somewhere as an adventure, that kids loved adventure and were denied it these days because they were so overprotected. She made endless cups of tea and it was just lovely having her there. A policewoman came round at about midnight to take down some more details and said that patrol cars had been notified. I rang every single hospital; Matthew went out on regular sorties on his motorbike, searching for her. Whenever he came back empty-handed, we simply sat and stared at each other, we even hugged and cried together at one point. The anger, the rows over who had Lola, now seemed so pointless when we had no idea where she was. I couldn't go into her room, and everywhere I looked there were her things, coats shed in the hall like caterpillar skins, shoes and pictures, toys and handwritten notes. Matthew and I searched through everything, looking for some clue as to where she might have gone but found nothing. She had taken her diary with her.

Frank and Chloe found her early this morning after a tip-off from a friend. She had spent the night in the cemetery off the high street, sheltering in the tomb beneath this rather amazing statue of a sleeping lion that I'd never even noticed before, but apparently she loves him, has been there often either in her imagination or for real (not quite sure which but probably a mixture of both), and says a boy is living there, although he wasn't there when we found her. She was cold, rather dirty and tired, hadn't eaten or slept much but otherwise she was perfectly OK, thank God. I'm so relieved and so tired that I never want to let her out of my sight again. She had a hot bath and some scrambled eggs on toast, Frankie then went to school, Toyah took Tom to the baby bounce and I tried to convince Matthew that he could now go back to work. But he won't, says he wants a really good chat with Lola when she wakes up, so I'm waiting rather nervously for that moment now. Whatever happens, Lola has to have the floor and Matthew has agreed to that. I'll let you know how it goes . . .

Oh and by the way, a bumper post this morning – Lola has a place at Frankie's school and is THRILLED ABOUT IT and Mum has a place at Clarice's at the beginning of June – but haven't told her yet. Thought I'd leave that until all this has calmed down a bit.

Much love,
Sxxxxxxxxxxxxxxxxxxxxxxxxxxxxxxxxxxxxxxxxxxxxx

Dear Diary,

Mum says I can stay home today and go back to school tomorrow or the next day when I feel stronger. Dad didn't go to work, which was nice so we all took Chloe up onto the common and sat outside in the sunshine at the café, eating ice cream. Dad asked me if I'd run away to bring them back together but it's not that simple. How can it be that simple because if I wasn't here, I wouldn't be with them being together? I don't know what I thought when I did it, just that it might be better for everyone if I wasn't here for them to fight over. Maybe everybody else's life would be easier if I just wasn't here to complicate things. But I didn't say that, I couldn't put all these mixed up feelings about everything into words so I just nodded and licked my ice cream and tried to wipe the tears from my eyes but they just kept pouring down.

Then Dad and Mum started on this lecture that dads and mums give when they split up, about how they both love us and how we can have two homes and two Christmases and birthdays and how they wish it could be different but sometimes grown-ups fall out of love and can't live with each other. Well, I wish it could be different too. And while I understand, sort of, what they mean, it doesn't take away that dreadful gnawing feeling I have sometimes of just missing my daddy. So I cried a bit more and said I understood and I knew they both loved me and that I'd try to be strong but that it was hard. And then Mum cried and then Dad stood up and walked about nervously like he does when he's upset and I felt a bit better because at least they said they understood how hard it must be AND they didn't row about it.

What About Me, Too?

Dear Diary,

Clare and her mum have just been round with a present. They bought me this really cool skirt and matching top from Gap and it was all wrapped up in a special presentation box. Mum invited them in and there was this rather difficult silence as they all watched me unwrapping the box. Then Mum thanked Clare's mum and told her that it had been the worst night of her life, which made me feel really, really bad. I didn't need to hear that. Clare then took me out into the garden and wanted to know everything that had happened so I told her but obviously didn't tell her about the boy because I knew she wouldn't believe me, and actually he's my friend, not hers. I think Granny must have gone round yesterday to talk to Clare's mum because otherwise why would they bother with a present? Clare stayed for a bit to play too after her mum had gone. That was the best thing because she hasn't been round since my birthday and it was the first time we've been here on our own for ages. She's just the same as she always was when she's not with Tanya, or her mum. Maybe I should run away more often.

From: Sue James
Sent: Tuesday 20 May 23:18
To: Angela James
Subject: Re: Sweet, darling, precious Lola

Thanks, Honey — I'll give Lola that lovely message in the morning. It's been an emotional roller coaster of a day and Matthew has only just left. He's been so shaken by Lola running away that he's managed to cap his anger and do the right thing. I had no idea that Lola had been under quite so much stress. It was Frankie I was worried about, what with GCSEs (the first one was today, great timing but Frank says it went OK) and her terrible relationship with Matthew, and splitting up with Chattie AND her love affair with vodka. With Frankie it all hangs out — she screams her unhappiness and frustration all around the house, daily. Lola just quietly gets on with things in her sane and sensible way. You think you know your children better than the back of your hand but as they grow older and more separate, more private, I wonder whether you actually know them less and less? It was Lola, who is always so good at looking after everybody else and pretending that everything is fine, who was actually suffering in more ways than she could say. I had no idea that she was masking such torment. I think she ran away to try and bring us back together, although I don't think that was necessarily a conscious act, more an act of desperation, the tween answer to chain-smoking a packet of fags in front of your mother or knocking back sixteen vodka and Cokes. And it's worked in a way. Matthew and I have agreed to try and be more cooperative around access and money. It was a warning and thankfully nothing bad has come of it, and maybe, just maybe, we'll be able to tread a smoother path towards divorce in the next few months. It's going to be tough though, he managed to push me close to the edge twice within hours of Lola's homecoming by promising her a mobile phone and ear piercing WITHOUT consulting me first. Bastard. Still, I guess on today of all days she's allowed anything she wants.

Feeling desperately tired in that way you do after an emotional crisis so must to bed.

Love you lots, Suexxxx

Dear Diary,

Monday the 26th of May

It's HALF-TERM and such great relief not to have to be at school. When I was there on Thursday and Friday everyone kept crowding round to ask me about what happened so I had to tell them over and over again about how creepy it was with all the spiders and rats and ants and worms and everyone listened to me transfigurated and asked questions and I probably did make a few things up to make them even more interested but basicly the story was as it happened. It was kind of nice being the centre of attention but then it also made me feel a bit claspophobic as well because it felt like everyone was looking at me or talking about me the whole time. It must be what Julia Roberts or Renee Zellwegger feel like when they go to Sainsbury's. But it's exciting, not the same feeling as when something bad happens and you don't want anybody to notice, like falling off a climbing frame or a horse or something, and all the adults come running from miles around, panicking and shouting 'Are you all right?' when all you actually want to do is hide the fact that you've just done something totally stupid. And THEN what adults do is they keep reminding you all day of the fact that you did something so totally stupid and didn't cry, when all you want to do is to forget what happened. Them reminding you makes you want to cry all over again, because of course it still hurts somewhere inside. Tanya and Clare didn't seem to think it was interesting though, they laughed at everyone else for

What About Me, Too?

listening. So I told them that I'd got into Frankie's school and how Mum had said they got better GCSE results than the posh toff school that Clare was going to and how my new school was ten zillion times better than the school that Tanya was going to and ran off with Camilla to play a fantasy game underneath the apple tree.

Dear Diary,

Wednesday the 28th of May 🖉

Dad came over to pick me up this evening to take me to see a film (a 12!!!) and he wasn't late and we didn't go out with Laura as well, it was just him and me, and Mum and Dad didn't row on the doorstep, in fact they even seemed pleased to see each other. Frankie's right, it's sort of more intense when you're just with him alone, even if he does find it hard to know what to say.

The really, really sad thing though is that Granny is going to have to leave again. She's going to a new home which is much nearer so that's good because we'll be able to see her more often and Mum says she can come for lunch lots. But I like having her here. I'm really going to miss her. I've asked her if she can teach me lots more recipes because that way she gets to feel useful and I learn stuff and I think it takes her mind off having to leave us again. I can see that she's sad in her eyes.

What About Me, Too?

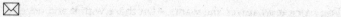

From: Sue James
Sent: Wednesday 28 May 19:23
To: Angela James
Subject: Re: 1 August

Fantastic news that you're coming – let's start making some holiday plans: Cornwall? Tuscan villa? French Alps??? And to have you and the boys for the whole of August fills me with nothing but the greatest pleasure. I'll see if I can get enough cover to be able to take most of the month off as well.

Lola's much happier. Even caught her singing and swinging her legs at the breakfast table this morning. Funny how long it's been since she's done that and funny, too, how I never noticed that it had stopped. Matthew and I still on our best behaviour although no nearer a resolution (meeting with the mediator next week). He's also making a different kind of effort with Frankie. He produced four tickets yesterday for Party in the Park which made her squeal with joy and throw her arms around his neck as she shouted 'THANKS, DAD!' which of course made everything all right in his eyes. She could have been a junkie on the game without a hope of a single GCSE at that moment and he would have forgiven her. I'm the one that has to cope with the prima donna stomping around the house. She's either hysterical and inconsolable, determined that she's going to fail every single exam or she's grumpy and demanding. So I run around the house, providing her with hot chocolates, face masks, massages, scallops, cups of tea, cheese on toast –

you name it whatever she wants – I'm there with it and never thanked, while Matthew just has to come up with some tickets (which the marriage-breaker bitch probably got anyway) and he's adored. Still, the timing's perfect – a week after her last exam so she can go bonkers there with her friends.

Mum's not happy about moving. She's sulky, and seizes every possible opportunity to drop hints about feeling unloved. Every innocent statement gets twisted, e.g., 'Supper's ready, Mum.'

'If it's not TOO much trouble for you to have another mouth to feed,' she'll reply as she heaves herself out of the chair. You know the sort of thing.

I just ignore it, but of course she manages to get under my skin in the way that only mothers can, and when she really pushes all my buttons I only feel more determined to get rid of her. I feel guilty, of course I do. She loves it here and if we had an extra bedroom and she was a different sort of mother I'd probably love having her here too. But what else can I do? She needs looking after and that need is only going to increase as she gets older. And we need our privacy here, and I need time to myself. After work and the children there isn't much time left for me and at the moment all of that goes on Mum, who never seems to need much sleep and is awake when I go to bed and up, clattering around and smashing crockery in the kitchen, when I get up. Plus there's the terrifying thought of her continuing to be alive, HERE, for another ten years or more, when I'll be about to draw my pension, if the strain of all this hasn't killed me first.

Much love Sxx

What About Me, Too?

Dear Diary,

I'm so bored of revising I could kill myself. Now I understand why teenagers hang themselves before their GCSEs. It's so that they don't have to do this any more – stare at facts and try to remember them and then feel like your whole life is totally pointless because you can't cram anything more into your poxy little oxygen-starved brain. If Lola had ADHD I could take her Ritalin to help me concentrate. I've eaten so much crap this evening I feel sick and will probably have a stroke once my blood pressure rises tomorrow morning when I turn over the paper and forget how to write my own name. I've stuck yellow stickies with science facts all over the walls of the house and I've read them standing on my head, in bed, on the loo, at the dinner table. I've got Mum to test me and Lola to test me and I'm still gonna fail, I know I am because THERE'S SO MUCH THAT YOU HAVE TO REMEMBER AND MY BRAIN HURTS BECAUSE THERE SIMPLY ISN'T ENOUGH ROOM IN THERE FOR ALL THIS INFORMATION. AAAAAAAAARRRRRRRGGGGGG-HHHHHH!!!!! I HATE GCSEs.

Ruby keeps ringing me and panicking which doesn't help, because like why should I care whether she passes or fails? Fran has just rung for a gossip – Saskia got a place at this really weird-sounding boarding school in the country for sixth form. There's a prayer room and it's vegetarian with only herbal teas, no caffeine at all and they treat eating disorders at the school and she'll only be allowed out on Sundays. Sounds like the sort of dumping ground that

*parents send their kids to when they don't know what else
to do with them and want to make sure they're safe until
they're eighteen. Then when they get out of there they just
go mad anyway, making up for everything they've missed.
I won't miss her, but good luck to the nasty bitch anyway,
with parents like hers it's really not her fault that she's so
horrible. It's 9 p.m. and just twelve hours until I sit Physics
so I think I'm gonna have a bath and relax with a bit of
OC and then get to school early and revise on the bus.
I mean, if I don't know it now I probably never will.*

What About Me, Too?

Dear Diary,

Sunday 🖉

Took Chloe for a walk in the cemetery although I didn't tell Mum because I don't want her freaking out about it again. It smells really fresh and sweet at the moment because it's full of wild flowers like elderflower and nettles and Granny says you can make drink and soup out of them. I don't know whether the boy knows that. He wasn't there to ask although most of his stuff was. I want to see him to thank him for looking after me that night and to make sure that he is OK. I feel kind of guilty because everything is so much better in my life now and I'm so lucky and he isn't. My mum and dad cared enough about me to look for me. I still have a mum and a dad even if they are getting divorced AND I have a home to go to but he hasn't. I left him a bar of chocolate and some bread. I'll go back soon to see if he is OK.

Dear Diary,

Monday the 2nd day of June

Granny left yesterday and the house feels really weird without her. We had a special dinner for her last night and Mum even invited HND (although she didn't come, she said she was busy but she never went out). Granny tried to be cheerful, said she'd lived through worse times than this, which made Frankie roll her eyes up to the ceiling but I understand. I mean, if you can't live with your own family when you're this old it's a pretty sad situashon. I miss her already although Mum doesn't. She says she's going to redecorate the sitting room now that Granny's gone and keeps saying isn't it wonderful to have the room back again when we never really used it much other than to store books and newspapers in anyway. We're always downstairs in the kitchen.

Everyone's talking about Sports Day at school, which is in two weeks' time. The whole school gets divided up into four teams with four different colours so you run to collect points for your team so that you're not running just for yourself. I'm always red, and red never wins. The teachers say it's to stop making us all so competitive but what happens is that we get even more competitive about the teams and who's in which team than we would do if we were just running for ourselves. Yellow always wins because the best runners are in yellow and they never mix the colours up. They should do to make it fairer and to stop people like Tanya and Clare from being bitches, because of course they are both yellow and Camilla and I are red. Of course she can't run because of her foot and they like to remind us of that fact all the time, like we can't help but lose because of Camilla, which, as Mum says, is not very kind. So Camilla and I have decided to practise. She's going to come over at the weekend and we'll get Mum or Dad to take us to the common because we can't do it in the garden in case Clare sees us out of her bedroom window. We're also gonna practise handing over the baton in the relay team because we'll be in the same team and that's where you can lose time and we need to be as fast as we can.

And I've had the best news. Dad has said we can go and choose a mobile phone at the weekend and then he'll take me to have my ears pierced. Mum's not pleased but she can't really argue about it although she has made me promise that I will only use the phone to send text messages and only ever put it to my ear in emerjensies because she thinks they give people brain ~~tuoomers~~ ~~tumors~~ tumers and she says that if my ears go septic because I haven't looked after them properly and the holes close up then I can't have them pierced again until I'm old enough to look after them, which seems fair enough. Only they are my ears, not hers.

✉

From: Sue James
Sent: Saturday 7 June 08:27
To: Angela James
Subject: Mum

Is a bloody liability. Clarice's have been on the phone three times this week and all the guilt and sadness about not being able to look after her here and make her final years memorable within the bosom of our family home have evaporated through sheer rage.

She's refusing to eat, she asked a volunteer to ring social services because she was not being looked after properly (the silly fool took her word for it and rang) and she's terrified a young child who was visiting her own granny by telling her wicked tales about what happens to the old people there at night after all the visitors have gone home.

So I went to see her at lunchtime yesterday and of course she denies all knowledge of the above. Says she likes it there much more than North Butting and that I mustn't worry about her. 'Go back to your work and all those other poor sick people who need you more than I do,' she said rather patronizingly, knowing it would drive me mad with rage and guilt and ruin the rest of my weekend. My hope is that these are just teething problems and that once she's settled and made friends things will improve. That's what I've told Clarice's, anyway. But if this continues I may well have to go in there and smother her with a pillow.

What About Me, Too?

The truth is that it's bliss without her, but she's been living here for so long now that I can in all honesty say that I miss having her around the place because she was such a massive presence in every respect. She followed me everywhere, talking all the time, complaining, fussing, interfering, so now that she's not here doing all of those things, the house feels like a mansion without her and it's SOOOO peaceful. I've sort of relaxed to fill the space left in her void. There's silence after the children have gone to bed (if I can get Frankie to go to bed, that is — I keep telling her that sleep is the most important thing before exams but she doesn't believe me). And I'm alone, wonderfully alone. I'm spending the rest of the weekend cleaning out the sitting room, chucking out clutter, sorting books for the charity shop and generally expunging the room of every last whiff of cigarettes and oil paints (which she has managed to splatter over half the carpet, and there are cigarette burns as well so that'll have to go too) by bringing in a team of decorators on Monday. Can't wait. Although am now in a blind panic about which colour to choose. Must press on.

Love, S

From: Sue James
Sent: Sunday 8 June 21:25
To: Angela James
Subject: Re: Can't go wrong with Farrow & Ball

OK, will take your word for it but just because they're more
expensive than every other paint doesn't mean they're always
right. I mean, should I go for a rich red because it's so warm
and cosy or is that going to be too dark in the summer when
there's less artificial light around? And I know, matricide is a
worry; Matthew would end up with everything – sole charge of
all three children plus the house – if I was found guilty of
manslaughter (surely not murder? I mean, how much does a
woman need to be provoked?). There has to be an easier way.
Perhaps a massive shot of morphine. Shipman got away with it.
Well, almost, but he was a psychopath. I'm just an
overburdened dutiful daughter, and by the time we get to that
age we should have euthanasia anyway, lucky us. Imagine the
pressure Frank and Lola will put on me then when they want
the house!

Yes, let's drive somewhere through France. Good idea –
much cheaper than flying, and we can listen to the entire works
of Harry Potter Unabridged in the car to keep the kids happy.
Have you got them for the boys?? Read by the wonderful
Stephen Fry and much better than the books because he does
all the voices so well. Gotta go. Matthew (BASTARD) took Lola
to have her ears pierced today and she's making a pig's ear of

cleaning them in the bathroom (excuse the pun but she is
squealing like a piglet every time the disinfectant goes anywhere
near the wound so I'd better go and help and try not to say,
'I told you so').

Sx

Kate Figes

Dear Diary,

Monday the 9th day of June

I feel really grown-up. Much taller even though my ears are now heavier and ought to really be dragging me closer to the ground. My ears are red, swollen and they hurt but I don't care because, as Frankie says, you do feel more pain in life as you get older. I mean this is not like when you just fall over and graze your knee kind of pain. This is the pain that comes from the more adult responsiblities that come with beauty like waxing the hairs on your legs, which Frankie says is agony but the only way to stop the hairs on your legs from getting so thick that you need a lawnmower to get rid of them. Frankie also says I have to use a deodorant when I start secondary school because all of the year 7s at her school stink. It took me ages to get to sleep last night because I couldn't turn my head on the pillow because it hurt so much, so I had to lie rigidly flat on my back which was a bit odd and I woke up with a stiff neck. But then when I went into school today I felt really proud because everybody noticed and Camilla thought that my studs were really pretty. They've got little blue shiny stones in them. I think even Clare was impressed because she didn't say anything, just stared at them and then walked off and if she didn't like them she would certainly have said so because she always does. I haven't dared show my mobile phone to anyone other than Camilla because you're not allowed them at school and if anyone sees it they might tell Miss Jennings and then it'll be confiskated until the end of

362

the week, but it felt kind of cool in my pocket. I knew it was there and just knowing that made me feel stronger, that whatever Tanya and Clare said or did wouldn't matter any more.

Mum is trying hard not to freak out about my ears or the mobile, which means she might be learning something finally, but what I really can't tell her is that Dad fainted when the woman put the gun to my ear and was absolutely no use at all. If I told her that she'd just have a go at him and then they'd start rowing again. He was out for at least ten minutes while the girl pierced my ears and then showed me how to keep them clean. She was really nice to me and just stepped over Dad when she'd finished to get me a leaflet and a discount voucher for some more earrings when the holes have heeled. I think I'm gonna get some of those big gold hoopy ones.

Dear Diary,

*Halfway through . . . I've got one more science, English
literature, one more maths paper, two history papers and
then I'M FREEEEEEEEE!!!!! I'm gonna get completely
pissed, spend an entire day in bed with Chattie and go
shopping. I deserve presents. Lots of presents.*

*I felt this total sense of exhilarated liberation today after
the last French paper because it meant no more French
revision EVER. And it went well, I know it did. I could
answer everything and finished in time, while poor Ruby
didn't notice that there was a page four on the back of the
paper and has missed out two entire questions so she was in
floods of tears because she wants to do French A level. It
was terrible for her and I hope this doesn't sound disloyal
but actually I just felt so stoned and happy because it was
over I could have kissed everybody, except Toby, that is.
He actually came to school today, even though he didn't
have an exam, just to bug me. He stood outside the school
gate with his pathetic cronies, wearing a hoody and yucky
jeans, thinking he looked cool when actually he looked just
like a weirdo wanker and then as we walked past he
produced this SNAKE from out of his pocket, a real live
snake, and started waving it around us to try and make us
freak, when all it did was make us think he was even
weirder. Fran asked him what sort of a snake it was and he
said it was a python, this minute little worm-like thing,
which just made us laugh. Like we don't know that pythons
are actually massive and squeeze you to death, so then he
tried to make out that this was a baby python and that he*

had a bigger one at home which was just such a lie we fell about laughing so he started chasing us around the streets waving this SNAKE!!!!! Fran reckons he was just doing that because he can't show us his pathetic little dick, only some of us have seen it although I didn't wanna point that out.

Dear Diary,

Wednesday the 11th of June

The boys have been lining everybody up in the playground and organizing races to try and work out who's gonna win which race next Tuesday. They're so competitive. Rory's even drawn up a list of odds and is making money taking bets from the parents. The good news, though, is that when he set me up against Tanya, I won. Camilla was so excited she couldn't stop going on about it, which of course wound Clare and Tanya up, and they've been even more bitchy as a result, teasing Camilla about not being able to run and about how she's the reason why reds never win, which is just so so SO mean. But instead of getting upset she just kept whispering to remind me that I beat Tanya in the 100 metres by at least two seconds. YESSSSSSS!!!!!

It's the 500 metres, right round the track, that's really worrying me. We've been trying it out in the playground and that's about twenty laps and I always get so breathless that I have to stop. No one has EVER done it before but this year they're going to try year 6 out with it, so of course everyone is being even more competitive about who's going to win. Camilla can't do that one, the teachers won't let her, but she really, really wants to do it even though that much exercise makes her leg stump sore from the rubbing. She doesn't wanna be left out. Her mum has written to the headmistress to ask her to let Camilla do it and they've had to agree but everyone knows she's going to come last.

I've been back to the cemetery two more times with

What About Me, Too?

Chloe and the boy still isn't there. I feel really guilty because now that things are so much better at home and Mum keeps telling me about how life is going to be with Dad not living here and hugging me all the time and buying me things to make me feel special, I sort of forget about the boy and that's just like what everybody else does. They forget about all the sad and lonely people because they don't want their happiness spoiled. I waited for a bit the first time but then I started hearing some really spooky noises so I ran away. But today when I went there after school I noticed that the remains of the chocolate I ate had been almost eaten away by rats and that the picture of his mother was gone. Toyah says that there are lots of young people like him who don't want to go home and have to move around so that they don't get found by the police or taken into care. I think he must have moved on, which makes me more sad than I can say because I really like him. I hope he's OK.

From: Sue James
Sent: Sunday 15 June 22:19
To: Angela James
Subject: Re: Re: Can't go wrong with Farrow & Ball

Gone for a vibrant, cheering, summery yellow. Lovely. Still heaps
of clutter around the place and can't actually sit in my new sitting
room because there are about 10,000 of Matthew's LPs piled
high on both sofas. I wish he'd move them out since I'll never
listen to them. He took Lola off for the whole weekend, brought
her back with a brand new pair of expensive trainers for Sports
Day on Tuesday without my even having to ask him and was
incredibly civil on the doorstep. Lola skipped into the house at
six, happy to say goodbye. It seems that so long as we avoid
every single contentious issue for Lola's sake, life is liveable and I
get to sleep at night. As to how long we'll be able to keep that
up, particularly since there is still the crucial issue of finance to
sort out, who knows . . . He's planning on coming to Sports Day.
I tried to talk him out of it because I'm not sure how we'll
manage an entire day together in public without rowing, but he's
never been to Sports Day before for either Frank or Lola, so if
he does show up it'll be something of a miracle.

I had Tom all to myself all weekend, absolute bliss since this
is the first time we've had alone together since Mum moved in.
No calls this week at all from Clarice's so maybe, just maybe,
Mum has settled (daren't ring). And Frankie threw a dinner
party for her sixteenth birthday, which was hugely entertaining.

What About Me, Too?

She still has two GCSEs to sit next week but you're only sixteen once, so I agreed to pay for dinner for ten here, plus candles, champagne, whatever she wanted, provided she did all the washing up before I got up with Tom on Sunday morning. After studying recipe books rather than her history textbook for most of the week, she managed to decide on two of the most dramatic and difficult dishes in the gastronomic canon: bouillabaisse followed by chocolate mousse. So we spent most of Saturday morning shopping for fish and most of Saturday afternoon scrubbing mussels and trimming off the yucky bits from raw fish, but we laughed, we really laughed, and it was as energizing as a two-week holiday in the Seychelles, I swear, Ange. When Frank's in a good mood she's the best company there is. Tom clattered about in his knight outfit, trying to inflict damage on the woodwork with his plastic sword, while Frankie squawked and squealed with disgust at the texture of squid. We talked about things, she told me stuff about her life that I never knew, like she'd been worried she was pregnant and now that she was on the pill it was a relief not to have that worry for a while. She's been selected by her science teacher to represent the school at an outside event to receive an award, which is just such an affirmation of her abilities that I can't believe she never told me. She asked me dozens of questions about Granny and what her life was like when she was younger and about Matthew and where we'd met and how had I known that he was the right man to marry and then we laughed a little over that. And we cooked together, and she listened to me and didn't criticize or slag me off once and I thought, my oh my, how things have changed. She's such a mature young woman now.

Dinner was sumptuous although I wasn't allowed to eat with them. I was allowed to serve and was instructed rather sweetly to get her a cake because those old traditions die hard and she wanted to be sung to. Quite right. And then a bike arrived at about nine, just as they were sitting down to eat, with a massive bunch of flowers and a schmulzy message from Matthew about how proud he was of his beautiful grown-up daughter and she burst into tears because he doesn't find that easy to say. Her first bouquet!!

She didn't manage the washing up – I had to do that, but what the fuck. I used to clear up after her birthday parties when she was small, so why not now? And you know what? This time when she and Chattie came down sleepily for breakfast at about two o'clock, she noticed and said, 'Thanks, Mum, it was the best birthday ever.'

Now my bath is probably overflowing (when that's usually Frankie's forte) so must go but will try and ping you in the week.

Masses of love, Suexxx

What About Me, Too?

Dear Diary,

Sports Day. Well, where do I start??? The best best thing was that I was expecting only Tom and Toyah to be there to watch but Mum and Dad and Chloe came too and they all sat together on a rug with a massive picnic basket, as far away from Clare's mother as they could manage. They waved at me as they arrived at the track and Mum ran down to give me a large bottle of water. It was a really hot day and she said that the more I drank before the race the faster I would run because the body needs to be hydrogenated to move. She should know as she's a doctor. I bet Tanya's Mum doesn't know that. The worst, worst thing was that I couldn't find my new trainers anywhere in the cloakroom and I knew that Tanya had taken them but she swore that she hadn't. I got really, really upset about it because Dad bought them for me, but we had to go and get on the coach before I could find them. Camilla wanted to lend me hers and said she couldn't run anyway but I didn't want her not to be able run in the 500 metres just because of me, when I knew how much it meant to her to run with the rest of the class, so I borrowed an old pair off Britney instead.

Anyway, Mum was right because I beat Tanya in the 100-metre race AGAIN. I've never run so hard or fast in my life. I could feel her just behind me in the next lane, breathing heavily, her feet pounding on the track and I just willed myself forward like my whole life depended on it. Dad ran down to the finish line and swept me up into his arms and twirled me round he was so pleased for me, and I waved at Mum who was jumping up and down with Tom in her arms. I can't tell you how good it feels to beat someone you really hate in a race.

Mum made the best picnic ever, all my favourite things – salami and strawberries and smoked salmon and cream-cheese bagels and macaroons, and Chloe of course had to sit right in the middle of the whole rug, pushing us all off onto the grass so that she could get the scraps from everyone. Tom's the worst, though. He would give Chloe his whole lunch if he could. He wouldn't share it with anyone else, mind, and Toyah just managed to stop Chloe from taking an entire bagel out of Tom's hand. When it came to the 500-metre race, the one we had all been dreading, the mighty marathon that was going to test the whole class to its most extreme limits, Clare walked right past me down to the track wearing MY brand-new trainers!!!! I ran after her and told her to give them back but it was too late for that, everybody else was lining up at the start line and all of the year 6 parents were standing up, ready to cheer their children on.

Miss Jennings asked Camilla quietly whether she wanted to run and she said she did so I stood next to her at the start line and squeezed her hand as Miss Grant said, 'On your marks . . . get set . . . GO!' I would have liked to have held her hand all the way round but you can't really run that way. Rory, Lucian and Harry sprinted off first because they're so competitive, which was just like so stupid because Miss Grant told them to pace themselves and to sprint at the end, so by the time it came to the final bit they collapsed and had to walk the rest of the way. Serves them right!!!!!!!

But it was when we got to the first bend and the sun was beating down and I couldn't hear Mum or Dad or anybody else screaming 'Re-Ed. Re-Ed,' only the sound of feet on tarmac and heavy breathing, that I felt something hard strike me across my shin and I fell smack onto the track. Tanya or Clare had tripped me up, I couldn't tell which, and I was out of the race for good.

Camilla helped me up and we hobbled back towards the grown-ups across the grass in the middle of the track. Dad ran down to me and gave me a hug and it was so nice just feeling him picking me up that I burst into tears and sobbed into his chest with disappointment and rage. But what I didn't notice because I was so busy crying and feeling sorry for myself was that Camilla had turned and walked back to the place where she had stopped running and picked up where she had left off, running slowly and not very well round to complete what she had started all on her own. Everyone else was cheering on the rest of the class as they came round to the last strait and ran as fast as their tired legs could carry them to the finish line, with Martha in the lead. They didn't notice Camilla with her high bunches and her false foot limping round on the other side of the track. But Dad did and shouted, 'Look how brave Camilla is, she didn't have to do that!'

I wiped my eyes and watched her run and I knew it wouldn't be long before her foot would start to hurt as the plastic rubs against her stump. So Dad and I crossed the track and ran along beside her, cheering her on. 'Come on, Camilla! You can do it, you can do it!' We shouted like we were her personal trainers or something.

By the time she reached the final strait, most of the rest of the school had noticed. Everyone from my class, except Clare and Tanya, ran down to the side of the track and started chanting her name, 'Camil-la. Camil-la,' and when she finally made it through the tape (which the teachers put up again in her honour) they all crowded around her and hugged her and told her how brave she was and most of the mums were in tears. The only person who didn't seem to be crying was Camilla's mother who just jumped up and down she was so happy to see her daughter achieve something so great. Clare and Tanya did not look at all happy. For once they were the ones who were feeling left out. I went over to Clare and told her to give me back my trainers. She sat down and started to undo the laces as we watched Camilla revelling in her triumph. All I said to them was, 'I think we know who won that race.'

It's been the most amazing day. Dad didn't come home with us but he asked Mum if it would be OK to take me and Tom out for the day on Sunday and Mum said yes. I kind of hoped that they might kiss each other goodbye to sort of round off this perfect day and make it even perfecter but they didn't. And then all the way home Mum kept talking about Camilla and how strong she was and how mean Clare's mum was not to offer us a lift home or share out any of her food, which was like way over the top – something called devils on horseback which looked disgusting, and about 6,000 quiches. Honestly, Mum. She should give the poor woman a break.

What About Me, Too?

Dear Diary,

Wednesday the 18th day of June

For the first time this year I woke up this morning and actually wanted to go to school. I couldn't wait to see the look on Clare and Tanya's faces while everybody else talked about Sports Day. The best news was that neither red nor yellow won. It was green this year so maybe all the best runners aren't in yellow after all. Maybe I was wrong about that. Anyway, Camilla has never looked happier and Miss Jennings mentioned her specially in assemberllee this morning and said that Camilla had shown the sort of sportsmanship that we should all aspirate too because it was the taking part that mattered, not the winning, which is true but we all know that winning helps. Miss Jennings also kept Clare and Tanya back at break time today and told them that she knew they had taken my trainers and if she ever caught them taking anybody else's property ever again they would be suspended from school, which is like really serious. Even Frankie never got suspended. So I'm happier now. Everything seems to be working out all right at home and at school, and soon I'll be going to a brand-new school and everything will be different.

From: Sue James
Sent: Sunday 22 June 21:54
To: Angela James
Subject: The miracle of children

Lola's Sports Day made *Chariots of Fire* look feeble. There I was,
worrying more about Lola's pierced ears (which have, of
course, gone septic) than whether she would actually win
anything. Then in the 500-metre race, Lola got tripped up by
the bitch next door. Little Camilla with the prosthetic foot
stopped to help Lola AND THEN WENT BACK TO WHERE
SHE HAD STOPPED RUNNING TO COMPLETE THE
COURSE ON HER OWN. I still find myself crying when I recall
it, me, the hardened doctor who breaks bad news to people
and sticks hypodermic needles into their arms and is so used to
taking smears that I rarely now need to even hold my breath to
avoid the smell. Yet I find myself walking along, thinking of
nothing in particular other than that I'm late or that Lola needs
a new swimming costume, and the image of Camilla hobbling
round a massive running track all on her own pops into my
mind and tears start running down my face. She had the perfect
excuse not to run, not to endure pain and humiliation yet the
little thing chose to do something brave and significant.
Children don't need to be taught right from wrong, they know,
they're born instinctively kind until they get corrupted by the
adult world. And then every now and again, a little angel pops
up to remind us, the adults, how to behave. Because on that

day, in that race, almost everybody else, including the adults, would have taken the easier, lazier route. Anyway, that was Thought for the Day . . .

Matthew and I managed (just) to keep a lid on our emotions in public. We have our third meeting with mediator next week and he tried to talk about it in between races, said that if we just agreed to splitting everything 50/50 we wouldn't need to carry on wasting our time with her. I ignored him at first but he went on and on about it, bullying me into saying something, so I said quietly between clenched teeth that only children believe that things in life ought to be fair and that since he couldn't even consult me on important issues like whether or not Lola got her ears pierced or had a mobile phone then how on earth could we share care, and he got cross. Thank God that Lola managed to win the 100 metres at that point and beat the horrible Tanya because he was so overjoyed he ran down to congratulate her, and thankfully the moment was lost and we were all smiles again for Lola's sake. Honestly a Martian looking down on us on that particular day would have concluded that the large people were the children and that the small ones were the grown-ups.

Frankies GCSEs finally over (she took a tub of Häagen-Dazs with her to bed last night and said she was never getting up again!). She's reasonably optimistic about how she did in them so now we just have to wait until August 26th for the results. She went out with a huge gang from school on Friday night and got so pissed that she can't remember how she got home. Still, at least she did get home.

Masses of love,
Sxxx

Dear Diary,

I wake up each morning now and all I have to think about is whether or not to get up and what to have for breakfast. Such perfect bliss. I can now see why the ultimate ideal is to be totally rich and idle. I can't actually see the point of marrying a nice poor man if you could marry a perfectly nice rich one instead.

And now that I'm sixteen I don't have to do anything I don't want to do. I don't have to go back to school (although of course I probably will, to do A levels), but it's nice knowing that nobody can make me. I could go and work as a receptionist in a record company and meet all the best-looking pop stars if I wanted to but actually that's just shallow and I'd be much better off saving peoples lives as a doctor. As Mum says, you're never out of work.

What About Me, Too?

From: Sue James
Sent: Thursday 3 July 21:29
To: Angela James
Subject: I think we may, just may, have sorted it . . .

Dearest Ange,

Meeting with the mediator today – she was ill last Thursday so had an excruciating week waiting and trying not to rise to any of Matthew's provocations. He's clearly a brilliant lawyer, like a pit bull. Once he's got his teeth into you he doesn't want to let go, and strikes well below the belt wherever possible in order to undermine the opposition. Which is me. Anyway, we've agreed to alternate weekends, when Frank and Lola want to go. Tom too, if he's not ill and seems to be able to cope with the change (which will be where arguments are likely to come because I will notice changes in his behaviour because I'm his mother, but Matthew won't acknowledge that and will accuse me of being neurotic/overprotective/biased, etc.). We've also agreed in principle to alternate Christmas and divide up the summer, so they should get two holidays if Matthew can get it together. It's Christmas that will break my heart . . . I'm sort of hoping that we might come to an arrangement where we agree to spend Christmas Day together for the sake of the kids, but if that doesn't work, I'll have to start bribing them with more excitements here than Matthew can possibly muster to make them stay. Anyway, we talked it over with the kids afterwards and they seemed cool about it. I think the most important thing is that they know that we're in agreement and are not fighting over them so that they don't feel torn, particularly for Lola. I feel really guilty about what she's been through. I can't stop cuddling her. She needs smothering with love. I think she found the whole thing harder than Frank because she's beginning to grow up, but has had nowhere to go to get away from the fact that her parents are separating. We justify it rationally in adult terms but she is still a child in so many ways and to her it must have felt like her whole family was falling apart.

Frankie made it abundantly clear to Matthew that Chattie and her social life came first but that if she was ever at a loose end she'd give him a ring to see what was on offer, which made me laugh out loud. I also offered Matthew shared care of Chloe which I thought was incredibly generous of me but he didn't seem interested. Lola says Laura doesn't like dogs and thinks them unhygienic. Hah! Toyah has finally handed in her notice and leaves just before you arrive. She has stayed much longer that she planned but she has now saved enough for that six-month tour with her boyfriend (a creep, can't believe they're still together because she's much too good for him) and she can sense that everything is much more settled and the summer is a good time for her to go but we will really miss her. So it's a childcare-free summer, and find someone new for September.

Planning on springing Mum from Clarice's on Sunday to bring her here for lunch so if you can JPEG some pics of the twins and maybe stay awake long enough to give us a call that would be fab. Must also start to get my head around your imminent arrival and make some plans with Mum. Won't have her here because there simply isn't room but we could maybe plan a short trip away somewhere all together . . . let me know your thoughts before I go anywhere on this.

Oh, and I almost forgot – you'll never guess who came into the surgery today. Mark (without the black Lab). He walked in and our eyes met and we both blushed because neither of us expected to see each other. He is registered here but with Bryson (who's off sick – he really ought to go and see a good homeopath). We sort of stammered into conversation, acutely embarrassed. And then I had to say the usual 'How can I help you today?' and it felt so odd stepping into a professional role when we've talked about our kids together on the common, and then for one awful moment it occurred to me that he might be coming in with a prostate problem. Actually it was a chest infection, so I could get right up close with the stethoscope and HEAR his heart beating at twice the normal rate, which was kind of exciting. AND WE'VE GOT A DATE!!!!! Next Friday! Gave him my number and he said he'd call next week and I'm so excited I feel quite alive, young and wanted again. Planning on a major body job next week – exfoliation, face mask, leg wax, maybe even a haircut if I can squeeze one in and I thought I'd eat nothing but carrot fingers and broccoli between now and then so that I can look thinner in bigger clothes. Probably just get bad breath instead. It's incredibly exciting but the thought that he might actually touch this flabby body fills me with such fear and trepidation. I don't think I've ever felt THIS nervous about a date. I've got to arrange with Matthew to have Tom and Lola that night without letting him know why. Talk about today being my lucky day –

one man out with the divorce almost sorted (finances to be debated next week), and the new man almost in. Must to bath and bed to dream . . .

Much love,
Sxxxx

What About Me, Too?

Dear Diary,

Sunday the 6th of July 🖉

Mum is SOOO much happier. She was singing round the house this morning and doing really weird things. She's started doing exercises on the living-room floor. She NEVER usually does that. Maybe it's because she and Dad are talking to each other again. They were even being nice to each other last week. I don't think that means they're back together because we had another one of those talks from them about 'arrangements' but there's always hope that they could be. I mean, being nice to each other is a good start.

I've decided to devote myself to Tom from now on. Toyah's leaving and that's going to be a big blow for him. So he's going to need me around a lot for konteenuwity. Particularly since Frankie does nothing. She's always asleep and then when she's awake she's on the phone or stealing my clothes. Bitch. Toyah thinks the boy must have moved on. I went back to the cemetery again after Sports Day, I wanted to tell him all about it, but he wasn't there and more of the stuff had disappeared. Either he came back to take it or somebody else did. I'm so lucky to have a nice home and the best Mummy in the world, who is still alive.

Only nine more days at school and then I'm totally FREEEEEE! I hate that place now. It's suffixicating. Camilla says she's feeling really sad about leaving and wants to be able to stay at primary school for ever and ever because she loves it so much but I don't. The sooner I leave and make a fresh start, the better. That's what Mum says anyway. She's still doing exercises and hasn't even made us any pancakes yet. Better go and ask her why not.

What About Me, Too?

Dear Diary,

Sunday. Chattie and I have been making plans for our gap year. We're gonna learn to drive and then fly to New York and then buy a car and drive all the way across America to the West Coast and then all the way down the West Coast through Mexico and then all the way down through South America. That should take at least a year. Then I'll come back, go to medical school and get serious. That's my plan anyway. Ruby says that anything could happen in two years' time, but what does she know.

    Dad wants to take me out for supper tonight to celebrate finishing GCSEs which is progress, because at the start of this year he didn't even think I was gonna get any. I said I'd only go if Laura didn't come, came straight out with it and he agreed. I hardly ever spend that sort of time with him alone. We've never been out to supper together like that, just me and him. We're always either all together here or out together or with other people, but this feels more grown-up, like we might even get to talk about things which are important, like ME and MY LIFE and how important Chattie is to me (because if he doesn't get that firmly lodged in his head then life is going to be really difficult between us from now on). I don't know what to wear. Mum says I can borrow her new dress which is nice of her since it's the only decent thing in her wardrobe and she only got it yesterday. Plus Dad won't know it's Mum's because he hasn't seen it. Might be kind of weird otherwise, him looking at me

across a candlelit table wearing his wife's clothes . . . Eugh
. . . Sooo Freudian.

Time to get up and try everything on in my wardrobe
now that Chattie's gone home for lunch.

What About Me, Too?

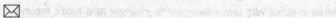

From: Sue James
Sent: Saturday 12 July 10:21
To: Angela James
Subject: Re: What about a nice country luxury hotel with child activ . . .

GOOD IDEA. With a lovely roaring fire for Mum to sit in front of, giant beds with chintzy eiderdowns, good food, babysitting, or at least an alarm, and they have to take dogs. I'll go onto the Net this weekend and let you know what there is, plus price, which is bound to be high but what the fuck. And I've nearly sorted our 'Thelma and Louise Take the Children on the Road to France Profonde' trip – ferry booked for Friday 15th, return on 1 September. Espace booked for all our kids plus things (another good idea and thanks for paying for that) and hotel booked in Orleans for our first night, then a week in this house at Felletin which sounds basic but cosy and very very rural, and after that we're free to roam hippy-style with our kids. Very exciting, it'll be lovely to be girls together again, can't wait to spend some time with you over a bottle of red wine once the kids are asleep.

Date went well . . . I think! Went out for dinner and talked. He's really funny, Ange, makes me laugh and gentle and considerate (so unlike Matthew) but fragile. There's a hurt behind those eyes. He found it hard not to talk about his wife and then got embarrassed when he realized that he had been, but I really like him. Don't fancy him in that heart-stopping, knee-melting way like when you're younger and more fecund but maybe that's not that important any more. I like him, he's a friend. We have another date next Thursday – he's taking me to the theatre – and I feel alive again, Ange, as if the emotional nightmare of the past two years with Matthew is at last abating, although we have yet to settle the money side. He's still holding out for no support. I'm saying over my dead body, so we may yet have to go to court on that front.

Much love, Suex

What About Me, Too?

Dear Diary,

Saturday the 12th day of July

Mum now lets me take Chloe out for walks whenever I like, which is funny because she never wanted me to before, she always took her herself, but she still won't let me go to the common on my own and she's really funny about the cemetery because she thinks I nearly died there, so I don't tell her that I go there. But I do. I go just in case the boy comes back because I'd like to see him again. I'd like to be able to thank him and help him. He could come and live with us. He's fit too, Frankie would LOVE him. He looks a bit like a young Anthony Horowitz who is really fit. Well, he isn't really. Well, he is for an old man. So I wander around the lanes with Chloe reading the names and dates on the tombstones and imagining what the people's lives must have been like. It also helps you feel so fortshunate about being alive when you remember that they're dead.

From: Sue James
Sent: Saturday 12 July 21:32
To: Angela James
Subject: August plans

OK, I figure you will need at least two to three days to just chill here after you arrive. There's a five-star hotel in Yorkshire, converted manor house, that sounds lovely and has two family rooms free for the nights of the 6th and 7th. It means one of us sharing with Mum but that's fine by me. Long way to drive just for two nights and it's expensive (£350 a night for room and breakfast) BUT I'm having trouble finding anywhere else that fits the bill. They're holding it for me for twenty-four hours. We could just ditch this idea and go for a cottage somewhere instead or a cheaper hotel for longer further away like North Wales or Scotland but it won't be as luxurious, plus we do have the drive through France to consider as well. Alternatively we could just take Mum out for day trips and feed her up with good tucker in lovely country restaurants.

Ping me soonest,
Suex

What About Me, Too?

From: Sue James
Sent: Sunday 13 July 20:43
To: Angela James
Subject: Re: August plans

Agreed ... we'll do day trips instead.

Had an extraordinary morning – nearly lost Chloe. A woman accosted me on the way back from the common with Tom and Lola and said it was her dog. She even snatched the lead from me and tried to run off down the road! I shoved the buggy in front of her and Lola grabbed Chloe's lead back and kicked the woman hard in the shins, which was a little over the top but you can forgive that in a child (clearly upset at the prospect of losing her beloved dog). So I accused her of being a thief, lied through my teeth and said we'd had her since she was a puppy and then felt profoundly guilty. BUT (and it's a BIG BUT) she has been with us since October and the vet reckons she's only three or four years old at the most which means we've had her for almost a third of her life, so doesn't that make her ours now anyway? I asked her why she was so sure. She said she knew it was 'Sindy' (yuk) in the way she would know her own child. Talk about racking up the guilt factor. So I constructed a scene reminiscent of *The Caucasian Chalk Circle*. I told her to call Sindy to see if she would follow; my whole heart was in my mouth at that point and I was praying to a God that I don't believe in that Chloe would be temporarily struck deaf at that moment. Mercifully she didn't follow. Lola called

'Chloe' and Chloe came to her obediently to be put back on the lead. The woman looked really disappointed but she did at least concede defeat. I tried to console her by saying that shaggy sheepdogs did look very much alike and that I hoped she'd find her dog soon but went home feeling terrible because she had a little girl with her who was desperate to find her own dog. If Chloe had responded to the name 'Sindy' we would have had no choice but to let her go and I would probably have had to console Lola with the promise of a puppy. But she didn't, so we were at least spared that nightmare. However, I still feel bad about it. Do you think dogs forget, that she could actually be Sindy and have been with us for so long that she has become Chloe?

Sx

What About Me, Too?

Dear Diary,

Thursday the 17th day of July and the last day of year 6 and the last day of primary school ever! ✏️

I can't wait to go and buy my new uniform. I've never had a uniform before. Loads of people, mainly the girls, were crying in the playground, wailing with greefe, which is just so totally stupid because most of them are going to see each other in September in their new school anyway, but I suppose it is kind of significant that we're moving on, waving goodbye to a part of our childhood that we will never see again. Mum was in tears, too, when she came to pick me up with Tom. I'm just so, so, so, so glad that I never need see Tanya again, and with any luck Clare will move and a much nicer family will move in next door. I can't believe how much has changed over the past year. At the beginning of year 6 I thought Clare was my best friend, now we're so different I can't believe we were ever that close, and what's more I don't mind. I also used to think that Camilla was just a saddo like the rest of the class did, but now that I really know her, she's the kindest, funniest person and I'm gonna miss her not being there when I start at Balham High, but Mum says we'll make lots of plans to take her out to places in the holidays and at weekends. This time last year Dad and Mum were rowing really so badly it felt like they were stabbing me over and over again with a knife but now they're not rowing and even though they SAY they are going to get divorced it doesn't feel quite so bad because I know I can see Dad whenever I like and I don't have to choose between them which would have been just so awful, and I know that we're not gonna have to move from here. I still kind of wish that they could live together and maybe after a while they will, because some people do divorce and then marry again. Camilla showed me an artikal about it in *Chat* magazine. Last year we didn't even have Chloe.

Six whole weeks of blissful emptiness stretch before me. Auntie Angela and the twins are coming to stay and Mum is planning this mega drive through France, which I am not looking forward to because I get carsick on long journeys. She also can't stop going on about Clare's mum, like she was some sort of psychopath. I mean I know she's a bit weird but she's not THAT bad. She talked practically the whole way through supper about how much make-up Clare's mum wears and how bad it is because it's full of petrokemikals and how deodorants give you breast cancer and how she hopes I never use either, and in the end it was Frankie who told her to shut up and grow up and asked why was she so fixated on the stupid woman next door anyway. She told her to stop frightening us with scare stories and that maybe I would need to wear make-up to hide the spots and to make me look less ugly (thanks, Frankie) and she should just relax about it because when you're young you need different things to when you're old like her. Yeah, right. Not much that make-up can do for Mum now anyway.

What About Me, Too?

From: Sue James
Sent: Sunday 20 July 21:34
To: Matthew Wilcox
Subject: The summer holidays

Matthew,

Angela arrives on the 3rd of August and is here for roughly a
month. We're booked onto a ferry on the 15th and return on
the 1st. Lola and Tom too, not Frankie who is planning on
holidaying with Chattie, probably on one of those InterRail
thingies. So if you want to take the kids somewhere for a few
days before then let me know. If you make it somewhere with
shops you just might be able to coax Frank along too.

You forgot to bring back Tom's beaker and his bear
yesterday. Could you perhaps drop them round on your way to
work tomorrow???

Thanks, Sue

From: Sue James
Sent: Sunday 20 July 21:53
To: Angela James
Subject: Re: Not long now

Sorry to hear the weather's been bad there, must be a bit of a
shock! It's hot here at the moment, a heatwave. Blissful. T-shirts
and tossing around with just a sheet at night. Spent all afternoon
with Tom and Lola, splashing about in the paddling pool in the
garden. HND has gone on holiday, thank the Lord, to their new
house in Tuscany and won't be back until the end of August. She
came over yesterday, talked for nearly half an hour about what a
nightmare it was dealing with Italian builders when she couldn't
speak Italian and how the house was still not finished and a total
mess – which means that it's probably fine – but they needed to
go there to try and sort everything, and would I water her
garden and take in the post and contact her if anything
happened!! Amazing that she feels able to bulldoze into our lives
without ever apologizing. So I told her that we would be away for
two weeks, hoping that she would say, 'Oh well, never mind, I'll
find someone else,' but she didn't. She asked me instead if I could
find someone to do both our gardens while we were away!!! She
really is amazing, you have to hand it to her, But OH, what bliss!!
We can make as much noise as we like, not worry about being
overheard in the garden, snoop for a laugh and when the door
goes I can answer it absolutely relaxed in the certainty that it
won't be her with an ailment of Clare's for me to examine.

What About Me, Too?

Second date went well, I think, thanks for asking. Dreadful play, one of those ones where you'd rather sleep and squirm from buttock to buttock in an effort to get comfortable. I felt guilty every time I yawned because he'd invited me, but he hated the play too so we left at the interval and went out for a drink. Not sure whether this is going anywhere. Lola didn't like the look of him one little bit when he came to the door to pick me up. She gave me one of her cynical looks when I told her he was just a friend the following morning, so there may be trouble on that front. She still wants me and Matthew to get back together. No pass yet. Not sure if he will, but maybe that's for the best. The idea of ANYBODY other than the kids seeing me naked is terrifying. Next date is Sunday lunch next week at his house; all of us are invited as a family so that'll be interesting.

Finding it hard to concentrate at work too because it's nearly happy holiday time with you. And work isn't busy for once. No major excitements and emergencies, just the usual round of run-of-the-mill aches and pains, summer colds, stomach upsets and sunburn. Had a classic on Friday though – man comes in with the whole of his upper body covered in nicotine patches, complaining about the fact that he didn't have any more room. He didn't realize you only need one at a time!

Got tickets for you to take Mum to a nice sounding prom on the 6th of August – John Eliot Gardiner and Bach's Mass in B minor, one of her favourites, so will babysit the twins. Let me know if there is anything else you fancy and I'll get tickets.

Longing to see you, and those boys,
Suexxxxxxxxxxxxxxxxxxx

From: Dr James
Sent: Tuesday 22 July 13:45
To: Matthew Wilcox
Subject: Re: Why didn't you tell me before?

I'm sorry, Matthew, but you never mentioned that you wanted
to go away that week and since you hadn't said anything I
assumed it was fine, plus Ange and I haven't seen each other for
a year and since she's here without Spike it makes sense for us
to go on holiday somewhere together. Our ferry is booked. You
have yet to book anything. Please don't make this any more
difficult than it need be. It's bound to take time for us to get into
a rhythm with the kids and this is only two weeks – they are off
school for six. And please don't turn this into an issue – we really
must be careful and try not to argue over the kids because it
upsets Lola so.

Once we have the finances sorted I suggest we go through
a diary and agree dates so that we can make proper fixed plans
and avoid confusion in future.

Thanks for dropping off Tom's things.

Sue

What About Me, Too?

Dear Diary,

Friday 25 July

I think Mum has a new boyfriend. This is a deesaster. He's got horrible pointy ears and he's small and bald. I can't believe Mum would choose this dwarf over Dad, but then again I don't suppose she's got much choice since she's old anyway. So I made a point of telling Dad when he took me to see *Mary Poppins* last night and he sounded really interested. He kept asking me questions about him like what did he do, when how should I know? And did he have children and where did he live and has he spent the night, which is like a really, really rude question and I wondered whether to lie and say that he had to make Dad really jealous but actually that is a lie so I said, 'Not yet but it's only a question of time before they move in with each other because Mum really likes him.' He started jiggling his leg really hard like he does when he's nervous or angry and then didn't hear anything I said for about half an hour so he's obviously thinking about it. Good. Maybe he'll come back to us before Mum makes a terrible mistake.

We have to go to his house on Sunday for lunch. I asked Dad if he'd have me on Sunday so that I could sort of protest my allegiance to Dad but he's busy, wouldn't say why but it's obviously got something to do with the marriage-breaker. She managed to burn Tom's mouth with some scorching hot lasagne in Pizza Express yesterday. Of course, she doesn't realize that babies need things cooling down. HAVEN'T told Mum that because she'll only tell Dad off and that'll cause another row.

Dear Diary,

I've brought you to Mark's house so that I don't have to
look interested in anything he says or does, and I can write
down everything that happens and then report it back to
Dad. The house is kind of nice. Modern and massive and
everything is really tidy and smart with these huge pots and
statues on every shelf, like a sort of museum. Two
bathrooms, one off the master bedroom, massive double
bed – not a good sign as Mum has always wanted a bigger
bed. Huge garden full of roses – Mum's favourite flowers
(also not a good sign). Plasma TV – OK.

Mum says he's an arkitekt and that he built this house
which is why it's so nice. He's got two sons, one's fifteen
and looks just like Brad Pitt – you should have seen
Frankie's face when they met, it went bright red and then
she got really embarrassed about it – and the other one is
thirteen and small, like the dwarf only without the pointy
ears. Only he was nice and taught me how to play ping-
pong. He's really good at it.

Number of ex wives – one.

Lunch was delicious, roast chicken and roast potatoes so
he can cook and he didn't touch Mum once which I'm like
really pleased about, because it means nothing has
happened yet and there is still time for Dad to come back
and say that he still loves her, but Mark's not that bad. He
has a really cool shelf of DVDs which Frankie and I
salivated over and Chloe really seems to like his Labrador
who is called Pip. They chased each other round the garden
and then curled up against each other to go to sleep on the

patio after Mark had given them the remains of the chicken, and Mum did look really happy so maybe, IF Dad doesn't come back, then maybe it won't be so bad after all.

From: Sue James
Sent: Sunday 27 July 22:35
To: Angela James
Subject: Mark

Well, where do I start???? His house is FANBLOODYTASTIC!!!
Could move in right now and leave this dump to Matthew, well
almost. AND he has a house near Padstow that sleeps eight!!!
He can cook, his sons are really sweet and went out of their
way to be nice to Frank, Lola and Tom when they could easily
have made life difficult for them if they'd wanted to. Unlike
Lola, who sulked in the corner of this massive leather sofa,
writing her diary and refusing to talk to anyone until Sam
persuaded her downstairs to the ping-pong table. Tom behaved
beautifully and spent most of the afternoon chasing the dogs or
splashing in this amazing high-tech paddling pool which I'm sure
Mark bought specially for him, which is so, so sweet. He's just
nice, Ange, easy to be with, funny, a family man trying to do the
best by his kids. Only one difficult moment when Lola asked
him how many times he had been married (brave of her, wasn't
it?) and Mark laughed. Frankie told Lola not to be nosey and
Mark said, 'No, no it's exactly the sort of question you should
ask someone at dinner.' She was sitting next to him. 'It's only
been once and once was quite enough.' That seemed to make
Lola happy and she wrote the answer down in her diary which
was positioned beside her at the table.

Plus there was a massage table down in the basement next

to the sauna (yes, I said SAUNA). You don't think he does, do you? Massage, I mean. Wouldn't that be simply heaven, someone who could massage you to sleep each night? I'm won over already.

Only trouble is, I don't know when we're meeting again. No plans made, so now I'm in that excruciating will-he-ring-me phase, or should I ring him?

Anyway to bed now to dream of massage, and maybe more.

Sxx

From: Sue James
Sent: Tuesday 29 July 23:19
To: Angela James
Subject: Re: Invite them back for supper

I couldn't possibly! To this dump! What would they think? No, it's time to play it a little cool, like he's a friend and so what. I'm not going to risk anything by making a move too early.

Can't sleep, though. Downloading maps of Limoges and it's environs and writing endless lists of markets and things for kids to do. Longing to see you and the boys, it's been too long, but not long now. Taking Mum to have her hair done on Monday just for you and she's insisting on coming with me to the airport to pick you up and since my three will be in Paris with Matthew I think I can manage that. So remember to make a massive fuss and pretend you didn't know she was coming. She's on very good form at the moment, Clarice's is a hit and she's made friends (honestly, it's more trouble than settling a child in school).

Much love, not long now, your ever-loving bossy big sister, Suex

What About Me, Too?

Dear Diary,

Friday the 1st day of August

Toyah left yesterday and even though I told myself I wouldn't cry, I couldn't help it. I'm going to really miss her. She's been like the rock keeping this family together through everything. She says she'll send us postcards from every country she goes to so that I can build up a collection. She gave Frankie a CD and me a photograph album full of pictures to remind me of the things we've done together but I can't look at it without crying.

Dad is taking me, Frank and Tom to Paris tomorrow for four nights. Laura's coming too which will be interesting because Frank definitely doesn't like her, but she likes the idea of Paris and the shops enough to come. It feels odd going on holiday with Dad and without Mum because we've never ever done that before and it feels like that really means the end of something and the beginning of something else that's new, like we're never going to have a family holiday again unless something totally extreme happens like Laura and Mark get killed in car crashes or fall in love with each other. Now that's a good idea. I wonder if I can get them to meet when we get back, ask Mum to make the peace by inviting them all round. How could she say no???? Four days is a really long time for Tom to be away from Mum so I'll have to make sure he's happy and well looked after. It'll be nice to be with Frankie though, we're sharing a room in a hotel!!! It'll also be good to DO something. The summer holidays get a bit boring although Camilla and I have decided to turn the Lion's Tomb into a really cosy den so that if the boy does decide to come back it'll be like home for him. Or maybe even a home for lots of other children who aren't as lucky as me or Camilla. But you know what I really feel guilty about? That I never asked him his name. He may be homeless but he had a name, and just like all the other people who are dead and buried in the cemetery, he deserves to be remembered by it.